Praise for A Red Dotted Line:

"Gervais brings back covert agents Mike Walton and his wife, Lisa, in this stellar follow-up to *The Thin Black Line* . . .. The personal stakes involving his protagonists and almost nonstop action keep the pages turning; his improved prose style reveals that Gervais is a thriller writer to watch. The next book in the series can't come soon enough."
— Library Journal

"*A Red Dotted Line* reminds us of what thrillers are supposed to be: thrilling. Gervais, a former anti-terrorist agent, knows the world that he writes about and illuminates the dark threats we all face on the global stage. *A Red Dotted Line* will entertain, educate, and engage even the most jaded reader of international thrillers."
— Nelson DeMille, *New York Times* bestselling author

"*A Red Dotted Line* is a taut and intelligent thriller chock full of excitement and authenticity. Simon Gervais shows off an expansive range of knowledge and an equally remarkable ability to keep a complex story moving along at a breakneck pace. The plotting is first rate, and the wide cast of standout characters memorable. Readers will find *A Red Dotted Line* reminiscent of the very best of Vince Flynn and David Baldacci."
— Mark Greaney, *New York Times* bestselling author

"Crisply plotted and highly entertaining, *A Red Dotted Line* hits the ground at a breathtaking sprint from the first page. Insider Simon Gervais writes with the clarity of someone who knows and a been-there-done-that expertise in the world of anti-terrorism that only an insider can give."
— Mark Cameron, *New York Times* bestselling author

A Red Dotted Line

A Red Dotted Line

Simon Gervais

Studio Digital CT, LLC
P.O. Box 4331
Stamford, CT 06907

Copyright © 2016 by Simon Gervais
Cover design by Barbara Aronica-Buck

Story Plant Hardcover ISBN: 978-1-61188-235-3
Story Plant Paperback ISBN: 978-1-61188-236-0
Fiction Studio Books E-book ISBN: 978-1-943486-96-0

Visit our website at www.TheStoryPlant.com

First Story Plant Printing: November 2016
Printed in the United States of America

0 9 8 7 6 5 4 3 2 1

To Lisane, for always being there, no matter what.

PROLOGUE

Federal Correctional Institution Otisville
New York

Louis Wall wasn't a patient man, but he was curious. When the guard told him he had a visitor, he didn't say a word. For the last ten years, no one had cared enough about him to visit, not even his only daughter. He didn't blame her; his stupid ex-wife had brainwashed her into thinking he was dangerous. He should have killed the woman when he had the chance.

"You know the drill," the guard said through the cell's door. "Turn around."

He obeyed and offered his wrists. Seconds later, he felt the cold steel of the handcuffs against his skin. As Wall exited his six-by-eight-foot prison cell, the guard dug his fingers into his bicep while pushing him in the back.

"What the fuck?"

"Shut the hell up and stop resisting," the guard said. To get his point across, he delivered a powerful punch to Wall's only kidney.

Wall winced in pain, but not a sound escaped his lips. He didn't want to give the guard the pleasure of knowing he had hurt him. A few years ago, Wall would have fought back and cracked a skull or two, but with only a few weeks left of his twelve-year sentence for manslaughter and drug trafficking, it was better to take it like a man. Plus, he couldn't help but wonder who his visitor was.

To his surprise, the guard didn't lead him to the regular visitors' room. Instead, he was escorted to an interview room where a man dressed in a three-piece suit was seated behind a steel table bolted to the floor. Laid open on the table was a yellow file to which Wall's headshot was stapled. Another file folder, a green one, remained closed.

"Remove his handcuffs," the man said.

The guard didn't look happy but obeyed nonetheless.

"You can leave," the man added.

Once the guard had closed the door, the man pointed to the single chair across the table. "Please."

Wall remained standing. The man seated in front of him didn't look dangerous. It was hard to say how tall he was. Five and a half feet, he estimated. Maybe less. Dark skin. Slight build. Nothing like Wall's own muscular six-foot-four-inch frame. But he did have an accent. Russian? It definitely sounded like that. He didn't like Russians.

"What do you want?" Wall grunted.

The man slowly looked up from the file he was reading, his brown eyes locking onto Wall's.

"Louis Wall, forty-seven years of age, born in Dickson, Tennessee. Only child of Claire Dolan and Peter Wooley. Attended Dickson County High School before enlisting in the US Army—"

"Was my jaw supposed to drop?" Wall cut in. "That's all public knowledge."

The man simply continued without acknowledging Wall's interruption. "You faced your first court martial before the end of basic training after assaulting your drill sergeant. After serving a month in a military prison, you were dishonorably discharged and spent the next two years living off the small inheritance you received after your father's passing. You met Isabella, your first real girlfriend, at the local tavern on the night of your twenty-first birthday—"

"What do you want?" Wall said for the second time in less than sixty seconds.

"Please have a seat," the man replied.

Wall shook his head from left to right, then crossed his arms, his biceps threatening to tear apart the fabric of his gray prison suit.

"I'm here to offer you a second chance."

"At what?"

"Revenge, Louis. Revenge."

A picture of his ex-wife hanging at the end of a rope appeared in his mind. "I'm listening."

"First you sit," the man said with an authority that couldn't be denied.

10

Wall sighed, then pulled the chair and sat. "This better be good."

"Or what?" the man replied. When he didn't respond, the man pressed on. "No really. I'm curious. Or what, Louis? What will you do?"

"I'm on my last stretch here, mister know-it-all. I have no intention of doing anything to fuck that up. Understood?"

The man cocked his head and looked at him as if he were some kind of undiscovered species. "And what exactly are your plans once you're out of here?"

The vision of his ex-wife at the end of a rope reappeared in his mind. "There are a few things I can think of."

"Of that I'm sure. But are any of them worth a quarter of a million dollars?"

That was enough money for Wall to live comfortably in Mexico for a couple of years. Once he'd taken care of his ex-wife, of course. "I'm listening."

The man slid the green folder toward him. "Open it."

A single picture of a man was attached to a white sheet. Wall recognized him instantly.

Mapother. Charles Mapother.

The bastard had killed his older brother three decades ago.

"I would have done it for free," he said.

CHAPTER 1

IMSI Headquarters
New York City, NY

Zima Bernbaum threw up a little bit in her mouth.

"Did you hear what I just said, Zima?" Charles Mapother asked.

Zima met his gaze. Mapother, like a stereotypical Zurich banker, was dressed in a custom-made Armani suit. His deeply tanned skin contrasted with the full head of silver hair he had combed back. His deep blue eyes, she knew, didn't miss much.

"Zima? Are you with me?"

"What do you mean I didn't make it?" she asked just loud enough to be heard by Mapother. The taste of her own bile in her mouth disgusted her. *Get a grip, Zima.*

"I'm sorry; you just weren't good enough," Mapother said, reading the final report his trainers had forwarded him the day before. "You missed too many benchmarks."

"I left CSIS for this job," she said, anger creeping into her voice when she thought about the chance she had taken leaving the Canadian Security Intelligence Service. "You know I can't go back."

Mapother closed the report and pushed it back toward the middle of his desk. "You knew the risks involved, Zima. The deal was that you had to go through the same training the others did last year. They were successful; you weren't."

Zima sank back in her chair, frustrated. She had sacrificed so much, had gambled everything. And now she had nothing to show for it.

Emotionally and physically, the last eight weeks had been the toughest of her life. The first four weeks, eighteen-hour days filled with weapons manipulation drills followed by geopolitics and foreign languages classes, had drained her energy. The next two had nearly killed her. The bruises all over her well-toned, five-foot-seven-inch frame were a testament to the countless hours spent in the dojo with Greg, the in-house Krav Maga expert. But it was the last two weeks—the ones spent learning a dozen ways to kill someone without leaving a trace—that had altered her forever. There was simply no way a sane human being could go through this training without suffering a psychological backlash. Fully aware of the potential repercussions it might have on her life, she had held nothing back and given her all. The worst thing about all of this was that she'd convinced herself that she was doing okay.

Heck, I thought I was doing great!

Two months ago, she had left her job as a CSIS operative to join the International Market Stabilization Institute—IMSI—following the successful takedown of a terrorist cell in Edmonton, Canada. As a privately funded organization run by Charles Mapother, the IMSI could do things that government agencies just couldn't. Her friend Lisa Walton, who was a trained emergency physician, and Lisa's husband Mike were part of the IMSI. They were field operatives, or "assets" in the IMSI's jargon. They had gone through the same training she just did.

They did better than me, obviously.

It wasn't difficult to understand why Mike had aced everything. He always did. A former Canadian Special Forces officer and Royal Canadian Mounted Police counterterrorism specialist, Mike was used to these sorts of things. But Lisa? Even though Lisa had done her medical training with the military, Zima didn't believe Lisa had any real experience handling a gun or shooting at a live target. One that fires back, that is.

How the hell did she pass the IMSI training? It doesn't make any sense! How come I failed and she passed? Not that I'm better than her . . . Actually, yes I am. For this type of work, I'm the best.

Charles Mapother must have known what she was thinking because when she looked at him, he was smiling.

"Oh, you bastard," she said, her voice a mixture of frustration and relief.

"Don't doubt yourself again, Zima," Mapother said, rising from his chair. "You passed everything with flying colors. Welcome to the team."

She rose, too. They shook hands. "Thank you, sir."

"You earned your place, Zima," Mapother said. "Glad to have you aboard. Now, let's celebrate."

CHAPTER 2

Grand Central Station, New York

Mike Walton laughed out loud. His wife Lisa, seated next to him, did the same. So much so that water came out of her nose. That made Mike laugh even harder.

"I can't believe you did that to Zima, Charles," he said, after he had regained control of his breathing.

"I knew he was kidding," Zima replied before Mapother could chip in. "I didn't believe it. Not for a second."

Mapother coughed, and then said, "If you say so, Zima."

"What are you talking about?" Zima said between sips of her Chardonnay. "I was playing along, that's all."

"Sure you were, dear friend," added Lisa. "But that doesn't matter one bit; you're in now."

"Cheers to that," Mike said, raising his glass. The others did the same.

When Mike's eyes met his wife's, he smiled. So much had changed in the last two years. The tragedy they'd faced should have been enough to tear them apart. And it almost did. But they had regrouped, found a common goal, and moved on. That didn't mean he didn't think about the terrorist attacks that had wiped out most of his family.

Far from it.

The gentle spirit of his two-year-old daughter Melissa visited his dreams almost every night as a stark reminder. Killing the Sheik, the murderer who'd orchestrated the attacks, was the first thing he thought about every morning. He wouldn't say that to anyone, not even to his wife, but recently, his thoughts about killing the Sheik weren't limited to simply putting a bullet in his brain. He aspired to skin him alive. He wanted the Sheik to feel the pain he had inflicted on his family.

Mapother's voice brought him back to the present. "Did you decide on your main course?"

"Not yet," Mike said, chasing the images of the Sheik out of his mind.

The four of them were having lunch at the Oyster Bar. Located inside Grand Central Station, it was Mike's favorite oyster place and the oldest business within the terminal. He had discovered the restaurant years ago while staying at the nearby Grand Hyatt during a training exercise between the Royal Canadian Mounted Police—the Canadian federal police service—and the Federal Bureau of Investigation. He loved the Guastavino tile vaults and the old-school charm of the restaurant. It was always buzzing with people, it was loud, and the waiters did their best to provide pleasant and prompt service. The restaurant had a killer clam chowder, and the oysters were always fresh and tasty. Mike made a point of having lunch here at least once a month. Sometimes more. Plus, they had his favorite beer, Chimay Red, a high-end, dark-brown Belgian beer with a sweet and fruity aroma he couldn't resist.

A few tables over to their right sat a tall, broad-shouldered black man wearing a tailored gray suit. His name was Sam Turner. Turner was charged with the personal protection of Charles Mapother, and Mike knew him as a loyal and capable operative. Mapother had handpicked Turner, a former member of the FBI Hostage Rescue Team, to be his personal bodyguard after Turner had sustained a back injury during an FBI training exercise.

The waiter, a thirty-something named Chuck, brought their appetizers. He put a huge portion of Cajun-style fried popcorn shrimp in the middle of the table next to a bowl of broiled Blue Point oysters. Chuck took their entrée orders before disappearing again.

Mike made sure the plates were passed around and that every-one had served themselves before digging in. In his opinion, the smooth and meaty texture of these particular oysters placed them in a category by themselves, but they really became divine with a touch of anchovy butter melted on top. Mike was about to taste his first oyster when his smartphone vibrated inside his jacket pocket. It was Jonathan Sanchez, the IMSI's newly appointed second-in-command and a longtime friend of Mike's.

"This better be good, buddy," Mike said. "I'm about to indulge . . ."

"It is," Sanchez interrupted. "We've heard from the Syrians. They have your father."

Mike stopped breathing. *Dad.* The oyster he was holding in his left hand fell onto his lap, soiling his pants. His father, a former Canadian ambassador to Algeria, had been kidnapped by the Sheik three and a half years ago.

"That's what Charles told me almost three months ago," Mike said.

"I know, brother," Sanchez replied. "But this time is different. We got this tip directly from the White House."

Mike's mind was spinning with the implications. "You didn't tell him?" he asked.

"No, I wanted you to hear it from me first," Sanchez replied. "I'm calling him now."

Mapother had his eyes fixed on Mike. "Everything all right?" he asked, his mouth half-full with popcorn shrimp.

"Just pick up your phone, Charles," Mike said.

Mapother raised an eyebrow when his smartphone started vibrating on the table. He wiped his mouth with a napkin and tried unsuccessfully to remove the grease from his fingers before answering his phone.

"Okay, we'll be there shortly," Mapother finally said before hanging up.

"Are you still hungry?" he asked Mike.

"What do you think?" Mike replied, standing up. He left four twenty-dollar bills on the table. "Let's go."

His wife was looking at him, a question mark on her forehead.

"It's my father, honey," Mike said. "Jonathan got a tip from the White House. You guys can stay and enjoy yourselves. I'll call you if this is serious."

But the two women operatives were already grabbing their purses and coats.

CHAPTER 3

Grand Central Station, NY.

Mike's mind was racing. His phone conversation with Jonathan Sanchez had only lasted a few seconds, and he couldn't wait to get back to IMSI headquarters to hear the rest of the story. Could this be it? The thought of seeing his father again was overwhelming. How would he react after all these years? So much had changed. For him and for his father.

Sam Turner was the first out of the restaurant's door. He kept it open for the others and took his position behind Mapother. With Zima and Lisa leading the way, they started on the ramp toward the upper level. Turner gave instructions to Mapother's driver, another former FBI agent named Frank, who was circling around the block in the modified black Yukon Hybrid Mapother used for transportation, to pick them up on 45th Street.

With people sprinting to catch their train, shoppers and diners converging in and out of the shops, and tourists taking pictures of the terminal's magnificent architectural details, Grand Central Station was a hectic place to be at this hour.

"We'll get him, Mike," Mapother said.

"I thought I had him four months ago. I'm not holding my breath," Mike replied. Four months earlier, he had led Lisa and Jasmine Carson, an IMSI support team leader, on a raid to seize and take control of the Sheik's mobile headquarters, an eighty-six-foot Azimut yacht located in Spain. He had been sure his dad was aboard the boat, but that wasn't the case. Instead, Alexander Shamrock, also known as Omar Al-Nashwan, murdered Jasmine Carson before Mike shot and killed him. To make matters worse, Mike discovered that Alexander Shamrock wasn't only a former US Special Forces officer; he was also the son of Steve Shamrock, a close friend of President Robert Muller and CEO of Oil Denatek, one of the larger publicly traded oil-and-gas companies in the United States.

"Did you hear from Richard Phillips?" Mike asked as they were reaching the main concourse. Richard Phillips was the director of National Intelligence and, with the president, one of the only bureaucrats to know the true purpose of the IMSI.

"I did."

"And?"

"They didn't find him."

Damn it. Following the raid on the Sheik's yacht and the death of Alexander Shamrock, Steve Shamrock had disappeared. That had made a lot of people nervous, including Charles Mapother. Steve Shamrock was one of the three billionaires who'd helped create the IMSI. Mike couldn't wrap his head around the reasons the oil executive had financed the IMSI if his plan had been to sink the United States all along.

"Maybe he's dead," Mike suggested. "The Sheik might have killed him."

"That would put many minds at ease," Mapother said.

"Not yours?"

"No, not mine, Mike. We have no idea what the Sheik knows about us. Are we compromised? What kind of intelligence did Steve Shamrock leak before he disappeared?"

"Did he have access to all of our classified information?"

"He didn't," Mapother said. "But he knew about the IMSI. He financed it, goddamn it!"

Mike opened his mouth to reply but just then Sam Turner's powerful voice reverberated through the main concourse, "Threat to the rear!"

Then the first shot rang out.[1]

. . . .

Louis Wall wasn't the best shot, but it was hard to miss when you were so close to your target. He had expected Charles Mapother to be alone. He wasn't. *Big deal.* He'd deal with Mapother first and if the others caused him any trouble, he'd deal with them, too.

19

Acquiring the Beretta 92 FS had been easy. Eight hundred dollars had been enough to convince a former contact to hand over his pistol. Two magazines of thirteen rounds were acquired for an additional two hundred dollars. A bit on the expensive side, but Wall didn't mind. He was a rich man now. *Two hundred and fifty thousand dollars.*

Wall drew the Beretta from its holster and brought it up to eye level, its muzzle pointed at Mapother's back. That was when the tall black man walking behind Mapother turned around and scanned his rear. For a fraction of a second, they made eye contact and Wall hesitated. It was enough for the man to sidestep to his left, effectively blocking Wall's view of his target. The man yelled something unintelligible at the same time Wall pulled the trigger.

. . . .

Mike Walton reacted intuitively. Pivoting toward the sound of gunfire, his left hand found the compact Taurus pistol holstered in the small of his back. By the time his eyes acquired his target, less than two seconds had lapsed since Turner's verbal warning. The man on the other side of his iron sight was built like a bulldozer. He was in a stable shooting position twenty meters away, and Mike could see the man's pistol go up and down as he fired rounds in quick succession.

No time to aim.[2]

Mike's first round hit the man in the abdomen while his second shot nicked his shoulder. The man dropped his weapon and took a few steps back before collapsing. Mike scanned left and right, looking for more targets—difficult to do with all the commotion the firefight had generated. Suitcases and other luggage were left on the spot as their owners ran for their lives. A woman, standing next to a baby stroller, screamed at the top of her lungs.

Did a stray bullet hit her baby? Mike saw Zima sprint to her. He continued scanning but a pit formed in his stomach when he saw Sam Turner sprawled on the floor, blood pouring out from under him. Lisa was already next to him with Charles Mapother, dragging Turner to safety, out of sight. The man Mike had shot was now less than ten meters away. He moved and managed to get on his knees, his eyes searching for his weapon.

"Don't move! Police!" Mike yelled.

A shot was fired. Then another. The man yelled, his hands clutching his neck in a failed attempt to stop the bleeding.

There's another shooter! Friend or foe?

Mike dove to the floor and then rolled to his left just as another round ricocheted to his right.

Definitely not friendly.

Where was the shooter? There were still dozens of people left in the terminal. Some had found concealment while some others simply lay down on the floor with their hands on their heads.

There. On the East Side balcony, right under the Apple Store, a short man with a gray hood jumped the last few steps and dashed toward the Lexington exit. It was hard to say from this distance, but the man seemed to be holding a small submachine gun.

Mike looked behind him. Lisa, Mapother, and Turner were nowhere in sight. Zima had grabbed the baby from its stroller and was running back toward the restaurant, the toddler's mother in tow.

Satisfied that Sam Turner was in the capable hands of his wife, Mike sprinted across the main concourse in pursuit of the man who had just shot at him.

CHAPTER 4

New York City, NY

Zakhar Votyakov was furious. He had never failed his father before. He had underestimated his opponents, and he was now paying dearly for his mistake. He should have known better. After all, he was the one who'd assembled the file on Charles Mapother. Mapother, a former FBI special agent, went to work as a freelancer for the Central Intelligence Agency in the eighties because he thought the FBI's policies were impotent to stop terrorists. Zakhar's research taught him that Mapother had the reputation of being a ruthless interrogator and that he had the habit of surrounding himself with capable and dedicated people. Still, taking down a single man should have been an easy task. Even for a fool like Louis Wall.

In one swift movement, he collapsed the stock of his Arsenal Shipka submachine gun. With that done, the Shipka was less than thirteen inches long and easily concealed. His last shot had missed its intended target, but he didn't have time to re-engage. Louis Wall was dead; that was all that mattered now.

Going down the steps two at a time, Zakhar jumped the last four and ran through the Grand Central Market toward the Lexington exit. Outside, police sirens filled the air and so did the smell of burnt peanuts from a nearby food cart.

Time to disappear.

Amid the commotion around him, he removed his gray hood and grabbed a loose-fitting beige jacket from his backpack. He put on the garment over the Shipka's sling so his weapon wouldn't be obvious but would remain accessible.

Going north on Lexington Avenue, Zakhar walked past the Verizon store before turning right on East 44th Street. He didn't dare look back when he heard the police vehicles roaring behind him as they raced on Lexington Avenue. His car, a navy-blue Chevy Impala, was parked in a public parking garage just east of Third Avenue.

The turmoil at Grand Central Station had somewhat diminished, but Zakhar spotted two uniformed police officers running toward him from further up East 44th Street.

They don't have my physical description. Stay calm.

Zakhar stepped down from the sidewalk and let the two officers run past him. His eyes followed after them, but neither gave him a second look. Once he was certain they didn't represent a threat, he turned around to resume his walk toward his car but stopped dead in his tracks. Less than two meters away, a tall, heavyset man wearing a dark, two-piece suit over a white shirt and blue tie blocked his way. The man's right hand was inside his suit jacket where a service weapon would be if he had one. The gold NYPD detective badge on the man's belt pretty much confirmed that assumption. *How did he know?*

"Don't move, and make sure your hands stay where they—"

Zakhar never hesitated. *Action's faster than reaction. Always.*

He closed the distance almost instantly and threw a powerful kick at the detective's right knee. The detective cried out but was successful at pulling his service pistol from its holster. Before he could fire, Zakhar was already on him, gripping the other man's wrist with his right hand while his left grabbed the barrel of the pistol, pushing it outward. A shot went off harmlessly, and Zakhar continued the outward movement of the pistol, effectively trapping the detective's finger inside the trigger guard. The finger snapped. An enraged scream came from the officer's mouth. Zakhar was now in control of the detective's pistol, but the other man wasn't beaten yet. A powerful left hook connected with Zakhar's chin followed by an uppercut that sent him flying in the air.

Zakhar forced his eyes open. He was on his back, spread-eagled on the sidewalk with no pistol in his hand. His vision was blurred, he was dizzy, and his jaw was throbbing. He tasted blood. He had cut his tongue on a broken tooth.

The detective's eyes were filled with rage. A pocketknife had materialized in his hand. With no other options, and still on his back, Zakhar brought up the Shipka and fired.

. . . .

Mike Walton's heart was racing. *Where did the bastard go?* Mike had holstered his Taurus to avoid unwanted attention. NYPD cruisers were now parked on Lexington Avenue. Mike guessed other police vehicles were also covering the other exits. Some uniformed officers had rushed in, while others remained outside.

What would I do if I wanted to escape? Lexington Avenue's traffic is to the south. If I didn't want to make it easy for a police car, I'd go in the opposite direction.

Mike jogged northbound on Lexington, but to no avail. No man with a gray hood. Aware his prey could have changed clothes, Mike estimated his chances of finding him from nil to very low.

Three shots fired in rapid succession changed his mind.

. . . .

Zakhar watched the detective stagger backward. A weaker man would have already collapsed. The detective was strong; his will to live even stronger, guessed Zakhar. But the three red dots on his white shirt told Zakhar all he needed to know; the police officer had only a few seconds to live. Disbelief, surprise, and finally fear registered on the detective's face. Then his eyes went blank and he fell.

Aware the sound of his Shipka had attracted attention, Zakhar, still lightheaded, pulled himself together and forced himself to his feet. A dozen or so pedestrians looked at the scene in shock, some of them frozen in fear. But a few had their smartphones out and were recording.

My face will be all over the news in less than an hour. I need to get out of here. Now.

He was disoriented. The detective must have hit him harder than he thought. He had difficulty focusing on anything. The world around him spun. His legs buckled under him.

"Hey, you!" someone yelled behind him.

Zakhar turned around. Two Arabic-looking men walked purposefully towards him. They wore red T-shirts, with the word "Security" written on the front. They carried baseball bats. He was about to get hit. He tried to bring the Shipka up but he had no strength left.

. . . .

Mike Walton ran as fast as he could. Less than eighty meters away, a man was down on the sidewalk. Two men armed with baseball bats were surrounding another man, but this one had a submachine gun.

Mike was sure he had found who he was looking for even though the gray hood had vanished. He had to take over the situation before anyone else got hurt. *What are these two bozos playing at?* Didn't they know you never brought a baseball bat to a gunfight?

Fifty meters.

Mike reached for his Taurus and slowed his pace to a brisk walk. He controlled his breathing so that he could analyze the situation.

Forty meters.

Radios crackling and heavy footsteps behind him had him take a quick look.

Mike cursed under his breath. Three uniformed officers, the same he'd seen standing right outside Grand Central Station's Lexington exit less than two minutes ago, were now running with weapons in hand in the same direction as him. They'd probably heard the same gunshots. His FBI identification wouldn't work with these guys. They wouldn't care. The best thing was to let the officers do their job and then use the IMSI to dig out the intelligence the NYPD got from the shooter.

It didn't please Mike, but he had no choice. Too many questions would be asked if he got involved. He holstered his Taurus and crossed the street to get a better look at the takedown that was about to happen.

Then the head of the man he'd been chasing exploded, and Mike was forced to hit the ground once more.

CHAPTER 5

New York City, NY

Igor Votyakov adjusted the scope of his Dragunov sniper rifle. He had a clear view of the scene. His brother was surrounded and he blamed himself for Zakhar's predicament. He should have shot the plainclothes police officer that had engaged his brother. From his sniper's nest inside the minivan's modified trunk, he could have taken the shot. The sound suppressor attached to the rifle would have ensured a clear exit.

But his father had given him clear instructions. He wasn't to intervene unless absolutely necessary. Zakhar had to prove himself in the field.

"More uniformed officers are approaching," Denis said from the driver's seat. Of course, Denis wasn't his real name. He was an SVR agent—Russia foreign intelligence service.

"How many?" Igor asked, his voice betraying his impatience. He wanted his subordinates to be precise. Denis wasn't cutting it.

"Five or six."

Five or six. How Denis had survived this long in this business was a mystery.

"Is it five, or is it six?"

"It's three."

Idiot. "How far from us are they?"

"Less than seventy-five meters," Denis replied.

What? "How did they get so close to us without you noticing them?"

"I don't know. Maybe they just—"

Igor wasn't listening anymore. He had a job to do. His window of opportunity was closing rapidly. He had three magazines of ten rounds. He could do a lot of damage before being taken down. But that wasn't the mission.

He cursed his father. Twice.

He took a few deep breaths, made one final adjustment, and started to caress the Dragunov's trigger. The 7.62 bullet exited the sniper rifle's muzzle at a speed of 2723 feet per second and took only slightly longer than a third of a second to reach its intended target.

Through his scope, Igor saw his older brother's head turn crimson.

· · · · · · · ·

Mike didn't hear the shot and had no way of knowing where it had originated. The NYPD uniformed officers were scrambling to find cover. He crawled forward to get a better view and yelled to the civilians to get down. Some did but most of them ignored him and remained standing, unsure what was going on.

Was the sniper waiting for targets of opportunity to pop up or was his mission completed already? Mike glanced at the NYPD officers across the street. One seemed to be issuing orders. Seconds later they ran to one of the fallen men, the one wearing a dark suit. A police badge was attached to his belt. One officer had his gun drawn in the general direction from which the shot had come, while the other two pulled their fallen comrade out of harm's way.

Mike tried to get up, to offer some kind of assistance, but he couldn't. His legs were like Jell-O, his breathing had suddenly become erratic, and his heart was pounding so hard it threatened to pop out of his chest.

Not now.

· · · · · · · ·

Igor Votyakov fought the urge to engage the uniformed officers. The one with his gun drawn was an easy target and Igor figured the officer was aware of this. He offered himself as a target while his colleagues rendered support to the man his brother had shot.

Igor respected bravery. An officer within the GRU Spetsnaz— an elite military formation under the control of the Russian military intelligence—he understood the strong bond between men fighting or serving alongside each other. His finger moved away from the trigger.

"We're done here," he said, heart heavy, his brother's exploding skull carved into his mind. He had no doubt, no doubt whatsoever, that his brother's soul would visit him in his dreams for a long time to come. But there was no time to dwell on what he had just done. He pushed the horror of his act to a faraway corner of his mind, where he had put so many similar thoughts over the course of his illustrious career with the GRU.

The minivan moved. Denis turned right onto 2nd Avenue. "Where to?" he asked.

"There's a safe house in Newark." He gave Denis directions. "We'll debrief there."

Manhattan traffic notwithstanding, the eighteen-mile ride to the safe house was uneventful. Igor wasn't surprised. He was confident the police would treat what happened at Grand Central as a criminal act rather than a terrorist attack. And that made sense. Only a handful of people would know that this was a direct attack on the United State's security apparatus. He doubted the IMSI—an organization that didn't even belong to the government—would go public with this. Nobody knew who they were and Charles Mapother wasn't about to put this in jeopardy by helping the police. No, Igor thought, they'd get their friend DNI Richard Phillips to put a lid on this.

When the van turned into the safe house's driveway, Igor stowed the Dragunov back in its hard case. The safe house was a nondescript dwelling in an even more nondescript, blue-collar community where neighbors knew to mind their own business.

"Stay in the car," he instructed Denis as he slid a backpack over his shoulder. "I'll let you know when I want you to come in. I need to make a phone call. Understood?"

"Yes, sir," Denis replied.

. . . .

Igor punched the code to disarm the alarm. The house hadn't seen an occupant in weeks and it showed. A lawn contractor had been hired to do the maintenance around the house but the interior was in poor repair. A musty smell and dusty furniture was the price to pay when you wanted a safe house to remain secured in a hostile foreign country. Unlike most safe houses he had stayed at in recent years, this one didn't belong to any of the shell companies used by the Russian government. No, this one was part of his father's network.

Igor opened the fridge and grabbed a bottle of water. He drank half of it before setting it on the kitchen table. From his backpack he removed three different burn phones, a wireless audio receiver, two pairs of zip ties and a PSS silent pistol with two magazines. He loved the PSS. It was the perfect weapon for a silent, close-up kill. Before making his phone call, he needed to confirm his suspicions. He turned on the audio receiver and plugged in a pair of earphones.

. . . .

Inside the van Denis was struggling. He should have contacted his FBI handler the moment he'd received Moscow's instructions two days before. That was expected of him. That didn't make it easy. He still had regrets about how easily he had been turned, how his personal well-being had taken precedence over his mission and his country. He had not been trapped; he had crossed over to his country's enemies for money. For greed. And to feed his gambling addiction.

But there was something about this GRU operative that scared him shitless. He didn't know why, but the operative didn't trust him. Denis had worked with this type before. They were arrogant, sure of themselves and dangerous. *Does he know?* Had he waited too long to sound the alarm when the three cops showed up on 44th Street? That thought forced him into action and he made the call.

"Lucie's bakery."

"This is Tony Twardorsky," Denis said, his hand becoming moist. "I'd like to leave a message for Mr. Dubois."

"Go ahead," replied the voice at the other end.

"I'm calling you from my wife's phone. I have no idea where mine is," Denis said. "I was wondering if Mr. Dubois would be kind enough to search for it?"

"I'm sorry to hear that, Mr. Twardorsky. Is the matter urgent?"

"Kind of."

"I see. Do you remember the last time you saw your phone?"

"In Newark. At a friend's house."

"That is helpful. Thank you, Mr. Twardorsky. We'll put a rush on this."

"Please do," Denis replied. Beads of perspiration had formed on his upper lip.

. . . .

Igor Votyakov removed his earphones. He had heard enough. He looked at his watch and set the timer. He had less than ten minutes to get out of there. And there was much to do. He slipped the PSS in his coat pocket and walked out of the house. He signaled Denis to come in.

"Shouldn't we bring the rifle inside?" Denis asked.

"It's secured in its case and we won't be inside for long. There's something I want to show you," Igor replied, closing the door behind them.

"Sure."

"Kitchen's this way," Igor said.

As Denis walked past him, Igor slid his arm under his chin and pulled him close. Hard. So hard that, for an instant, Denis' feet actually left the ground. Igor didn't say anything. He simply started choking, counted to six in his head, and then slightly relaxed his hold.

"Do I have your attention?" he whispered in Denis's ear.

Denis nodded but nevertheless kicked back, the sole of his shoe connecting with Igor's tibia. Pain shot through Igor's lower leg. Enraged, Igor responded by flipping Denis around and delivering a powerful punch to his solar plexus, followed by a left hook that landed on his temple. Denis's knees buckled under him, but Igor wasn't through. He pulled Denis by the hair and forced him into one of the dining table chairs, where he used the zip ties to secure him.

"Who's Mr. Dubois?"

"Who?"

Igor punched Denis directly on the nose and felt the bones shatter on impact. The effect was so rewarding that he did it again. And again, and again, while visions of his dead brother flashed in his mind. He only stopped once Denis' face was a gruesome mess of flesh and blood. Igor drank the rest of his water then looked at Denis. His chest was still moving but his breathing had become erratic.

"I despise you," he spat. "I can't stand traitors. But you already knew that, yes?"

Without further ceremony, Igor removed the PSS from his pocket and put a bullet in Denis's forehead. He washed his hands in the kitchen sink and used a dishcloth to dry them off. He inserted a battery in one of the burn phones and punched in his father's number.

"What happened?" Igor's father said. "It's all over the news."

"Zakhar's dead."

There was a pause at the other end. "What about our target?" his father finally asked.

"I don't know."

Another pause. "Get out of there. I need you in Damascus."

"The Newark safe house is burned. You can't use it anymore."

"I see."

"Denis was a traitor. I dealt with him," Igor said, looking at the lifeless body of Denis.

"Then there's no time to waste, son," his father said. "I can't afford to lose you too. As I said, I need you in Damascus."

"I'll go." *Once I make sure Charles Mapother's dead.*

"Not tomorrow. Not when you're ready. Now," his father insisted.

When Igor didn't reply right away, his father added, "I know what you're thinking. We'll have another shot at him. Trust me."

"Okay."

Father or not, the Sheik wasn't someone you said no to twice.

CHAPTER 6

Biopreparat research facility, Koltsovo, Russia

Tired of the screams escaping from her test subjects, Dr. Lidiya Votyakov had unplugged the speakers from her computer weeks ago. But even without sound, she was mesmerized by the video feed coming through her computer screen.

Can this be it?

During her ten-year tenure as the head of the Biopreparat Koltsovo Facility, she'd never seen anything so fascinating. There could be no doubt; subject 131 was in agony. His body thrashed against the restraints used to keep him immobile on the iron bed. Subject 131 was different from the 130 before him. He was tougher, stronger, and, for a moment, Dr. Votyakov feared he would break free. An impossible task, really. Nobody escaped from this part of the complex. Even if he did break free of the steel braces locked tightly around his wrists and ankles, there was nowhere for him to go. In addition to the army regiment guarding the complex, former Spetsnaz troops, now working private security, patrolled the building and its surrounding neighborhoods to detect any suspicious activities.

At fifty-nine, Dr. Votyakov had been the head of the Biopreparat Koltsovo Facility for just over a decade. Cigarettes and stress had deepened the wrinkles around her eyes and her once bright blond hair was now a strange, yellowish color. But her mind remained sharp.

Most western intelligence agencies thought Biopreparat, the former Soviet Union's biological warfare agency responsible for the research and the production of pathogenic weapons, had been officially closed in the mid nineties. They were right, *officially*. But like everything else in Russia, things weren't always as they appeared. A skeleton crew, a fraction of the fifty thousand former employees of Biopreparat, had remained employed and had continued to look for the perfect bio-weapon. And one month ago, Dr. Lidiya Votyakov had found it. Or so she thought.

"The incubation period of the virus is exactly the length we've been hoping for," Dr. Yegor Galkin said, standing behind her and looking at the same video feed. Wearing his glasses low on his nose, he nervously pushed them back higher with his index finger. Older than Votyakov by at least a decade, Galkin was one of the few remaining scientists who'd been with Biopreparat since the glory days of the late seventies.

"I know," Votyakov replied.

"Congratulations, Doctor," Galkin said. "You did it."

"We're not done, yet, Dr. Galkin. We'll need to confirm our results with subjects 132 and 133."

"Of course, Doctor Votyakov, but I don't foresee a different outcome."

Votyakov allowed herself a rare smile. Blood was now pouring from subject 131's nose and ears at an alarming rate. She didn't enjoy seeing other humans suffer. She wasn't a sadistic person but, as a scientist, she appreciated what she had accomplished.

"How long do you think he has?" she asked.

"Hard to say." Galkin scratched his head. "Less than ten hours, I'd say."

Votyakov closed her eyes. *Finally.*

"I've been summoned to the Kremlin two days from now," Votyakov said, standing up. "And, for once, I'll be the bearer of good news."

CHAPTER 7

IMSI Headquarters, New York.

Mike Walton had spent the last twenty minutes on the phone briefing Charles Mapother on what happened on East 44th Street. He left out the part where he hadn't been able to get up to render assistance to the NYPD officers. At the end of the call, Mapother had requested his presence at IMSI headquarters. News regarding Sam Turner's condition wasn't good. He was still in surgery.

Mike drove his Volvo S80 right up to the ten-foot-high chain-link fence that surrounded IMSI headquarters at the Brooklyn Navy Yard. A few seconds later, a double gate opened and Mike slowly drove forward. Beyond the gate were dozens of concrete wall panels that had been aligned on each side of the road, forcing any vehicles entering the premises to follow a single, preapproved route that led to another gate—this one made of steel—and a security checkpoint.

A man in a dark security guard's uniform and sporting an MP5 approached the vehicle. Mike lowered his window.

"Good evening, Mr. Walton."

"Good evening," Mike replied, his eyes moving to the passenger-side window where another security guard was peeking inside his vehicle with a flashlight. Another guard, this one holding a German Shepherd on a short leash, had taken position behind the vehicle.

"Open the trunk, would you?" the guard asked.

Mike obliged. With word of the attempt on the director's life, the guards were understandably on edge. Once satisfied Mike wasn't carrying anyone in his trunk, the guard signaled someone inside the guard hut. The steel gate rose slowly and Mike moved forward. Just beyond the gate stood a medium-sized concrete building with no windows. Multiple antennas of difference sizes could be seen on its rooftop. Mike maneuvered the Volvo down a ramp leading to the only entrance of the building, a large, solid, double-garage door. He parked in his assigned space and walked to a steel door with no handle. He swiped his ID card in a small black electronic keypad and entered his seven-digit code. The door opened with a soft click and Mike started down the long, marble-floored hallway. He passed many abutting hallways, each lined with a series of black doors— none of them had knobs or handles, just keypads—and continued until he reached a large brown door. He once again entered his seven-digit code and the door opened, revealing a spacious conference room.

Already seated around the large table were IMSI director Charles Mapother, IMSI second-in-command Jonathan Sanchez, IMSI asset Zima Bernbaum and the IMSI's chief analyst—an attractive, black-haired woman in her thirties named Anna Caprini.

"Any developments for Sam?" Mike asked, holding his breath.

"Nothing," Mapother replied with steel in his voice. "As you know, he was hit three times. The first two rounds lodged in his gut while the third shattered his femur. Lots of blood loss. It's complicated."

Mike sighed. Gut wounds were the most painful, but often enough weren't fatal. Sam Turner had a chance.

"Lisa's with him, Mike," Sanchez said.

"Why aren't we all?" Mike asked. "What are we doing here? We—"

"Don't you think I know that, Mike?" Mapother roared. "You think it makes me happy to be here while he's under the knife?"

Mike was taken aback. He'd never heard Mapother raise his voice before. Before he could muster a reply, Mapother continued in a more reasonable tone, "I owe Sam my life. Without him, I would be the one with three holes in me."

"Sir—"

"Don't 'sir' me, Mike," Mapother said. "We all feel the same, but we need to move on. The existence of this organization might depend on what we do next."

"What do you mean?"

Mapother turned to Sanchez. "Would you mind explaining to Mike what we've been through?"

"We believe the IMSI may have lost part of its cover," Sanchez said. "The good news is that we're confident the leak didn't come from within the Institute."

Mike certainly hoped so. He knew Charles Mapother had handpicked all the employees because of their excellence in their respective fields and their loyalty to their country. All of them, without exception, were former law enforcement officers or military personnel.

"That's only true if you don't consider Steve Shamrock part of the IMSI," Mike said.

"He was never one of us," Mapother said. "He helped finance the whole thing but he had no access to the intelligence we collected or the operations we conducted. Only the president has unlimited access."

"But did Shamrock know who you are?" Zima asked.

"He did. He and the other two financiers recruited me to head the IMSI," Mapother answered. "But the only people outside this organization who know of our existence are Director of National Intelligence Richard Phillips and the president. That's it."

"May I continue?" Sanchez asked.

Mapother signaled that he could.

"We have no idea for sure how deep the penetration is inside the IMSI. Having said that, Anna and Jonathan are confident they were only able to scratch the surface."

"Why are you so sure?" Mike asked, pouring himself a glass of water from the carafe.

"Our cover goes pretty deep," Sanchez answered. "As you know, the IMSI does extensive foreign-market analyses for real clients. It has good revenue and pays its taxes on time. If the opposition had anything substantial against us, Anna and I believe this information would have been leaked to the media."

Mike pondered what his friend had said. It made sense. The IMSI's cover was everything. Especially when it came to the identity of its assets in the field. That thought brought him to his next question. "What happened at the Grand Central? Who's in charge of the situation?"

"Homeland Security took over the NYPD investigation, including the murder of one of their own."

"Really? I'm surprised the NYPD agreed to this. That's their jurisdiction," Mike said. As a former cop he knew how bitter turf wars could be.

"DNI Phillips can be persuasive when he wants to be," replied Mapother. "And you should know the Homeland team is actually a joint taskforce that includes more than one detective from the NYPD."

"I guess that softened the blow," Mike said.

Mapother's phone started vibrating on the table. He picked up. Nobody spoke while Mapother listened. "Thank you, Lisa," he said after a few seconds.

Mapother pinched his nose and Mike realized he'd been holding his breath for the last half minute. When the IMSI director looked up, his eyes were tearing up.

"Sam Turner didn't make it. He died on the operating table." With that said, and without another word, Charles Mapother walked out of the conference room.

CHAPTER 8

The Walton's Penthouse, Brooklyn, NY

Mike studied the instruction manual for the espresso machine Lisa had bought the week before. They'd both been so busy the last few days that the coffee machine had remained packed in its box until tonight.

"Just put milk in the plastic container, plug in the machine, and press the damn button, Mike," his wife said from the comfort of their living room. "It shouldn't be too complicated."

"You forgot the capsule, Lisa," Mike replied. "Without the capsule, there's no coffee."

They'd bought the penthouse three weeks after he'd been discharged from the Johns Hopkins Hospital following the Ottawa terror attacks. Financially speaking, the purchase made sense. In the last year or so, the value had gone up more than five percent. But what Mike loved the most about their place was the fact that they were close to IMSI headquarters. A short commute to work was one of the secret keys to happiness.

Mike made three cappuccinos and sprinkled cinnamon on top of Lisa's frothed milk. His wife accepted the hot beverage with a smile. Zima, who was seated next to her on the love seat, nodded her thanks.

"Gratitude, honey," Lisa said, taking the cup with her two hands. She took a careful sip and nodded appreciatively. "Perfect."

Mike sat in front of them in one of the armchairs. The floor-to-ceiling windows afforded them a beautiful view of the Manhattan skyline. Being on the top floor definitely had its advantages.

"I can't stop thinking about Sam," Lisa said, placing her cappuccino on the coffee table.

"Were you with him when he passed?" Zima asked.

Lisa shook her head and then said, "He was in so much pain."

"You did what you could, baby," Mike said. "You ran to him and pulled him to safety."

"So did Charles."

"Yeah, he did."

Mike closed his eyes as he relived in his mind what had happened earlier in the day. The attempt on Charles Mapother's life had been well-orchestrated, with many fail-safes. But they had failed, somehow. Or had they?

Once Mapother had walked out of the conference room, Jonathan Sanchez had continued with his briefing. Sam Turner's killer was an ex-con named Louis Wall, a former soldier who'd spent the last twelve years behind bars. At first, the IMSI hadn't found anything to link him to Mapother. Digging a little deeper, Sanchez, with the help of Anna Caprini, did manage to establish a possible motive. During his time in the FBI, Mapother had shot and killed Wall's brother during a drug raid. So it was possible that Wall had taken upon himself to kill Mapother as retribution for his brother's death. But this line of thought didn't hold, not after Wall was finished off by another shooter who was then himself killed by a sniper. The IMSI was now operating under the assumption that the attack at the Grand Central Terminal had been planned and ordered by an outside organization with powerful means.

"Could it be the Sheik?" Mike asked out loud.

"I'm sure it crossed Mapother's mind," Zima replied.

"It's the only thing that makes any sense," Lisa said. "Who else would know about Mapother?"

"So this is revenge for the damage we've done to his organization?" Mike asked, convinced this was the case.

"I'm sure the fact that you guys killed the son of his trusted mole played a role too," Zima added.

"So what's next?" Lisa drank the last of her cappuccino. "Are we gonna go after this bastard or what?"

Mike appreciated his wife's enthusiasm but he knew Mapother wouldn't send them on a wild-goose chase. "I know we will, honey. Charles will let us know when."

"I'm ready," Lisa said. She stood and made a move toward the kitchen. "Anyone want something stronger than coffee?"

"Not for me," Zima replied. "It's been a long day and I'm dead tired. I'm heading home."

Mike escorted Zima to the door. "Any news regarding your dad?" she asked.

"With everything that happened today, there was no time. Jonathan sent me an email, though. He said Mapother wants to meet with me tomorrow morning."

"Okay, then," Zima said. "Fingers crossed for good news." She gave him a hug.

"See you in the morning," Mike said.

"Yeah, see you."

With Zima gone, Mike joined Lisa. She poured two glasses of Pinot Noir and offered one to Mike. "To what are we drinking?" he asked.

"Not to what, but to who," his wife replied. "To Sam Turner."

Yes, to Sam.

. . . .

Lisa Walton emptied what was left of the bottle into Mike's empty glass. It had been a while since she had drunk so much wine in so little time and she was feeling the buzz. A pleasant one. It reminded her of the long evenings she and Mike had passed together entangled in each other's arms watching television or reading their favorite authors, while drinking a whole bottle of wine, sometimes two. She missed that time. A time before tragedy decimated her family, when all the dreams she shared with Mike were still alive. When everything was possible.

But that world, that bubble of theirs, had shattered when the Sheik had killed almost everyone she had ever loved. Only Mike remained.

She looked at him, lying in their bed, his shirt unbuttoned and out of his jeans. His eyes were on her. Devouring her. She became aware of how she looked in her nightgown. She felt her nipples grow harder against the soft satin fabric. Her heartbeat accelerated and she wondered what he was thinking. A quick look at the bulge in his shorts told her everything she needed to know. At thirty-nine, he was still hot, and she wanted him. Badly. Now. She desperately wanted to feel him against her bare skin. She slipped the strings of her gown off her shoulders, exposing herself to him.

He bit his lip.

. . . .

His wife never ceased to amaze him. She was, at least to him, the most beautiful woman in the world. They had gone through so much together, shared experiences that had tested their relationship to its limit, but they had survived. Just when the elastic was about to snap, it had pulled them back together. Now they were one, at home and at work, the bond between them stronger than ever. Their common loss, and now their common objective, had transformed their love into a sanctuary that had grown into a sacred sense of intimate unity.

Aroused by the softness of her lips on his neck, he let himself relax as she freed him from his Andrew Christian underwear. A moment later, she was on top of him, her hair cascading around his face. She pressed her breast to his chest, her hips to his, and her lips to his ear.

"I want you," she whispered, her voice dark and raspy.

He kissed his wife fiercely, his own desire taking over. He rolled Lisa onto her back. Passion filled her eyes. He sensed her hand behind his neck, pulling him closer. They kissed again, softly, then more ardently. He let his tongue run the contour of her neck. He felt her quiver. He gently turned her around so her back faced him. He kissed the back of her neck and made his way slowly—oh so slowly—down her spine to the hollow of her back. Lisa was shaking now. She gasped as he entered her. His hands reached for hers. Fingers entwined, they made love with total abandon.

CHAPTER 9

IMSI Headquarters, Brooklyn, NY.

Mike Walton entered Mapother's office right on time at seven o'clock. Following the frolics of the previous night, he had slept like a baby. Well rested, Mike hoped Mapother had called him in to talk about his father. He was only half right.

"You look energized, Mike," Mapother said for greeting.

"I am. Six hours of undisrupted sleep will do that to you, Charles. You should try it sometimes."

"I will. One day." Mapother walked to his percolator. "Coffee?"

"Please." Mike looked around Mapother's office. By no means large, Mapother's work place felt comfortable. Mapother had recently had his office repainted and the previously light-gray walls were now navy blue. The furniture hadn't changed and the one-way mirror showing the control room—the IMSI's nerve center where the analysts worked—had now been covered by a privacy screen.

As usual, the coffee served in Mapother's office was piping hot.

"Let's start with your father," Mapother said, sitting behind his desk.

Mike took a deep breath. *Here we go.*

"Richard Phillips confirmed the Syrian government has your father."

"Where did he get the info this time?" Mike asked. Four months ago, the IMSI had received intelligence regarding his father's whereabouts, but nothing had panned out. His father was nowhere to be found.

"From the Canadians," Mapother replied. "They were contacted through some obscure back channels they've been keeping with the Syrians."

It wasn't easy to understand the politics surrounding the Syrian conflict. Mike even wondered if the Syrian president knew if ISIS was on his side or not. It seemed that everyone with a stake in Middle Eastern geopolitics had declared that ISIS had to be defeated, but nobody agreed on the best way to achieve it. Saudi Arabia had made it clear that ISIS couldn't be defeated unless the current Syrian president was removed from power. Israel, an ally of both the United States and Canada, saw only one way to defeat ISIS: through the destruction of Iran's nuclear program. And Turkey swore that their Kurdish opponents needed to be neutralized first.

With all this shit going on, I'm not surprised the Canadians kept a back door open with the Syrians.

"And they're ready to release him?"

Mapother shrugged. "You know as well as I do it's impossible to understand the reasoning behind any decisions the Syrians make. But yes, at least for now, they seem to be willing to release him."

"Any idea where they kept my father for the last month? Or why the exchange didn't go as planned the last time around?"

"Your guess is as good as mine, Mike."

"When am I leaving?"

"You're not going to Syria—"

"Why the hell not?" Mike asked. What was Mapother thinking?

"Zima's going. You and Lisa are needed somewhere else."

Mike took a deep breath and forced himself to control his anger. "She's going to Syria by herself?"

Mapother nodded. "She left early this morning."

Mike wondered if Zima had known she was about to be deployed to Syria when she was at their place yesterday night. He hoped not. Because if she did, that meant she had flat out lied to him and Lisa. And that wouldn't pass. Mapother knew how important it was for him to go after his father. After the close call they'd had a few months back, this was the biggest lead they'd received about his father's whereabouts. Still, without Mapother's support, there wasn't much he could do.

Mapother must have seen he was worried because he added, "The Canadians are in charge of the operation. Zima's only objectives are to observe the exchange and try to collect as much intel as she can about your father's captors."

43

Mike shook his head. "I'm the one who should go. Not her."

"As I said, you and Lisa are needed somewhere else."

"What could be more important, Charles?"

"Russia."

Russia?

"What does Russia have to do with my dad?"

"As far as we know, nothing at all," Mapother replied.

"All right. Is that supposed to make any sense to me?" Mike asked.

"It will soon enough," Mapother replied, before taking a sip from his cup. "Twenty-four hours ago, the FBI received a message from a long-forgotten source they had inside Russia in the eighties," Mapother said.

The FBI wasn't known to share its contacts or intelligence sources so Mike wondered how Mapother knew this.

"The source is a seventy-year-old Russian scientist named Dr. Yegor Galkin," continued Mapother, reading from another file on his desk. "He started working for Biopreparat, the former Soviet Union's biological warfare agency, in the mid seventies. Smart and ambitious, he quickly rose to the rank of major and was put in charge of a team of scientists tasked with weaponizing one of the most infectious diseases known to man, smallpox."

"When was that exactly?" Mike asked.

"In the eighties."

"Right after the World Health Organization declared smallpox eradicated," Mike said.

"Exactly," Mapother said. "Although we knew Russia kept a small amount of the disease in the Ivanovsky Institute of Virology in Moscow to match our own legal repository of the strain here in the US, we had no idea that only a half-hour drive away from Moscow, in the famous Russian cathedral city of Zagorsk, they were cultivating tons of smallpox in a secret lab."

Mike didn't know much about this particular subject and he was fascinated. "I guess we did learn about it somehow."

"Yes, we did," answered Mapother. "By Dr. Yegor Galkin himself."

"Really? How?"

"I turned him."

"You what?"

"I recruited him during one of his visits to Berlin," Mapother said.

Mike could see that Mapother was clearly enjoying himself as he remembered this particular story from his past.

"In the name of scientific research, trafficking in germs and viruses was legal then, as it is still today. Russia was known to send KGB agents to scientific fairs to purchase strains from universities laboratories and biotech firms."

"Just like that? Russia bought viruses on the open market? That's insane," Mike said.

Mapother raised his hands. "Don't be so naïve, Mike," he said. "We were doing the same damn thing. Everybody was doing it. I'll give you this, though: the Russians pushed it to another level. In fact, representatives of the Soviet scientific and trade organizations based in Africa, Asia and Europe were asked to look for new and unusual diseases."

"It's hard to believe they did so with such impunity," Mike said.

Mapother shrugged and continued. "For example, it was actually from the United States that Russian agents picked up Machupo, the virus that causes Bolivian hemorrhagic fever. And it was in Germany that they got their hands on the Marburg virus—"

"I know about this one," interrupted Mike. "A Ugandan health worked died of Marburg hemorrhagic fever in 2014."

"Correct," Mapother said.

"It's also a category A bioterrorism agent," Mike said, now on the edge of his seat. "And there's no cure that we know of."

"That's one more reason why the Russians wanted to weaponize the virus," Mapother said.

"Were they ever successful?"

"Yes, they were. Dr. Galkin's team quietly added the Marburg virus to the Soviet arsenal in the mid eighties."

"And how did we learn about it? From him directly?" Mike asked.

"You've heard about Chinese and Russian agents using honey traps to trick our diplomats or firm executives into working for them?"

"Of course, Charles," Mike replied. "This technique is still being used, I believe."

"You're right, and we used it too," Mapother said. "That's how I caught Dr. Galkin in Berlin."

Interesting, thought Mike. *Everyone at the IMSI knows Charles Mapother was a former FBI agent but not much else. Am I about to discover what he really did with them?*

"But that's a story for another time," Mapother said after a moment of silence.

I guess I won't.

"What's important for you to know is that a friend of mine at the FBI called me to let me know Dr. Galkin tried to contact me yesterday."

"How?" Mike asked. "What did he want?"

"Patience, Mike," replied Mapother, "I'll get there in a minute."

Mike waited while Mapother walked to his espresso machine. "You want one?" he offered.

"I'm good, thanks. Two cups are enough for me." Like most mornings, he had stopped by a Starbucks drive-through on his way to the office and ordered a Venti vanilla latte which he drank in his car before arriving at IMSI headquarters. If Lisa were to ask, he'd say he had a tall skinny vanilla latte. She'd been giving him hell recently about his extra calorie intake.

I gained a kilo. That's not the end of the world.

Even though they worked at the same place, Mike and Lisa did the twenty-minute drive from their Brooklyn penthouse to IMSI headquarters separately. They worked similar hours but they preferred using different cars in case one of them was deployed without warning.

Mike watched Mapother add two sugar packs into his tiny espresso cup.

"Maybe I should tell my wife you're a sugar addict, Charles," Mike said. "See what she'll have to say about that."

"Is she on your case because you've gained weight?" Mapother countered, looking Mike directly in the eyes while stirring his espresso with a small silver spoon.

"Will you guys give me a break?" Mike said, his temper flaring. "I gained a kilo, Charles. One kilo!"

Mapother carefully wiped his spoon clean of any remnant of coffee before setting it next to his espresso. "When was the last time you went for a run, Mike?" he asked.

Caught by surprise, Mike had to think before replying. "It's been a few days," he admitted.

"More like a couple weeks, wouldn't you say?" Mapother said.

"Did Lisa tell you this?" Mike asked. *What the hell was she thinking?*

"She had nothing to do with this," Mapother replied in a severe tone. "It's my job to know if my assets are deployment-ready or not."

"I'm ready," Mike said.

"Are you?"

"What the hell is going on here?" Mike asked. Whatever game Mapother was playing, he didn't like it. "Have I done something wrong? Didn't I prove myself yesterday?"

"You haven't done anything wrong, Mike," Mapother replied. "But you're not the same since you came back from Spain four months ago. And I can't stop wondering if I didn't ask too much too soon from you."

Mike sighed. A year and a half ago, his two-year-old daughter Melissa and his mother were murdered by a suicide bomber at the Ottawa train station. His wife Lisa had been spared but she'd lost the unborn child she was carrying. Her mom and dad had also been butchered in the same terrorist attack. Mike and his former RCMP partner Paul Robichaud had thwarted a simultaneous attack at the Ottawa international airport. Paul had lost his life while Mike, critically injured, had barely escaped with his. It was then that Charles Mapother had approached him, promising vengeance and justice. With Lisa already on board, Mike accepted Charles's offer and joined the IMSI. Unconvinced that his wife was made for this line of work, Mike had fought both Lisa and Mapother against her becoming an asset, or field operator. In the end, conscious that the eight weeks of training ahead of them would most certainly temper her enthusiasm, he'd acquiesced.

What came next had startled Mike like nothing before. After only a couple weeks of training, it became obvious that his wife, the most caring and loving person he'd ever known, was a natural-born killer. Not only did she successfully pass all the challenges and training scenarios thrown at her, she also managed to impress the cadre of instructors.

Be that as it may, tragedy hit again a few days after the end of their training. Lisa, on their first mission together, was stabbed twice while fighting a suicide bomber at the Nice international airport. While she was recuperating from her wounds, Mike was sent to Antibes to follow up on a lead. Embedded with a French special operations team from the GIGN, Mike had witnessed the merciless killings of a number of French law-enforcement officers, including their commanding officer, by terrorists belonging to the Sheik's network. Mike had no choice but to take command of the GIGN team and pushed through with the assault. What the surviving members of the assault force found in the dwelling occupied by the terrorists had stunned them all: a small tactical nuclear device only seconds away from being detonated in the heart of the French Riviera.

Upon his return to New York City, Mike had reconnected with his wife and had made peace with the fact that Lisa was now a fully fledged IMSI asset. He took comfort knowing that she'd be with him most of the time and that she'd been trained by the best. Unfortunately, as hard as it was to admit, all this had taken a hard swing at his psyche. He started having sporadic panic attacks. At first they were mild, but following the fiasco in Spain, the severity of his attacks had spiked.

No way I'm admitting this to Mapother. He'll pull me out of active duty and send Lisa in the field by herself.

Mike's mind wandered to Benalmadena, Spain, where he had led an ad hoc team of three on a raid on the Sheik's yacht. Thinking that his father, who'd been kidnapped by the Sheik two years prior, was on the yacht, Mike had rushed the assault and Jasmine Carson, an IMSI support team member, was killed in the process. Although the team had killed two of the most sought-after terrorists, neither the Sheik nor Mike's father had been on the yacht at the time. And, to make matters worse, a lead the IMSI had received about his father's whereabouts only a few days after the raid in Benalmadena had run cold.

Mapother's voice brought Mike back to reality. "I know you're blaming yourself for Jasmine's death," he said. "I've read your after-action report."

Just the mention of Jasmine Carson sent his heart into palpitations. "I'm not looking for your sympathy, Charles," Mike said, louder than he intended. "I know what I've done. I'm mission-ready for Christ's sake!"

For a moment, the IMSI director remained silent and Mike feared he had crossed the line.

"All right," Mapother said, playing with his espresso cup. "Back to Dr. Galkin, then."

Mike, glad to change the subject, breathed a sigh of relief.

"You were saying that a friend of yours at the FBI contacted you," Mike offered.

"Right," Mapother said. "What you have to understand here, Mike, is that I've always believed that Dr. Galkin knew what he was getting into when he fell for the honey trap."

Mike chuckled. "Yeah, I guess he did."

Mapother offered a smile. "That didn't sound right, did it?" he said, before continuing. "What I meant was that even though he displayed all the outrage and denial expected from someone caught in this kind of scheme, there was something that didn't feel right."

"Like what?" Mike asked.

"It felt like . . ." Mapother hesitated. "It felt as if it was all part of a show."

"You think he wanted to deceive you? That maybe his mission was to give you bad intelligence?" Mike said.

Mapother drained the rest of his espresso and carefully replaced his silver spoon in his cup, and the cup in the saucer, before continuing, "At the beginning, that's what I thought. But not for long. It turned out that Dr. Galkin was the real deal and not a big fan of the Communist party. He might have been one of the privileged individuals of a totalitarian regime, but his sister wasn't, and when the same government he was working for sent her to prison for an article she wrote on the lack of funding in education, he became disillusioned."

"I get it," Mike said. "His original behavior was so as not to make you suspicious. He didn't want you to think he was a spy sent to give you disinformation."

"Exactly," Mapother said. "Dr. Galkin is a scientist, and a damn good one. But he isn't a spy. He didn't know how to approach us. He did it the only way he knew how."

"By tasting the honey trap," Mike said, suppressing a smile.

"The last time I spoke to Dr. Galkin, some twenty-five years ago, he told me that cheating on his wife had been the most difficult thing he had ever done."

Mike nodded that he understood before asking, "You didn't talk to him for twenty-five years?"

"Dr. Galkin saw that the Soviet Union was about to collapse. Paranoia was running high everywhere and he didn't want to take unnecessary risks."

"I see," Mike said, unconvinced. "What did he want with you after so many years?"

"He had information he wanted to share with me. Information so mindboggling that he couldn't trust it with anyone he didn't know."

"I'm all ears, Charles," Mike said.

Mapother reached inside his jacket and pulled out a piece of paper folded in two. He handed it to Mike. "Read this."

Mike did. "That can't be true," he said, his eyes moving from the note back to Mapother. "How do you know he isn't dead? How do you know it's him?"

"I don't, Mike," Mapother said. "That's why you and Lisa are going to Russia. And here's how we're gonna do this . . ."

CHAPTER 10

Moscow, Russia

D r. Lidiya Votyakov saw Victor, the FSB agent assigned to her during her visits to Moscow, waiting by the luggage carrousel. Bald headed and six feet four inches tall, he was hard to miss. She smiled at him but he simply nodded back. Victor was a man of few words and he didn't offer to carry her suitcase. He led her to a black Mercedes S-Class idling at the curb. Moments before they reached the vehicle, Votyakov felt one of Victor's powerful hands on her right shoulder as he placed himself between her and a middle-aged lady who had just gone flying in the air after slipping on a patch of ice. Votyakov heard the woman grunt as she fell on the cold pavement. Before she could render assistance, Victor opened the back door of the Mercedes and shoved her in. *Poor lady. I hope she didn't break a bone.*

In sharp contrast to the crisp, chilly Moscow air, the interior of the Mercedes was like a sauna. "Would you mind turning the heater down a little?" she asked.

"My apologies, Dr. Votyakov," the driver said as Victor settled into the passenger seat seconds later. "It's not functioning properly, I'm afraid. We'll get that fixed right after we drop you at the Kremlin."

"Please do. This is unbearable."

The driver activated the blue emergency lights of the Mercedes and merged into the exit ramp, cutting off a taxi in the process.

It was Votyakov's fourth trip to Moscow in so many months and she could barely contain her excitement. She'd been given six months, and an unlimited budget, to create the perfect biological agent.

And I did it in four.

What she had created wasn't pretty. It wouldn't cure cancer and it wouldn't make the world a better place. *Quite the contrary.*

Nevertheless, Votyakov was proud of what she had accomplished. If used properly, her discovery would bring back the balance of power between Russia and the West. Like most scientists, she had dreamed about making research contributions that would help develop gene therapy cures for people infected with HIV or different types of cancer. But that wasn't to be the case. And she didn't mind one bit.

With my help, Russia will be great again.

CHAPTER 11

Moscow, Russia

Luc Walker strolled casually to the end of the line. In front of him were a dozen people waiting for a taxi. Like most of them, Walker was heavily dressed. Wearing a scarf covering half his face and a tuque low on his forehead didn't seem inappropriate in this inclement weather. Only his nose and eyes were visible. A picture taken from the right angle and run through a biometric program could identify him, but he wasn't worried. A Google search on Luc Walker would bring up many articles about how efficient he was at brokering deals between his wealthy North American clients and Russian vodka makers. A sharper than normal Russian customs officer, who called to verify his story with vodka producers, would be told that Walker was the real deal and a man with much influence in some close circles, both in Moscow and New York. What Google wouldn't say, though, was that courtesy of a tip provided by a covert organization named the International Market Stabilization Institute, Luc Walker had been arrested three days ago in San Francisco for tax evasion as he was boarding a plane to The Bahamas. The backstop identity wouldn't be enough to sustain a thorough investigation, like the one the Russian police do when they arrest a foreigner, but Mike Walton wasn't planning on getting arrested.

· · · · · · · ·

The window of opportunity was so small that anything from bad weather to a mechanical problem with any of their flights could have caused the mission to fail before it had even begun. Prior to embarking on their first flight, Mike and Lisa had spent a full day preparing for their assignment. Neither of them spoke Russian fluently, but if everything went according to plan, they wouldn't need to.

"Got her," mumbled Mike into the small mic attached to his collar. The encrypted radio they used to communicate with each other was voice activated so there was no need to press a button in order to transmit. "She has a bodyguard. Tall man with a black coat. He's a few feet behind her." Mike angled his body toward the Russian doctor and her escort. The miniature camera installed in lieu of one of his parka's buttons provided a video feed that was instantly broadcast to the control room of IMSI headquarters in New York.

"It has to be Dr. Votyakov," Charles Mapother said from New York. Because of the encryption used, Mapother's voice sounded robotic in Mike's earpiece. "So far, Dr. Galkin's words have held true."

"She's heading toward a black Mercedes parked at the curb," Mike said, scanning his surroundings.

"I see her," Lisa said. "I'm twenty seconds away."

"There's no way you'll be able to plant the device on the target, Lisa," Mike said. "Don't risk it. Abort."

"I'll be fine, Mike. Trust me."

Mike's eyes stopped on an older lady pulling her carry-on behind her. She was walking slowly in the direction of the Mercedes.

"Ten seconds," Lisa's voice announced.

Mike knew his wife was committed. There was no turning back now. His hand moved to the inside pocket of his parka where his Smith & Wesson M&P Shield was concealed.

C'mon, Lisa. We have only one shot at this.

As if she had slipped on a patch of ice, the old lady tumbled to the ground next to the Mercedes. The Russian giant walking next to Dr. Votyakov reacted instantly and placed himself between the fallen lady and his charge. Mike's heart skipped a beat when he realized the old lady wasn't getting up. With the cold butt of his compact pistol in the palm of his hand, Mike took a few steps toward the fallen woman.

Seconds later, once Dr. Votyakov had been safely hurried into the waiting car, the Russian bodyguard approached the old lady and offered his hand. With what seemed to be a lot of pain, the old lady slowly got back to her feet. She thanked the tall Russian in his language before picking up her carry-on and continuing on her way.

Mike relaxed and his hand came out of his parka.

"You're okay, Lisa? You fell hard."

"I'm fine, Mike."

"Don't worry about the tracker, we'll find another way," Mike said, already walking to their car, which was parked in the short-term parking garage. In fact, he had no idea what to do next.

"The device is on the bodyguard's coat. We're good."

Well done, baby. Well done.

CHAPTER 12

The Kremlin, Russia

D r. Lidiya Votyakov looked out the window of the Mercedes. A blast of polar air had gripped Moscow, forcing people to pull their hoods and scarves tight in an effort to protect exposed skin from nearly instant frostbite. The snow made the road slippery and Votyakov was glad she wasn't driving in these conditions. Due to a major collision involving a school bus, the usual sixty-minute drive from the Domodedovo International Airport to Moscow had turned into a three-hour ordeal.

"You're going directly to the Kremlin, Dr. Votyakov," Victor said from the passenger seat. "We don't have the time to stop by the hotel."

He didn't need to explain further. They were late, and the Russian president wasn't the type of man you kept waiting. Votyakov reached for her purse and the emergency makeup kit she kept for exactly these kinds of situations. Her heart fluttered at the sight of her reflection. She angled the mirror differently but the result was the same; the last four months hadn't been kind to her. She did the best she could with what she had, but the makeup couldn't hide that she'd be sixty in a few months. She snapped shut the pocket mirror and put it back in her purse with a sigh.

I was pretty, once.

The traffic had once again moved to a crawl and Votyakov could see that Victor was becoming more agitated.

"Not your fault if the traffic is backed up, Victor," she said.

Victor grunted a reply she didn't understand.

Four months ago, she'd been beckoned to the Kremlin for the first time. A major general from the Ministry of Defense had called her at home and requested her presence in Moscow. Even though she didn't answer to him, or to anyone else in the military for that matter, she needed to keep a good working relationship between Biopreparat and the Ministry of Defense. The next morning, a young army captain had picked her up from her office in Koltsovo and driven her to the airport. Waiting for her in Moscow was Victor the Giant. He'd been polite, as he was now, but not much of a talker. Not knowing why she'd been called to Moscow, she'd tried to prod some information out of him. Victor had simply kept his mouth shut, not even acknowledging her questions. Not used to this sort of treatment, she'd raised her voice. When that failed too, she had told him she would complain to his superior officer. That had made him and the driver laugh.

"You'll complain to Veniamin Simonich?"

"Your superior officer is the Russian president?" she had asked incredulously.

"Da."

Not sure if he was pulling her leg or not, she'd stopped bitching. She didn't want to piss off the most powerful man in Russia, let alone someone who could shut off her funding.

. . . .

The black Mercedes pulled up in front of the Kremlin Grand Palace twenty minutes later. Exiting the Mercedes, she took a moment to look at the sky. White snowflakes cascaded from above and melted on her exposed cheeks as she took in a few deep breaths. The cold air entered her lungs and she felt instantly revitalized. She followed Victor up the stairs and into the palace. It might have been her fourth time at the palace but she gasped nonetheless. With its one hundred-and-twenty-five-meter façade, decorated with carved white stones, it was simply grand. Formerly the tsar's Moscow residence, the Kremlin Grand Palace had been built to emphasize the greatness of Russian autocracy.

Who would have thought a peasant girl, born in an obscure part of Russia, would have reached the highest echelon of her country's scientific circles? Dad would be proud of me.

Her father, a sailor in the Russian Navy, often deployed at sea for months at a time, had missed most of her birthdays and school plays. Still, he had loved her in his own way; and her mother, a marine biologist, had made sure that school had remained her number one priority. After graduating from the Moscow State University with a degree in biology, she'd joined Biopreparat as a junior biologist. A quick intellect and a sense of self-preservation had seen to her selection to graduate studies. After a masters in biochemistry and a doctorate in virology, she'd returned to Biopreparat as a fully fledged scientist. From there, her ascent to the pinnacle of the Russian scientific field had come easily. Her sons, Igor and Zakhar, born from a short but passionate relationship with the son of a powerful sheik from the Emirates, were the only family members she had left. Not that she saw them much.

Security inside the Kremlin Grand Palace consisted of heavily armed men in black uniforms with a variety of high-tech security measures similar to those found in an international airport.

Victor bypassed security but she had to go through a metal detector and a biometric retina control while her shoes and purse went through an X-ray machine. After a final quick but comprehensive hand search, she was let through. Grabbing her purse and low-heeled shoes from a gray bin, she walked to Victor who stood next to the waiting elevator that would take her to the third floor where Veniamin Simonich's office was located.

"You've done well, Dr. Votyakov," Victor said as she walked past him and into the elevator.

Surprised by the sudden burst of vocabulary gymnastics displayed by Victor, Votyakov turned to look at him before asking, "What do you know of my work, Victor?"

"Enough," he replied, pressing the third-floor button. Votyakov didn't push the issue. Tasked with creating the ultimate bioweapon, Votyakov's research and lab results were known to only a handful of men. If Victor knew, he was much more than a simple bodyguard. He had the ears, or the confidence, of Veniamin Simonich. Something she could maybe use at a later date. Victor led the way out of the elevator and nodded to the two plainclothes agents from the Presidential Security Service standing next to the door leading to Simonich's office.

"I'll wait for you here," Victor said.

She knocked on the heavy wooden door and waited. A few second later, another plainclothes agent opened the door from the inside and let her in.

"Please have a seat, Dr. Votyakov," he said, pointing to a red leather sofa positioned against the wall. "The president will be with you shortly."

"Thank you," she replied, sitting down. Facing her, on the opposite wall, hung a portrait of Veniamin Simonich. Even painted he looked powerful. Welcoming green eyes, black hair, tan skin with a smile displaying teeth as white as porcelain gave Simonich the appearance of someone approachable. And maybe he was, but Votyakov didn't know him enough to say for sure. A former KGB political officer, Simonich had climbed the echelons rapidly and had done so not because of whom he knew, but because of his efficiency. He had no tolerance for incompetents, and anyone even suspected of corruption was sent to prison. He had campaigned as a man of the people and they had rewarded him by electing him to the highest office. Under his presidency, Russia had prospered and had somewhat restored the glory of the former Soviet Union.

But not anymore.

Russia's economy was now imploding. With oil prices plummeting, the unemployment rate was back to double digits and climbing every month. So far Simonich, with the help of the army and the police forces, had managed to retain control. Nevertheless, Votyakov knew it was only months before riots would erupt across the country. That was why her mission was so important.

The sound of a door opening jolted Votyakov back to reality. She jumped to her feet as Veniamin Simonich approached her.

"Dr. Votyakov, thank you for coming on such short notice," Simonich said, offering his hand.

"Of course, Mr. President," she said, shaking it. *It's not as though I could have said no.*

"Please follow me." He led the way into his office. "Close the door behind you and have a seat."

Votyakov complied.

"Would you care for a cup of coffee?"

"No thank you, Mr. President. I'm fine." Votyakov watched Simonich unbutton his suit jacket and hang it on the back of his chair. He then took a few steps towards the single large window and rolled up his sleeves.

"Four months ago, I gave you a mission," started Simonich, now working on his left sleeve. "A mission vital to the interests of the Russian Federation."

"Yes, Mr. President."

"Do you know the current unemployment rate across our country?"

"It's at thirteen percent, I believe," Votyakov replied.

"That was three months ago, Doctor. It's now at fifteen point five percent," Simonich said solemnly.

Votyakov knew things weren't going well, but a rise of two and a half percent meant that the situation was even worse than she thought. "I'm sorry to hear that, Mr. President. This is certainly not your fault."

Simonich's head snapped in her direction. "I know that." His eyes drilled hers. "It's the Americans and their puppets from Saudi Arabia that are responsible for the situation Russia finds itself in."

"Of course, Mr. President," Votyakov replied quickly. "I didn't mean to insinuate . . ."

Simonich interrupted her by raising his hand. "You, Dr. Votyakov, were tasked with providing us an option in case everything else failed."

Votyakov's stomach became a knot. *Did everything else fail? Already?*

Simonich sat down behind his desk and said, "I know you were given six months to do the impossible, but I'm afraid Russia is running out of time, and money."

Votyakov swallowed hard. *Is he about to cut my funding, now that we're within days of a potential breakthrough?*

"Mr. President," Votyakov said, "I believe that within the next few days I'll be able to present you with the option you were looking for."

For a fraction of a second, Votyakov thought she'd seen distress on Simonich's face. *Or was it fear?* But it went away immediately. "I see," he said. "You're positive you've found something we could mass produce?"

Votyakov nodded. "Dr. Galkin and I need to run a few more tests but we're confident we've found it. As for mass producing the Malburg virus thread we're working on," Votyakov added, "it shouldn't be an issue."

"I see."

There it is again. His eyes. Sadness. That's it! Simonich isn't afraid, he's sad.

Simonich opened one of his desk drawers and pulled out a bottle of Baikal Vodka with two glasses. He unscrewed the cap and filled her glass with more alcohol than she had consumed during the last two months. He poured himself the same quantity.

"To your discovery," he announced without fanfare.

She touched his glass with hers. "Thank you, sir."

She took a sip and he did the same. The vodka burned her throat but tasted good. *Maybe I should start drinking more often,* she thought to herself.

"You do realize what we'll do with the virus you've created, right?" Simonich said, after taking another swallow that drained more than half of his glass.

Of course I know, you idiot! I'm the one who's been killing off prisoners by injecting them different mixtures of pathogens. Or did you forget about them, Mr. President? Maybe you did. You're not the one who has to live with the sight of them dying tied to a chair burned into your brain.

But she bit her tongue and said, "Yes, sir, I do."

"And you don't mind?" he asked.

"I do my best to serve the Russian Federation, Mr. President. I understand what must be done." *Do you?*

Simonich offered to refill her glass but she put her hand over the top. She shook her head. Simonich shrugged and poured himself some more.

"From now on, you'll be working directly with one of my associates," Simonich said. "It is best that I remove myself from the equation."

"I understand completely, Mr. President."

"Whatever my associate says, you can take it as if it had come directly from me."

"Of course."

"Good luck then, Dr. Votyakov." Simonich rose from his chair.

Votyakov started to rise too but Simonich motioned her to stay seated. "My associate will be here shortly," he said. With that, he topped up his glass with more vodka and left the room.

She understood why the president was torn. She felt the same way. The thrill of her discovery was clouded by the fact that she knew exactly how it would be used. But she had known from the beginning. Why was she feeling so sad now? Would she be able to sleep at night, knowing that the strain she had created had killed hundreds of thousands of innocent Americans? But they weren't innocent, were they? The United States had conspired with the Saudis to plunge Russia into a deep recession. One that could very well send her country to its knees for the next decade. No, she'd do what must be done. Russia hadn't started this war. She wouldn't stand still while her countrymen starved to death.

The opening of the door behind her brought her mind back to reality. She turned to see who it was. A tall, still-muscular Arabic man she knew to be in his mid sixties stood a few steps behind her. Her heart stopped.

"It's been too long, my dear Lidiya," Sheik Qasim Al-Assad said, buttoning his suit jacket. "I've missed you."

CHAPTER 13

Moscow, Russia

Mike Walton glanced at his rearview mirror more from habit than anything else. The traffic was heavy and there was no way he could have detected surveillance. Support Two had informed them a traffic accident involving a school bus was causing this delay. Lisa was seated next to him with an open laptop. An application installed by Support Two allowed them to track Dr. Votyakov. Support Two team leader James Cooper had assured them the device had a range of at least twenty miles, maybe more. That was a necessity. Unlike the Mercedes, the BMW they were driving wasn't equipped with blue emergency lights to clear the way.

Having Support Two with them was a blessing. They had provided them with Luc Walker's car, two pistols, with one spare magazine each, and secure communication gear able to keep IMSI headquarters and its assets in the field linked. Support Two had also supplied local currency, the tracking device they had used on Dr. Votyakov's bodyguard and its accompanying laptop. Mike and Lisa had learned to appreciate having a support team with them. James Cooper, formerly from Support Five—the team based in Europe— had helped Jonathan Sanchez extract Lisa from a difficult position a few months back in Nice after she'd been stabbed by a would-be suicide bomber. IMSI assets like Mike and Lisa were partnered with a support team whenever possible. Each assigned to a specific geographical region, support teams delivered the logistics the assets needed to complete their missions.

"They've reached the Kremlin," Lisa said.

"How far away are we?" Mike asked.

"About four miles."

"How precise is this application?"

A few keystrokes later, Lisa said, "Enough to determine that the bodyguard entered the Kremlin Grand Palace."

"Are you getting this, Charles?" Mike asked.

"Charles had to step out, Mike," Jonathan Sanchez replied from the control room of IMSI headquarters. "But we're getting the same feed you're getting from your laptop."

"What do you want us to do?"

"Stand by, Mike," Sanchez replied.

The IMSI had sent them to Moscow to verify Dr. Galkin's information that Dr. Votyakov, the director of Biopreparat, was to travel to the Kremlin to meet with a high-ranking politician regarding a potential biological attack on the United States. As far as Mike knew, that was the extent of the information given by Dr. Galkin to the FBI.

"We need you to ascertain that Dr. Votyakov is inside the palace, not just the bodyguard," Sanchez said a minute later.

"We'll need to buy tickets to access the Kremlin," Lisa said.

Mike nodded.

"Traffic's getting lighter," he said as they passed a marked police vehicle parked on the shoulder. "We should be able to reach the Kremlin within the next thirty minutes."

"Mike from Support Two," heard Mike in his earpiece.

"Go ahead."

"Someone's running Luc Walker's license plate."

Shit! That wasn't good. "We just passed a marked cruiser," Mike explained. "It's probably a random check."

Support Two's reply sent an electrifying shiver down his spine. "It doesn't matter. A warrant for Luc Walker's arrest just appeared on our screen."

Mike's eyes shot to his rearview mirror. The marked vehicle had activated its emergency lights.

· · · · · · · ·

Lisa Walton didn't waste time. As soon as she heard that their car was being investigated, she started typing the code that would automatically erase her laptop's hard drive.

"I guess going for a tour of the Kremlin is now out of the question," she said, half joking. "We need to lose him before additional cars are added to the chase."

"I know," her husband replied. "Hang on."

Lisa's seatbelt tightened again her chest as Mike braked hard and cranked the wheel to the right in order to take the next exit. He accelerated rapidly once the car reached the exit ramp. Lisa looked behind them. The Russian police car cut two lanes of traffic but managed to follow them out of the highway.

Lisa smiled. She couldn't help it. This was exciting. The adrenaline rush felt good.

Too good.

"We have a better chance of losing them in the city streets than on the highway," Mike said.

"Support Two, Lisa," she said over her mic.

"Go ahead."

"Anything you can do to help?"

"We don't have enough time to hack the Moscow police system to modify the arrest warrant—"

"That wouldn't change anything," Lisa cut in, holding tight as Mike made a hard left followed by another left. She didn't have time to adjust to the sudden change and banged her head heavily against the window. "They're already after us. We need another vehicle."

"We'll see what we can do, Lisa. Stand by."

She said to Mike, "Luc Walker speaks Russian fluently. We don't."

"I know," Mike replied. "We can't get caught."

"Whatever the cost," she said before grabbing a Walter P22 from the backpack she kept at her feet.

"What the hell, Lisa?" Mike said.

"Don't worry, Mike," Lisa replied, retrieving a Gemtech Outback suppressor from the glove compartment. "I'm not planning on using it on the cops."

Mike looked confused. "Put it away if you're not planning on using it. You'll get us killed."

"Who said I wasn't planning on using it? I might need it to scare someone away from his car." She pulled a loaded magazine of ten rounds from her backpack. She inspected the magazine, making sure the first cartridge was in position, before pushing it up into the handgrip. She racked the action.

"What do you want to do?" Mike asked. Her husband's voice was calm, in control.

"Drop me at the next corner," she said. "I'll get us a new ride."

Mike looked at her as if she was crazy. "You're sure about that?"

"Yeah," she replied.

. . . .

His wife was gutsy. She was also right. Their only option was to ditch Walker's BMW and escape with another car. It would have been better to steal a car from the long-term parking lot at the airport but that option had come and gone.

The police car was still chasing them with lights and siren.

"I'll try to lose him, if only for a few seconds," Mike said. "It will give you time for a clean exit out of the car."

"Okay."

"Be careful, baby."

"You too, Mike."

She squeezed his leg. "I'm good to go. Whenever you're ready."

Mike checked his rearview mirror once again. The police car was only a few cars back and gaining ground. It was only a matter of seconds before other police vehicles joined the chase.

"Support Two from Mike."

"Go ahead."

Mike searched for a street sign. "I'm presently somewhere between 3rd Ring Road and Velozavodskaya Street."

"We see you on our screen," Support Two replied. "There's a supermarket a few streets down. Might be in good place to drop off Lisa."

"Agreed," Lisa said. "Let's go."

With the cruiser right on their tail, Mike wasn't sure how he was going to pull that one off. It wasn't easy to lose a police car, especially in a city you didn't know. The traffic light ahead turned yellow and Mike punched the accelerator. The BMW 550 leaped forward and was three quarters across the street when a small Lada SUV hit it at full speed. The impact spun the BMW and Mike lost control and smashed into a parked vehicle across the street. His airbag deployed and smacked against his head, stunning him.

He looked over at his wife. "You're okay, Lisa?"

She nodded. "We need to get out of here. Now!"

Before they could extract themselves from the vehicle, a police officer appeared next to Mike's door. He was holding a pistol, and it was pointed directly at Mike's head.

. . . .

Lisa scanned her surroundings to make sure there was only one police officer. Once she was certain, she raised her silenced Walter P22 and fired five rounds through the driver's side window. The first three rounds hit the officer square in the vest while another hit his pistol, before ricocheting aimlessly to his left. The last round punctured his left hand.

"Go, Mike, go!"

. . . .

Mike saw his wife raise her weapon and knew what she was planning. He pushed himself back against his seat. As soon as she told him to go, he unlocked all the car's doors and jumped out of the vehicle. He pounced on the officer, who had moved backward a few paces. The officer's eyes were those of a terrified man, fearing for his life. With his pistol out of reach, he tried to reach for his telescopic baton but Mike was too fast. He kicked the officer on the inside of his right knee. The officer bent forward and received Mike's right knee on the nose. He collapsed. Mike used the officer's handcuffs to secure his hands behind his back. He grabbed the police radio and picked up the pistol.

"Let's go!" his wife told him before sprinting across the road.

Mike took a quick look at the Lada SUV. It was totaled. Its driver was slumped against the steering wheel, his eyes open but lifeless.

CHAPTER 14

IMSI headquarters, New York, NY.

C harles Mapother entered the control room and made a bee-
line to Jonathan Sanchez.

"Talk to me, Jonathan."

Mapother couldn't believe how fast the mission had turned to
shit. A simple intelligence-gathering, fact-finding mission was now
a total clusterfuck, with two operatives running for their lives.

"We're still trying to reconstruct exactly what happened, sir,"
Sanchez started. "But what we know so far is that the BMW Mike
and Lisa were driving was investigated by a police cruiser belonging
to the Moscow City Police."

"Was it a random check or were they actually targeted?"
Mapother asked.

"Nothing is pointing toward a targeted investigation," Sanchez
said. "Seems like a routine traffic check."

Mapother scratched his head. "What happened next?"

"For reasons unknown to us at this time, a warrant for Luc Walker's arrest was initiated earlier today."

"God damn FBI," Mapother cursed. "They couldn't keep their
mouth shut." It was easy to figure out what had happened. To gain
some brownie points, the FBI had publicized the arrest of Luc
Walker. Words of his arrest had reached Moscow. Russian officials,
not wanting to look soft on crime, had also issued an arrest warrant.
Probably not even knowing why they were doing so . . .

"A chase followed and our assets' vehicle was struck by an
incoming SUV," continued Sanchez.

"Good God."

"Before they could escape, a police officer approached the
vehicle and threatened Mike with his sidearm."

Mapother pinched the bridge of his nose. *Not good.*

"Lisa used a Walter P22 to fire five shots at the officer," Sanchez said, before quickly adding, "He sustained only minor injuries to one of his hands."

At least they hadn't killed the officer.

"Where are they now?" Mapother asked.

Sanchez asked an analyst to put up Mike and Lisa's location on one of the control room's huge flat screens.

"They stole a moped from one of the witnesses at the scene," Sanchez said.

"A moped?"

Mapother looked at the two blue dots representing Mike and Lisa. They had put more than three miles between them and the crash site. They were now traveling westbound using small roads.

Sending them to the Kremlin was now out of the question. Could they reach Dr. Galkin, though? Confirming the presence of Dr. Lidiya Votyakov with a high-ranking Russian politician would have been enough to convince him his former informant was telling the truth, and he would have ordered Mike and Lisa to snatch him. But without being absolutely sure he was telling the truth, he could be sending Mike and Lisa into a trap.

"Do you know if their act was caught by CCTV?"

"We're still at least fifteen minutes from being able to hack into Moscow's CCTV system. The quality of their system isn't comparable to what the British have in London. Videos are usually grainy at best," Sanchez said.

"If they work at all," Mapother added. "They couldn't even find CCTV footage of Tadeas Chuchnova's murder when he was shot four times in one of the most secured locations in Moscow."

Tadeas Chuchnova, a former deputy prime minister and opposition leader, had been a fierce critic of Russian president Veniamin Simonich. He had been assassinated on a bridge in central Moscow after having dinner with his mistress, a young Ukrainian model.

"There's good news, though," Sanchez said. "Just before you walked in we found this."

Sanchez handed Mapother a piece of paper.

"That's good news indeed," Mapother said. "Patch me through to Mike. I'll give him a new set of instructions."

CHAPTER 15

Moscow, Russia

Mike Walton parked the borrowed moped in the parking lot of the Vremena Goda shopping center. He'd taken it away from a terrified teenager who had witnessed the entire ordeal with the police officer. His wife had climbed behind him and had held him so tightly that Mike thought she'd cracked one of his ribs. A moped wasn't his first choice of getaway vehicle but that had seemed less risky than forcing someone out of his car.

"Mike, this is Charles."

"I'm listening, Charles."

"We've got you at a shopping mall."

"Lisa and I will make a few purchases," Mike said. They needed to change clothes, buy some makeup and try to alter their appearances as much as possible.

"Neither of you was injured in the crash?"

"We're fine, Charles," Mike replied, but his thoughts were with the driver of the SUV who'd rammed them. "What about the guy who ran his SUV into our car?"

"I can answer this one," came in the voice of Support Two team leader James Cooper. "He's dead."

Mike sighed. Pictures of children growing without their father flashed in his mind. *Not now, Mike. Focus.*

This wasn't good. Not only had they shot a cop, they'd killed someone. The mission had turned into a nightmare. Lisa was gesturing him to get moving and he followed her in the direction of the shopping mall.

Mapother continued, "I need you to bring in Dr. Galkin, Mike."

"Back to New York, you mean?"

"Correct."

Lisa, who was getting all of this through her own communication system, looked at him and shook her head. "Charles, this is Lisa." She continued walking toward the mall. "Your brief indicated that Dr. Galkin's working at the Biopreparat Koltsovo Facility. That's like three thousand miles away."

"I know," Mapother replied. "But we came across some intel that indicates Dr. Galkin's name is on tonight's flight from Koltsovo to Sheremetyevo."

Built for the 1980 Summer Olympics, Sheremetyevo airport was the second largest airport in Russia and located eighteen miles northwest of Moscow.

"Do we know why?" Mike asked.

"I'm afraid we don't. The only thing we know with some certainty is that his name is on the flight manifest of an Aeroflot flight scheduled to land tonight at Sheremetyevo at a quarter to nine local time."

Mike looked at his Tag Heuer. It was just passed five o'clock in the afternoon. Lisa shrugged. *Why not?*

"We'll need transportation, a new set of IDs and an exfiltration plan."

"We'll work with Support Two to provide you with a new set of wheels, but you can forget about getting new identity cards."

"Luc Walker is now a marked man in Russia, Charles," Mike said.

"Maybe so," Mapother replied. "But the real Luc Walker doesn't look like you and if nobody captured the incident with the cop, you might be okay."

Might be okay . . . Mike didn't like this one bit. But what choice did they have?

"What if Dr. Galkin doesn't want to join us?" Mike asked. This was a real possibility, especially if the Russian doctor asked them how they intended to bring him out of the country. They had yet to come up with a plan. "Do we force him?"

"He'll go, as long as you tell him his family's safe."

"Aren't they still in Koltsovo?"

"For now," Mapother replied. "Lisa will need to pick them up."

. . . .

Lisa wasn't sure if she'd heard Mapother correctly. "Say again."

"We need you to pick up Dr. Galkin's family in Koltsovo."

71

Didn't I mention it was three thousand miles away?

Mapother continued before she had a chance to respond. "There are no indications that you've been compromised, Lisa. You came in on a different flight and you didn't link with Mike until you took possession of Luc Walker's BMW at the airport."

She glanced at her husband. He didn't look pleased. His eyes betrayed his anxiety.

"There must be another way," Mike said.

"The moment Biopreparat realizes Dr. Galkin's gone, they'll go after his family. We might be too late already," Lisa replied. *And if that's the case, I'll end up with a bullet in the head or, worse, in a forced labor camp.*

"We need Dr. Galkin, Mike, and he won't go without assurances that his family's safe," Mapother insisted. "He might be the only ally we have inside Russia and there's no time to send another team. Lisa's our best chance, and you know it."

"I'll go," Lisa said, staring into Mike's eyes. *Was that panic I just saw?*

"By the time you reach Koltsovo, we'll have an exfil plan for you."

That's if I reach Koltsovo at all.

CHAPTER 16

The Kremlin, Moscow, Russia

The Sheik approached his former lover and the mother of his children. She had changed in the last few years. Her waist had become a little thicker and streaks of gray could be seen within her blond hair. But her kind blue eyes, the ones that had conquered his heart so long ago, hadn't changed. They were still able to pierce his defenses and, for a brief moment, he wondered if they'd still be together if the CIA hadn't killed his father by mistake four decades ago.

The slaughter of his family had changed his life. In fact, this tragic event had not only transformed his life, it had altered the lives of thousands. Sometimes he wished he could go back to change his past and better orient his future. But he was a realist and, truth be told, he actually enjoyed being the Sheik. Four months ago, when Charles Mapother's men had raided his mobile headquarters—an eighty-six-foot Azimut yacht anchored in Spain—and killed his most valuable and trusted man, Omar Al-Nashwan, he had been forced to kill Al-Nashwan's father, his partner and long-time associate Steve Shamrock. This saddened him, and he placed the blame directly on Mapother's shoulders. Steve Shamrock had studied with the current American president and had earned his trust. Shamrock, an oil tycoon, had informed him about the creation of a new counterterrorism entity named the International Market Stabilization Institute. His friend had been furious when the president decided he'd be the only one with control over the IMSI, and that he wouldn't share operational details or the intelligence acquired during missions with the three financiers who'd funded the IMSI in the first place. Nevertheless, Shamrock had shared one important aspect of the IMSI with him: a name. Charles Mapother. And if there was one positive thing to come out of the attack on his mobile headquarters, it was the discovery of another name associated with the IMSI.

Mike Powell.

Mike Powell was the son of Canadian ambassador Ray Powell, the man he had abducted in Algiers more than two years ago. The successful kidnapping of the Canadian ambassador to Algeria gave him instant recognition amongst other terror groups. Within a year, his network became the most feared among the western hemisphere intelligence agencies. No countries were safe, with the exception of Russia. With the death of Steve Shamrock, he had lost access to the majority of his funds. His network had been shaken by the loss of many of his top lieutenants but was still operational.

Mike Powell. The two words Omar Al-Nashwan had said before dying. The ambassador's son was supposedly killed during a coordinated attack he had orchestrated at the Ottawa international airport and train station. But he had survived, or so it seemed.

As for Mapother, he wasn't easy prey. The fact that he had to take a step back following the attack on his yacht hadn't helped either. It had taken longer than expected to find the IMSI director. It had only seemed fair to take Mapother's life in exchange for Al-Nashwan's and Shamrock's deaths. To accomplish this, he'd tasked his older son Zakhar to formulate a plan that wouldn't implicate him. Zakhar, an accountant who'd been through a terror camp in Sierra Leone, led by a former associate named Major Jackson Taylor, came up with the idea of asking someone with a previous connection with Mapother. He had agreed with his son's plan and sent him on his way. The Sheik had been under no illusions about the difficulty of the mission. That was why he had asked his younger son Igor to shadow Zahhar's movements and to report back to him. Everything had worked like a charm, until Igor's phone call.

"Qasim?" Dr. Votyakov's voice sliced through his unpleasant thoughts.

"How are you, my dear?" he asked.

"I didn't expect to see you here," Dr. Votyakov replied.

"You don't look pleased to see me," he said, taking a step in her direction.

"You're usually the bearer of bad news, Qasim," she said. "What are you doing here? Don't you have some jihadists to brainwash?"

It took all his will not to slap her. How dare she judge him? *Damn bitch*. She knew him. She knew what he had been through and why he did the things he did.

She must have seen something change in him because she quickly apologized. "I shouldn't have said that." She sat down in the armchair facing the Russian president's desk. "I've been under tremendous pressure."

She had a way of affecting him like nobody else. A single word from her could change his humor in a heartbeat. One minute he wanted to choke her, the next he wanted to embrace her.

Standing behind the mother his children, he placed his hands on her shoulders. "I do have bad news, Lidiya." He felt her tense. "Zakhar has been killed."

She jumped to her feet to face him. Her eyes drilled into his. Her upper lip twitched, then she slapped him. Hard. He let her do it again on the other cheek, embracing the burning sensation. *If she only knew what I did, she'd kill me. Our first born, a fallen peon on the battlefield of revenge. My revenge.*

He grabbed her wrist on her third swing. "Enough. Get a grip." She slowly shook her head, a single tear gliding from the corner of her eye. He watched as her face crumpled into a mask of sadness and hate. "What did you do?" she hissed.

Her words speared into his soul. Why was he always the one she held responsible for any misfortune? The fact that she was right didn't subdue his anger.

"Your words hurt me, Lidiya," he said in the most compassionate voice he could muster. "I had nothing, absolutely nothing, to do with this." He didn't flinch when her inquisitive, teary eyes gored through his.

"Who then?" she whispered a full minute later. "Who?"

"An American spy named Mike Powell." *Someone whom I thought died months ago.*

"Will you kill him for me, Qasim?" she asked, her voice pleading.

"I'll do better than this, my love." The Sheik held her tightly against him. "I'll pierce his eyes, cut off his genitals and feed them to him before cutting his throat."

"Yes," she said between sobs. "I'd love that very much."

75

CHAPTER 17

Damascus, Syria

Ray Powell was seated in the backseat of Syrian General Fuad Younis's armored Range Rover. Younis was the commanding officer of the Fifteenth Special Forces Division of the Syrian Army. Four months ago, after Powell had been in the Sheik's custody for over two years, Younis had liberated him from his captors. Powell still remembered their first conversation that took place in his filthy cell:

"What are you planning to do with me, General?"

"We're here to send you home, Mr. Ambassador."

That had been bullshit. He hadn't been allowed even one phone call. The sad thing was that even if he'd been permitted a quick overseas call, he had no family to contact. One of the Sheik's men, a sadistic bastard called Omar Al-Nashwan, had told him about the death of his wife and only son. Powell had spat in Al-Nashwan's face. Al-Nashwan's response had not only been to savagely beat him. He was also shown numerous newspapers confirming the death of his entire family.

Younis had kept him in isolation. With no access to radio or television, Powell had no idea what was going on in the outside world. The only reason his will to live hadn't wavered was because he had gained access to intelligence that could dramatically change the face of Washington DC. Just before his capture by the Sheik, he had discovered that Steve Shamrock, a close friend of President Robert Muller, was in fact working with the terrorist mastermind.

At least compared to his time in the Sheik's custody, where he had lost a finger—cut by Al-Nashwan—and been forced to shit and urinate in his clothes, the Syrian general had fed him properly and

76

Powell had regained some of his strength. This morning, when he opened his eyes after a surprisingly restful sleep, Younis had been standing next to him. In his hands was a fresh change of clothes.

"You're leaving," Younis said. "Get dressed, shave and eat."

"That's what you told me four months ago."

"Not my decision, Mr. Ambassador."

After a breakfast of coffee and toast, Powell was escorted to a three-vehicle convoy. He climbed into the middle vehicle.

"Where are we headed to, General?" Powell asked.

"A Canadian delegation landed a few hours ago. You're going home."

Powell did his best to control his excitement. After years of solitude and despair, his brain had a hard time comprehending that the nightmare he'd been living in was finally coming to an end.

As the convoy moved slowly through the Syrian capital, Powell couldn't help noticing the destruction around him. Damascus had changed drastically since his last visit in the early nineties. Once a beautiful city, Damascus's five thousand years of history was being destroyed and slowly buried by rubble.

Four years of civil war will do that to any city.

"Sad isn't it, Mr. Ambassador?" Younis asked from the front passenger seat.

"I remember Damascus as a magnificent city, General," Powell replied, his eyes glued to the outside. "Picturesque, tree-lined streets, bustling, open-air markets with gourmet rooftop restaurants—"

"Did you know that Damascus is one of the oldest continuously inhabited cites in the world, Ambassador?"

"No, I can't say I knew that."

"We'll live through this. We'll rebuild. Come back and see for yourself," Younis said, looking at Powell.

Powell nodded. *This city will never be the same. Not in my lifetime anyway.*

The convoy came to a halt. A checkpoint. It was the fourth one, and they had traveled less than one mile. *No, I don't think I'll come back here. Ever.*

CHAPTER 18

Damascus, Syria

Zima Bernbaum drank the last of her energy drink. Using her binoculars, she scanned the roofs of the buildings surrounding the square where the exchange was to take place. Looking for threats wasn't as easy as it would have been in New York City, or Ottawa for that matter. Four years of civil war had changed the face of Damascus. Once a peaceful city, it was now one of the most dangerous places on the planet. Zima recalled a time not so long ago when she had explored Damascus with only a backpack and a few tourist books. The nightlife had been sensational, even better than Paris. Now the city lived in fear of car bombings and to a soundtrack of artillery salvoes. Tourism had died, and the reasons were painfully obvious. During her pre-mission briefing she'd been told that the financial losses since the beginning of the conflict were upward of eighty billion dollars.

Getting into Syria, let alone Damascus, had been a challenge. Zima flew on the IMSI's Gulfstream from New York City to Beirut. From there, she took a cab and had to cross two Lebanese security checkpoints before reaching the Syrian border. The IMSI had prepared the proper documentation and her forged Croatian passport—with a suitable visa—worked like a charm with the Lebanese. The Syrian border guards were more thorough. But after a methodical search of the taxi and a short interview where she talked about her credentials as an agricultural expert, they let her through but warned her that the road to Damascus wasn't safe and that the government couldn't ensure her safety. To her surprise, the taxi was stopped only twice on their way to Damascus. The government troops were respectful and, after a cursory inspection, they were given the green light to continue their journey.

With so many Syrians fleeing their country, it had been easy for the IMSI to find a suitable apartment with views of the square. She was perfectly positioned to observe the whole process and had already identified the Canadian contingent. The fact that she knew one of them had facilitated her effort. She transitioned to her camera and took several pictures of the man she knew to be Joachim Persky. Persky was the deputy assistant-director of the CSIS—the Canadian Security Intelligence Service—collection division. He was a hard worker who wasn't afraid to get his hands dirty. The fact that he was in Syria, personally taking charge of the operation, proved she'd been right about him. She then pointed the camera and zoomed on the two men seated next to him. Dressed in gray cargo pants and black, short-sleeved polo shirts, Zima guessed they were probably JTF-2 operators—Canadian Special Forces soldiers specialized in counter-terrorism—tasked with protecting Persky.[3] Both operators were carrying fanny packs that Zima was pretty sure weren't holding candy. They looked alert and ready to go. A waiter—a tall, good-looking man with a muscular build and dark skin—brought them espressos and water. She snapped a few pictures of him too. She'd always loved tall, handsome men, even bald ones like him.

If all went according to plan, she would take pictures of Mike's father and of the Syrians involved in the exchange and would be on her way back to Beirut before the end of the day. She looked at her watch. Ten minutes left before the scheduled meet.

CHAPTER 19

Damascus, Syria

Ray Powell's nerves were being tested. He wondered who would be there to collect him. He doubted they would be Canadians. That would be too good to be true, and he knew as well as anyone that the Canadian government didn't negotiate with terrorists. But were the Syrians considered terrorists? And what did his country agree to give back in exchange for his freedom? He would know soon enough.

"We're almost there, Mr. Ambassador," General Younis said. "Less than two minutes."

Since the last checkpoint, the motorcade had slowed down. Traffic was a bit heavier and Powell could see more pedestrians. Small shops, cafés and restaurants lined the street. There were only a few people seated at their tables but at least they were open. From the SUV's windows, he could see they were approaching a nondescript square close to the old city of Damascus. Orange trees gave the landscape some much-needed bright colors, as the rest of the city seemed rather drab to Powell. The motorcade stopped in front of a leather shop and General Younis said, "Stay in the vehicle, Mr. Ambassador. I'll be right back."

The Syrian general exited the vehicle and several plainclothes and uniformed officers did the same from the other two SUVs. Even though Powell couldn't hear what Younis was saying to his men, it was clear he was giving them directives. Less than a minute later, they left in different directions in groups of two.

"What's going on?" Powell asked as Younis climbed back in the SUV.

"I'm deploying my men around the perimeter. This area is one of the most secured in all Damascus, but the rebels have eyes everywhere. Your security is paramount."

He looked sincere enough.

"I appreciate this, General."

Younis nodded. "Time to go."

CHAPTER 20

Damascus, Syria

Igor Votyakov brought the espressos and the glasses of water to the two Canadian security men. He was careful not to make eye contact with them. Tier-one operators had a tendency to recognize one another. With only a few minutes before the beginning of the operation, he didn't want to draw any unwanted attention.

His father, the Sheik, had briefed him on exactly what he wanted. There were no rules. Only the successful completion of the objectives counted. The Sheik wanted Ray Powell. He wanted him badly. And General Younis had to die. Younis had betrayed his father and that wouldn't stand. No one betrayed his father and lived.

No one.

Case in point was the assassination of one of his father's closest associates, Major Jackson Taylor, at the hands of Omar Al-Nashwan. With Al-Nashwan dead and his father in bed with the Russian president, Igor had been chosen to assist his father in accomplishing a task that would allow his country to take its revenge on the United States. Igor doubted his father's motivation was to see Russia prosper once again. The Sheik wasn't known to take other people's wishes under consideration when plotting his own retaliation. But if his objectives were aligned with Russia's, why not?

His phone chirped in his pocket.

"We've identified six Syrian security officers on foot," one of his men said.

"Wait for my signal before engaging," Igor replied.

"One more thing, sir," the man continued. "I've spotted a women observing the scene from a fourth-floor window across the square. I didn't see any weapons but she does have a camera."

"She'll be your first target. Do it quietly."

"Understood."

The motorcade parked on the other side of the street and Igor watched a smiling Younis opening the door for the former Canadian ambassador. Younis's attitude pissed him off. How could he ever think that betraying his father wouldn't bring any consequences? Younis's driver had remained loyal to the Sheik and would be handsomely rewarded for his services.

Time to play.

Igor blew his nose in a tissue, giving the signal to begin.

CHAPTER 21

Damascus, Syria

From her vantage point, Zima Bernbaum caught sight of the plainclothes Syrian security officers before the JTF-2 operators did. Their presence was to be expected, but it wasn't reassuring to see them. Being the eternal optimist, Zima wanted to believe they were there to protect the ambassador. The Canadian operators rose from their chairs the moment they realized they were being watched. They didn't look too concerned, so maybe they already knew to expect company.

Zima took as many pictures as she could of all the Syrian officers she had spotted before continuing her security scan. She focused on the windows facing the square. Some of them were open but she couldn't see deep enough inside to know if a threat was lurking or not. There was only so much she could do by herself. She returned her attention to the Syrian officers and was happy to see that they weren't focusing on the Canadian delegation but on the perimeter. They too were looking for any signs of danger.

A convoy of three Range Rovers in tight formation made its way slowly toward the square. Zima's heart started beating faster. *This is it.*

She grabbed her camera and started taking photos of the Range Rovers. There was no doubt in her mind that Mike's father was in one of these vehicles. Movement on one of the rooftops on her left grabbed her attention. She used her camera to zoom in.

Not good.

A man carrying a sniper rifle was crawling toward the edge of the building. For a moment, Zima thought the man was part of the Syrian security detail but she dismissed the idea once the man reached his firing position.

His rifle was aimed at the Syrian security detail. Zima remembered the one-plus-one rule. If you see one, there's another one you don't see. It was a basic police concept that had saved her life more than once.

Only seconds remained before the motorcade carrying Ray Powell reached the café where the Canadians were waiting. *The motorcade is waiting for the green light from the security officers they deployed.* Her gut told her something was wrong but she couldn't see another sniper.

Wait! There! Fifty meters to the right of the café, a group of six men, all of them Caucasians, split into three groups of two. *Shit! Something's happening.* Zima used her secured satellite phone to call the IMSI headquarters as the motorcade stopped in front of the café, partially obscuring her view.

Jonathan Sanchez picked up the phone on the first ring.

"All is well, Zima?"

"Contact the Canadians," she said. "Something's not right. They need to pull back. Now."

Then the window in front of her shattered and a bullet struck the satellite phone she was holding to her ear. Plastic fragments peppered her face as the bullet continued its trajectory and ripped away her middle finger, sending blood and bone fragments into the wall next to her.

· · · · · · · ·

Ray Powell couldn't believe it when the motorcade stopped across the street from the café. He didn't know personally the three men who were waiting for him but they looked the part. It was clear that two of them were security while the one wearing a gray suit was probably a diplomat from the Canadian embassy in Beirut. By their looks, the two men providing security were either from the RCMP Protective Division or they were members of JTF-2. It didn't matter. He was in good hands.

General Younis was the first out of the Range Rover. He personally opened Powell's door.

"Please, Mr. Ambassador."

Powell stepped out and followed the general. The Canadian diplomat was smiling and Powell waved at him. He was halfway across the street when he heard the familiar sound of a pistol being drawn out of its holster. He turned around to face the barrel of the driver's pistol. The Syrian soldier already had his finger on the trigger. Powell's training, honed from years spent in the RCMP Prime Minister Protective Detail, kicked in. His left hand swiped from right to left and connected with the driver's wrist just as he was firing. Powell heard a grunt and saw General Younis clutch his abdomen. He tried to grab the gun but the soldier was well trained and kicked him in the stomach, creating the distance he needed to readjust his aim.

For a fraction of a second, Powell was sure he was about to die. He was unarmed. Powerless. Then a multitude of shots rang out from behind him as the JTF-2 operators opened fire on the soldier. The Syrian collapsed, his torso turning red. Powell ran to him and picked up the pistol just as a full-blown firefight erupted all around him. The first to fall was the Canadian diplomat. He was hit multiple times from fire coming from two shooters forty meters to their right. One of the JTF-2 operators returned fired and the two shooters went down. Then the JTF-2 member fell face first as a bullet entered the back of his neck. Powell scanned the rooftops and saw the barrel of a sniper's rifle. He fired a few rounds at it.

"Sir!" yelled the remaining JTF-2 operator who had run to him. "We need to go."

Powell nodded. A quick look at General Younis confirmed he wasn't dead, but he wasn't going to make it if he didn't receive immediate medical attention.

"We don't have time to help him, sir," the operator said. "We move or we die."

Powell didn't understand what was going on. The Syrians seemed to be engaging another group of men that had apparently come out of nowhere.

"We have a car and a driver at the back of the restaurant," the operator said. "We'll go through the café. Stay on my heels, and check my six. Let's move."

. . . .

Zima Bernbaum's face was on fire. The plastic had cut through her flesh, and blood was pouring from the open cuts. At least her vision wasn't affected. But her hand was a mess. The middle finger of her right hand was missing and blood gushed out.

Need to stop the bleeding.

She looked around for a medical kit she knew wasn't there. The apartment was empty except for a couple of dirty couches and a dining table. She had to move. People might already be on their way to her location. Her mind snapped back to her mission. Ray Powell. A firefight was raging outside. She needed to know what was going on, but her instinct told her to stay down, not to show herself. The sniper knew her location and his next shot wouldn't miss. She crawled to the main door of the apartment and made her exit. She climbed down the stairs two by two. She was already feeling lightheaded. She needed to stop the bleeding. She had only a few minutes before she would lose consciousness. And that would mean certain death, or torture. An explosion from somewhere near the square told her the fight raging outside wasn't over.

She reached the third-floor hallway and rammed, shoulder first, into the first door she saw on her left, knowing the apartment wouldn't be facing the square. Pain rushed through her upper body as the door ceded. Zima crashed to the floor and found herself in the middle of a small living room. A man ran at her with a butcher's knife and took a swing at her. The move was telegraphed and Zima had no problem ducking and counter-attacking by punching the man in the solar plexus. The man doubled over and Zima finished him off by delivering a powerful elbow behind the man's head.

Behind the fallen man stood three young children who looked terrified. A woman was standing between Zima and the children, screaming in Arabic, her eyes filled with hatred.

Zima said in Arabic, "I'm sorry. I'm sorry. I want you no harm. I'm injured and I need your help." She showed the woman her injured hand but that didn't calm the woman. Zima couldn't blame her as she had just knocked down her husband.

"Go. Leave this place," Zima said, pointing to the open door of the apartment.

The hysterical woman wasn't leaving. Her husband was sprawled in their living room and she wasn't about to abandon him.

Zima had wasted enough time and went in search of the bathroom. She found it next to the master bedroom. She located a small emergency kit under the sink filled with medicine and bandages. The pain had become unbearable and she had trouble focusing. She turned on the faucet and poured antiseptic where her finger used to be. Adrenaline rushed through her body and her knees buckled at the agony.

Movement behind her startled her. She looked in the mirror. The Arabic woman was standing behind her holding the butcher's knife in the air.

CHAPTER 22

Damascus, Syria

R ay Powell tailed the JTF-2 operator through the café. His heart was racing, pumping blood into his brain. This, mixed with the adrenaline rush that came with combat, gave him a feeling of ecstasy. The operator was moving fast, his pistol flashing left and right, looking for threats while Powell concentrated on their six.

"Kirk, this is Travis," the JTF-2 operator said into a mic attached to his collar. "Dan's down. The ambassador and I are moving to you. We're one minute out."

A quick scan to the rear told Powell they weren't followed by armed men into the café. The cacophony outside had somewhat diminished in intensity but Powell wasn't sure if this was good news or not. When he had followed the JTF-2 operator into the café, Younis's men didn't seem to have the upper hand. What had just happened? Who were General Younis's men fighting? Rebels? It didn't matter now. Whoever they were, they had killed two Canadians. Someone would pay for this. But first, he had to live through this.

· · · · · · · ·

Igor Votyakov walked through the café's back exit just as Powell and the Canadian operator entered by the main entrance. One of his men, a sniper positioned on the rooftop of a building with a clear view of the back exit, had informed him a car with diplomatic plates was parked less than fifty meters from the back door.

Conscious the driver might be watching him, Igor made sure his pistol was pressed against his leg, concealed from view. From the thickness of the windows, Igor concluded the car was armored and he had to change his plan. Shooting through the side window to kill the driver wouldn't work. With only seconds before the two Canadians made their exit, he had to act fast.

Igor pressed a key on his cell and it autodialed the person he wanted to talk to. His man answered on the first ring.

"The car is armored. Engage it as soon as I'm done with the ambassador," Igor ordered. His man would know what to do.

He then placed his back against the café's exterior wall and waited. He didn't have to linger for long. Less than five seconds later, the exit door was kicked opened and the Canadian operator's head appeared.

Igor pulled the trigger.

. . . .

Ray Powell saw the red sign over the door indicating the exit that would lead to the street where a car was supposedly waiting for them. The JTF-2 operator kicked the door opened. Rays of sunlight blinded Powell and he heard a pop. A warm mist speckled his face and he fell forward over the fallen corpse of the man in front of him. Powerful hands attempted to wrestle his pistol away but Powell used his forward momentum to push his attacker into the street. His assailant lost his footing and fell backward with half his body still on the sidewalk. Powell tried to fire but the man, who was wearing a waiter's uniform, had jammed one of his fingers inside the trigger guard behind the trigger.

A loud explosion broke Powell's concentration. A black vehicle, located less than fifty meters away, burst into the air as an RPG hit it. Glass fragments flew everywhere and a heat wave engulfed Powell. The man under him seized the moment to slash Powell's wrist with the outside of his hand. Powell yelped in pain as the pistol was knocked away. But the man wasn't done. He sent a series of jab into Powell's sternum, stunning him.

Then Powell felt something cold behind his neck.

. . . .

Igor Votyakov was surprised by the older man's strength. He was about to plunge his left index into Powell's right eye when one of his

90

men emerged behind the ambassador. Igor saw the surprise register in Powell's eyes. But the former ambassador wouldn't quit and, with shocking agility, pivoted on himself and deflected the gun that was pointed at his neck with his forearm.

With Powell off him and engaged with someone else, Igor grabbed Powell from behind and started to choke him by compressing his carotid arteries. Powell kicked his shin with his heel, causing so much pain Igor nearly lost his hold. Powell elbowed him, but the ambassador's strength was fleeing rapidly. Seconds later, Powell become limp in his arms. For good measure, Igor held the choke for three more seconds.

"Secure him," Igor said to his man. "We're leaving."

CHAPTER 23

Damascus, Syria

Zima Bernbaum pivoted one hundred and eighty degrees and grabbed the woman's wrist with her injured hand just as the butcher's knife was about to slice into her shoulder. Zima yelled in pain, as if her hand had caught fire.

"Stop!" Zima shouted. She understood the woman was scared, but hadn't she proven she didn't want to hurt her or her family? She continued in Arabic, "Please, stop this nonsense before someone else gets injured." *Or I pass out . . .*

"Just get out of my house, I beg you." The woman let the knife go and it fell less than an inch away from Zima's right foot.

Was losing a finger not enough for one mission? I'll keep all my toes if I can. Thank you.

"Give me one minute," Zima replied, doing her best not to sound threatening. "I need to take care of my hand."

The woman's eyes moved to Zima's hand, which was still clutched around her left wrist.

"Let me," the woman offered.

Zima wasn't sure why the woman suddenly wanted to help her but she suspected it was because she believed it would be the quickest way to get rid of her.

"Thank you," Zima said.

The woman worked well and fast. *I'm not the first person she's patched up, and probably not the one in the worst shape.* Still, the bandage around her hand wouldn't go unnoticed. From now on, it would be much more difficult to blend in. With her hand taken care of, she needed to find out what had happened during the exchange. Was Mike's father safe? Did he get away? Her secured satellite phone gone, she had no direct way to contact the IMSI. Hopefully, the Canadians had been able to contact their embassy to give them a situation report. It was time to go.

Zima thanked the woman and gave her two hundred dollars she dug out of her jeans pocket. The woman started to shake her head but Zima used her left hand to close the woman's hand into a fist. "You keep it. For your troubles."

Zima walked past the fallen husband. He was slowly regaining consciousness. His pride had taken a beating but he would be okay. She nodded her thanks one more time and exited the apartment, closing the door behind her. She hurried down the stairs but slowed right down once she reached the ground floor. There was nobody else in the simple lobby. The door leading outside had a small window and Zima peeked into the plaza.

She was shocked at the carnage that had taken place. And then she saw him. An immense sadness overwhelmed her. Joachim Persky was sprawled on the road, only meters away from the coffee table he'd been seated at less than ten minutes ago. The body of one of the Canadian security men was also in the street, face first. He wasn't moving. People were starting to move in closer to the downed Syrian soldiers. Zima wasn't sure if it was to render assistance or to steal any valuables from the dead men. One of the soldiers was still moving, though. Zima waited a few more seconds to make sure no one was going to start shooting again. When it became clear that whoever had done this was gone, she broke cover and ran to the soldier she believed was still alive. Bystanders were within feet of the man when Zima reached him.

"I'm a medical doctor," she said. "Call an ambulance." Nobody made a move, but she could hear sirens in the background. The police would be here in less than a minute. She needed to act fast if she wanted to learn anything.

The soldier's mouth was filling with blood and Zima placed him on his side to help him breath.

"Who did this?" she asked the wounded man in Arabic.

The man tried to speak but only managed to cough blood in her face and ear.

Not good.

The man had merely seconds to live. Zima looked around for any signs that someone else had survived the shootout but had no luck.

The soldier grabbed her arm, his fingers digging into her flesh. His eyes were bloodshot but were still burning with rage.

"Who . . . are you?" he said.

"I'm a friend of Ray Powell," she said without blinking. She knew he wouldn't say anything to a simple Syrian citizen. This was her best shot.

His grip relaxed slightly. "The . . . The Sheik did . . . this."

The Sheik? That didn't make any sense.

"Are you sure?"

"Yes," the man replied in English. His voice was only a whisper.

"Do you know where he is?" she asked. The soldier didn't reply. Death had taken over.

CHAPTER 24

Moscow, Russia

M ike Walton's chest tightened as they approached the Sheremetyevo International Airport.

"You sure you want to do this?" he asked his wife, who was seated in the passenger seat of the Toyota Camry Support Two had unearthed for them.

"We've been through this before, Mike," Lisa replied.

"I know."

"So why are you asking me this?"

Mike could see his wife wasn't happy about him questioning her willingness to go to Koltsovo by herself. They both knew the issue was with him, not with her.

"I'm sorry, honey. I shouldn't have said anything." Mike maneuvered the car between two taxis parked curbside in front of the departure terminal.

The simple intelligence-gathering mission had now turned into a rescue mission. To make matters worse, he and Lisa had to go their separate ways. It hadn't fared well for Lisa last time they split like this. Mike only hoped his wife had learned from her past mistakes and that she wouldn't rush into situations before analyzing all possible options and outcomes.

His wife unbuckled her seatbelt and placed her hand behind his neck. The warmth of her hand against his skin felt good and he wished they were home instead of in Russia. But they had a job to do.

"I love you, Mike." She pulled him towards her once he had parked the Toyota. Her lips were soft and moist and fit so perfectly against his. Her left hand slipped into his left and her fingers curled around his, their palms touching in the most natural way. She gazed up at him, tenderness in her eyes. "I'll be okay, but I need you to believe it."

Mike had never been afraid of anything. But he was now. Lisa was the only remaining connection to his previous life. She was everything to him and to see her go, all by herself, broke his heart. The only reason he'd agreed to her becoming an asset with the IMSI was because Mapother had promised he'd be her partner. She might have gone through the IMSI's training, but she didn't have the experience he had. Good training was crucial, but experience was what would save your life.

"I do believe in you, Lisa," he said, chasing away the negative thoughts that threatened to overwhelm his psyche. "Just be careful."

"I will."

Mike watched his wife grabbed her carry-on from the backseat and disappear into the crowded terminal.

. . . .

Lisa Walton watched the electronic board to confirm her flight was on time. She had booked her flight less than two hours ago. To diminish the scrutiny a last minute purchase usually brought, she had paid for a return ticket. Aware that two hours would be plenty of time to position agents all over the airport, Lisa half expected to be caught by the FSB— the Russian internal security service. Her heart was racing but it helped her remain focused. She fought the urge to buy a coffee as she wanted to be able to sleep on her two-and-a-half-hour flight to Koltsovo. She had no idea what kind of opposition she'd be facing once in Koltsovo, though she suspected it wasn't going to be a walk in the park, and she wanted to be sharp and hit the ground running. A tired mind and body was one of the easiest ways to make a mistake. Lisa had no doubt what kind of pain she'd find herself in if she made a mistake. Her medical training had taught her to listen to her body and, right now, it was screaming, "I'm tired." The last few hours had brought their share of excitement and danger, and now that the adrenaline had left her system, she needed to rest before plunging into action again.

Lisa spent the next twenty minutes trying to spot any surveillance. She did identify a two-man team but they weren't after her.

They had their eyes on a well-dressed, thirty-something woman traveling with a toddler. The agents weren't discreet enough to be conducting surveillance and Lisa guessed they were some kind of protective detail. She yearned for them not to be on the same flight but she wanted to be prepared in case they were. She used her smartphone to snap a picture of the good-looking woman and sent it to Support Two with a note asking for a quick identification. With less than thirty minutes before boarding time, she crossed her fingers Support Two would come through.

And they did, ten minutes later.

· · · · · · · ·

Mike Walton swore under his breath.

"What do you mean?" he asked Jonathan Sanchez.

"She's pretty sure these guys are with the FSB," Sanchez replied from the IMSI control room. "But she's adamant, Mike, they didn't once look at her."

Mike slammed his fist on the steering wheel. "Were you able to identify the woman in the picture?"

"Not yet," Sanchez said, "but we will."

"She can't be on that flight, Jonathan. Why would two FSB agents be on a late flight to Koltsovo?"

"For a number of reasons, Mike," Sanchez replied. "Lisa's a big girl. She can take care of herself."

"I'm heading back to the airport," Mike said, looking for the next exit. "She needs to get out of there."

"Don't do this," came in Charles Mapother, who'd been listening in on the conversation. "You have your objective, she has hers."

"What if they're on to her, Charles? What then? She'll be taken and we'll never be able to get her out of Russia." Visions of his wife being handcuffed in a dirty cell flashed into his mind.

"Listen to me carefully, Mike," Mapother said, steel in his voice. "Lisa will be fine. You need to stop worrying about her and you need to do this now. Can you do this for me?"

Mike wasn't sure he could. He loved his wife more than anything and losing her would mean the end of his own life. He had suffered enough, had lost too much just to let it go. Maybe they should never have worked together in the first place.

"No, I can't," Mike said, bringing the Toyota to a stop. He put on his blinker and turned left onto the overpass.

"We need you to get Dr. Galkin, Mike," Mapother continued.

Mike knew the IMSI director wasn't pleased, but right now he didn't care. His wife needed him. He had failed her in the past and wouldn't allow it to happen again. Family's first.

"You need to understand—" Mike started, but Mapother interrupted him.

"No, Mike, *you* need to understand something. I don't know what's got into your head but you'd better fix it, because if you don't, thousands of people might die. Is that clear enough for you? You want American kids to die?"

"What the hell does that mean, Charles?" Mike asked, accelerating back toward the airport.

"You fucking well know what it means," Mapother said. "You remember the letter I showed you in my office before you and Lisa left for Russia? Or are you so messed up in the head you forgot about it?"

Mike hadn't forgotten about it. The letter written by Dr. Galkin had clearly stipulated that Russia was on the verge of fabricating and maybe mass producing a virus intended to be used against the United States.

"I didn't forget, Charles."

"Good. Do you also remember what you told me when I asked you if you were mission ready?"

"I do."

"And there's one more thing I want you to consider, Mike," Mapother added. "The IMSI's main objective is to protect the financial well-being of our nation. What do you think will happened to our already fragile economy if we are on the receiving end of a major biological attack?"

The last six months hadn't been so kind to the US economy. It was true that the unemployment rate had gone down, but most of the newly created jobs were part time. The stock market had lost over ten percent and the average publicly traded company had slashed its R&D budget by half. You didn't need to be an actuary to understand that the path to an economic recovery didn't include a full-scale biological attack on US soil.

"Nothing good," Mike said.

"Do your job, then. And trust your wife to do hers. She's quite good at this game."

Don't I know it.

. . . .

Lisa Walton certainly didn't expect this. *Russia's Got Talent? To how many countries did this infection spread? Too many, that's for sure.* She glanced again at the lady with the stroller and looked downed at the picture Support Two had provided her. There couldn't be any mistake. It was her. Her name was Olesya Slutzky and she was the main judge of the *Russia's Got Talent* television show. Why in hell she needed a protection detail was incomprehensible to Lisa.

But at least she knew she wasn't the reason these FSB agents were at the airport. Lisa allowed herself to relax. When the announcement to commence the boarding of her flight was made, Lisa realized she and the Russian star would share the same airplane. But that wasn't what worried her. What bothered her was the fact that the two Russian FSB agents had stopped watching Slutzky and weren't acting like bodyguards would. They were too far from the TV star to offer any real protection and didn't even trouble themselves scanning the area.

If they weren't there for Slutzky, who were they there for?

She should have gone for that coffee after all. She wasn't going to get any sleep on the flight.

. . . .

Mike Walton glanced at the dashboard clock. He had a decision to make. Should he drive back to the airport to get Lisa or listen to Sanchez and Mapother and head to the Domodedovo airport in an attempt to grab Dr. Galkin? There was no right or wrong here. Only confusion. He knew his wife. There was no way she'd listened to him. She'd made her decision and she'd even asked him to believe in her, to stop worrying about her.

Why can't I do that?

He knew why. France. Their first mission together had turned into a bloodbath. Pictures of his wife, stabbed in the back by a terrorist, flashed in his mind. If it hadn't been for him, she'd be dead.

Dead.

But she hadn't died. She had lived. And, truth be told, she had saved countless lives on that chaotic day. She had made a judgment call and gone for it. She'd been courageous. No, fearless. She'd been fearless and her bravery had saved the day.

"We've identified the picture Lisa sent us," Sanchez said over the comms system. "She's a Russian TV star. The men are probably some kind of private security hired by the studio."

"But you don't know that for sure, do you?"

"Mike," Sanchez replied, "we need you at Domodedovo."

If Dr. Galkin really had information on a potential biological attack on the United States, they needed to know. His awareness that he was the only man in a position to do something about it tore him apart. He had to let Lisa go, and if he wanted to have even the slightest chance of pulling Dr. Galkin's kidnapping off, he'd need all of his concentration. *Trust your wife, Mike. She trusts you to trust her.*

"I'm on my way," Mike said. "I'll get it done."

CHAPTER 25

New York, NY

Charles Mapother looked at his second-in-command. "You know him better than I do, Jonathan. What do you think?"

"He's confused, Charles," Sanchez said after a moment. "The last two years have been challenging for him. But he's one of the toughest sonofabitches I know. You should have seen him in Kosovo . . ."

"That was then, this is now," interrupted Mapother. "I'm aware of what he's capable of. We all are. With what he did in Ottawa before joining us, and then in Europe, nobody will ever doubt his tenacity as a warrior. But my question is this: with Lisa in harm's way, does he have the mental strength to focus solely on his mission?"

"The stakes are too high for him not to. He knows that," Sanchez said. "He'll come through. He always does."

CHAPTER 26

Moscow, Russia

The traffic wasn't as dense as it had been earlier in the day. Mike made good time and arrived at the Domodedovo airport with enough time to spare to conduct a small recce. He parked the Camry at the short-term parking and walked to the terminal. The sun had set for the day and a cold wind from the north motivated him to walk faster. That didn't mean his eyes weren't moving and probing for threats.

His gaze stopped on a Mercedes S-Class parked curbside. It looked exactly like the one Dr. Votyakov had climbed into that morning. Exhaust smoke came out of the Mercedes's mufflers, but even though the road in front of the terminal was well lit, the tinted windows of the vehicle prevented him from seeing the interior.

"Support Two from Mike," he said into the mic hidden inside his coat collar.

"Go ahead."

"Please pinpoint the location of Dr. Votyakov's escort."

"Stand by."

Mike entered the terminal using one of the swivel doors. A blast of warm air hit him as soon as he set foot inside the terminal. The difference in temperature brought him back to his childhood when he was still living in Canada. During the long winter months, he remembered freezing his ass off waiting for the school bus to pick him up and drive him to the private school to which his parents had decided to send him. Fifteen minutes standing on the street corner had been enough for his toes and fingers to feel as if they'd been cut off. His schoolmates standing next to him at the corner always fought to see who'd get in the bus first. Mike was always the last to climb aboard. He'd stopped participating in the fight the day after his friend Jeremy accidentally stepped on his glasses in a struggle to jump in front of the line. The warm sensation of finally entering the bus gave rise to mixed feelings. It was nice to be sheltered from the cold, but the physical pain from the pins and needles associated with the return of regular blood flow to his extremities wasn't fun. Plus, fog would form on his glasses, limiting his field of vision to a few feet. He'd be forever thankful to his father for agreeing to pay for his laser eye surgery when he was sixteen.

"Mike, Support Two."

"Go for Mike."

"We have a weak signal but it seems that whoever's wearing the tracking device is just outside the terminal."

So it is indeed the same car I saw earlier. But what did it mean? Was Dr. Votyakov already on her way back? Or maybe they were here to pick up Dr. Galkin. He needed to find out.

Mike located the electronic board and searched for Aeroflot flight 1405.

Delayed.

The board didn't provide a new landing time but it did indicate the gate the flight was supposed to land at. Unfortunately, he didn't have a boarding pass and couldn't access the secure area of the terminal without one. Since Luc Walker was a wanted man, the IMSI had decided against booking him on a flight. It would have certainly attracted the unwanted attention of the police or, worse, the SVR. Taking another look at the board, Mike noticed there weren't any flights to Koltsovo departing for the remainder of the night. That could only mean that the Mercedes, and the giant bodyguard, weren't here to drop off Dr. Votyakov. They were here to pick up Dr. Galkin. Dr. Galkin having an escort changed everything. The plan he had quickly concocted on his way to the airport wasn't feasible anymore. He had to think of something else. And fast.

He made his way to the Starbucks he'd seen on entering the terminal. He ordered a large dark roast and added a bit of sugar. He threw the stirring sticks in the trash and selected a table far from the entrance that still allowed him to see who was coming in and out of the café. At this hour, there were less than a dozen clients in the Starbucks, but Mike decided not to risk exposure and used his secured smartphone to communicate with Support Two. In less than five minutes, he had outlined his plan to Support Two and CCed the IMSI headquarters to make sure they knew what was going on.

While waiting for a response, Mike dug into his pocket and retrieved a bottle of go-pills. He popped two in his mouth and washed them down with a sip of coffee. It would be a long night.

. . . .

Charles Mapother, Jonathan Sanchez and Anna Caprini were in the bubble—the soundproof area overlooking the IMSI control room—trying to make contact with Zima. Since their last communication had broken down, they had been unable to reach her and Mapother feared something had gone terribly wrong.

Mapother had contacted DNI Phillips to know if he had heard from the Canadians but he hadn't. The DNI told Mapother he'd look into it but had not gotten back to him yet.

"We just received a secured email from Mike," Caprini said, cutting into Mapother's conversation with Sanchez.

Mapother's eyes moved to Caprini's screen. It took the decryption program less than five seconds to make Mike's message readable.

"What do you think?" Mapother asked once he was sure Sanchez and Caprini had read the message.

Sanchez was the first to speak. "It does complicate things a little."

"A little?" Caprini asked. "There's no way he's gonna pull this off by himself."

"You don't know him as well as I do, Anna," Sanchez said. "Mike wouldn't say he could do it if he had any doubt about his ability to do so."

"C'mon, Charles," Caprini pressed on, looking at Mapother for support, "don't tell me you're seriously considering giving him the green light?"

The plan *was* a little over the top, and extremely risky even for an experienced operator like Mike. But they were running short on time. "I get what you're saying, Jonathan," Mapother said. "I'm sure

Mike convinced himself he could do it but I don't agree with his assessment."

"Do you have any other suggestions on how to snatch Dr. Galkin from the grasp of his Russian babysitters?"

Mapother's second-in-command was getting flustered. He had fought alongside Mike in Kosovo and, with the exception of Lisa, knew the man better than anyone else at IMSI. A former tier-one operator himself, Sanchez had a tendency to overestimate what he and his former colleagues could do.

"Actually, I do," Mapother said. Sanchez and Caprini both looked at him expectantly. "I'd like to bring James Cooper into the fold."

They all knew what had happened last time a support-team leader had joined an asset to conduct a mission outside the scope of their area of expertise. The death of Jasmine Carson at the hands of the Sheik's former right-hand man Omar Al-Nashwan was still fresh in their minds.

"Charles, are you sure about this?" Sanchez asked. "We both know why Mike didn't propose this in the first place."

"Because he doesn't want to feel responsible for someone else if the plan falls apart," Mapother said. "I get that, and I'm all ears if you have any other suggestions."

Caprini shook her head, and so did Sanchez.

"All right," he said, "let Mike know."

. . . .

Mike slowly sipped on his coffee. The amphetamine pills he'd swallowed hadn't started to work their magic yet. It would take another ten minutes or so.

The IMSI headquarters had just sent a reply to his last message. *That was fast.* It was something he loved about working for the IMSI. Decisions were made quickly.

No red tape. No bullshit.

How different it was from his time with the RCMP. Even though the Mounties were renowned worldwide for their professionalism and for always getting their men, the number of times he and his team had missed a target because of a lack of decisiveness from their superiors was mind-blowing. Mike entered his password and waited for the email to go through the decryption software.

Someone at the IMSI headquarters had figured out the reason behind Dr. Galkin's flight delay. It had been a mechanical problem. One of the bathroom doors wouldn't close and the pilot refused to take off until the door was fixed. The situation had taken more time to resolve than everyone had anticipated but the flight was now airborne and would land in approximately eighty minutes. Mapother had more or less given him the green light for his plan. But the IMSI director had decided to burden him with James Cooper, Support Two team leader.

James was a good kid. He had done well in France. But he was a nerd. Mike appreciated everything Support Two had done for him and Lisa in Russia, but he had his doubts about James's ability to operate outside his Support Two team-leader role.

What choice do I have? Being totally honest, Mike could see why Mapother wanted him to use James. He had to admit it would make his job easier. That didn't mean guaranteed success, though. Far from it. But adding a player might even the odds. A little.

Mike sent his reply to Mapother, took one more sip of his coffee and walked out of the café. He needed to make sure he and James Cooper were on the same page.

CHAPTER 27

Moscow, Russia

D r. Lidiya Votyakov reached once more for the box of tissues next to her on the back seat of the Mercedes. The news of her oldest son's death had hit her like a sledgehammer. The sweet comforting words of Qasim—she couldn't get herself to call the father of her children the Sheik—had not done much to appease her rage. The panoply of used tissues by her side was proof she still had a heart. The last few months had definitely played on her psyche. What she had to do to conduct her research had made her sick—she'd had about enough of the torture—but she had pushed through like a good soldier, knowing her country counted on her to exit the hole they'd been put in by the Americans.

Seeing how disappointed she was not to see her youngest son Igor, Qasim had told her the truth about his whereabouts. And that worried her even more.

Syria. What a hellhole that was.

The silver lining was that Igor's mission had been a success. He had managed to grab Ray Powell from the Syrian general who'd betrayed Qasim's network. Igor was now on the run, trying to make contact with members of ISIS who'd help him get out of Syria. Qasim seemed confident that Igor would find his way to their Greek safe house within the next forty-eight hours. She hoped so. She'd do anything to spend a few minutes with the bastard responsible for her son's death, including flying to Mykonos herself. She shivered with pleasure at the thought of what Qasim would do to the man.

Victor's voice brought her back to the present. "Galkin's flight is delayed. We'll wait."

She sighed. "Could you be more specific, Victor? How long till it lands?"

"Ninety minutes, maybe. They'll let us know," Victor replied, showing her his cell phone.

She opened her laptop. At least she'd get some work done. An urgent message from one of her associates popped up on her screen. She clicked it open.

She gasped. Patients 132 and 133 were having exactly the same symptoms as patient 131. And that wasn't all. Dr. Galkin was bringing samples with him.

"I did it," she said, her voice little more than a murmur.

"Why did you say, Doctor?" Victor said, twisting in his seat.

"I was talking to myself," Votyakov replied, her spirits lifted by the unexpected email. She wrote an email to Qasim informing him of the latest developments. She was about to send it when she had second thoughts. Qasim didn't expect the virus to be ready so soon. He was planning on spending the next few days dealing with Ray Powell and Charles Mapother. Something she really wanted him to take care of. If she were to send him the email right away, wouldn't he concentrate on the mission Simonich gave him instead of bringing his wrath down on the people responsible for their son's death?

What about her? Wasn't she a patriot? Or was she a mother first?

Can't I be both? She clicked the send button.

. . . .

The Sheik was impressed. *Lidiya never ceases to amaze me.* He didn't think she would have told him so soon about the findings of her associates. She, of course, had no idea that he had access to all her data and research material. Simonich had seen to that. He had honestly believed that she would let him take care of Ray Powell before informing him that the new thread of Marburg virus she had developed was working.

There was no doubt in his mind that Lidiya was a strong woman, and someone he really cared about. Did he still love her? After all these years fighting the people who had ruined his life, he wasn't sure there was any kindness left in him. But seeing Lidiya again brought back memories he had long ago locked away. And, to his utmost surprise, it felt good. Maybe there would be a time for him and Lidiya, but it wasn't now. He was fighting a two-front war that required all his attention.

Through the Russians, he had a shot at accomplishing what he had failed to do with Steve Shamrock. They had come very close to breaking America's back and, in some ways, they had somewhat won the first round. The North American economy was still struggling and he was in total agreement with Simonich: a biological attack on US soil would push them over the cliff. The trick was to make sure the Russians wouldn't be blamed. This was why Simonich had come to him. The Sheik's network remained strong enough to lead one more attack against Russia's sworn enemies. But the Sheik was under no illusions; his network wouldn't survive the aftermath. Simonich had been very clear about it. He would kill everyone associated with the Sheik to assure that Russia's involvement would remain secret. The Sheik had started this whole thing to get his revenge by crumbling the United States' economy. With that done, he'd be happy to retire. Simonich had promised him asylum anywhere in Russia, with a dacha on the Black Sea.

But is this really what I want? A year ago, he was on top of the world. The mere mention of his name would strike fear into the very hearts of everyone who knew of him. But word of his failed attempt at destroying the Edmonton Terminal—the starting point of the mainline system of the world's longest and most complex crude-oil pipeline—four months ago had greatly diminished the flow of young Muslims wanting to join his terror network. Most of them were now lining up to join ISIS. With the death of Al-Nashwan, and the assassinations of his top lieutenants, he had lost more control than he cared to admit. That was why he wouldn't rest until he had Charles Mapother's head in a bag. The dacha on the Black Sea would come later.

CHAPTER 28

Moscow, Russia

J ames Cooper was out of his depth and he knew it. His hands were sweaty and a migraine had started to creep in. They always came when he was nervous.

Who are you kidding? You aren't nervous. You're terrified!

Trained as a software engineer, he'd always been a geek. Not too good at sports, he'd excelled in science and mathematics. The day he graduated from MIT—the Massachusetts Institute of Technology—with a master's degree in system design, the Boston Police Department offered him a job to head the unit in charge of integrating their newly acquired gunshot detection technology. His work ethic got him noticed by Homeland Security and he started working for them exactly eight months after his graduation. Everything was going his way. He had lots of money, a girlfriend who actually loved him—or so he thought—and a job he enjoyed. That was until Charles Mapother knocked on his door with proof that he'd cheated at online poker and defrauded other players of more than half a million dollars over the previous six months.

Never in his lifetime did he think he'd get caught. When Mapother offered him a clean slate, he took it. He didn't want a criminal record or, worse, to spend time in jail. Guys like him didn't last long in jail. And the moment the money disappeared so did his loving girlfriend.

Truth be told, working for the IMSI was a dream come true. He'd always wanted to be a spy. When he was a kid, he had watched all the James Bond movies and was pleased that he and his hero shared the same first name. He'd learned a lot from Jasmine Carson, the former Support Five team leader who had lost her life on the raid against the Sheik's yacht. She'd been a mentor to him and losing her had been a terrible blow to their team. Shortly after her death, Charles Mapother had disbanded Support Five and assigned all its members to new support teams. Originally assigned to Support Two as its second-in-command, James Cooper was hastily promoted to team leader when his predecessor broke his leg in a skiing accident while away on vacation with his family.

For this mission, Mapother's orders were clear. He had to do whatever Mike Walton wanted. And what Mike wanted right at this moment was for him to sit inside the terminal and keep watch on the black Mercedes parked curbside. He was to take pictures of anyone climbing in or out of the vehicle and send electronically said pictures to the rest of his Support Two team, parked not too far away from the terminal. That had seemed easy enough.

The problem was that with only a few flights left for the evening, the pedestrian traffic inside the terminal was minimal. Staying too long at the same place would make him look suspicious. The Mercedes had tinted windows that forbade Cooper from seeing inside, while the interior of the terminal was well lit. Whoever was in the Mercedes could see him but not vice versa. And that made Cooper nervous, and sweaty.

God damn it! I'm not trained for this. This is exactly how Jasmine Carson was killed. She shouldn't have taken part in the raid, and I shouldn't be conducting physical surveillance in Moscow.

"Calm down, James," came in Mike's voice through his secured Bluetooth earpiece. "You're doing fine."

"Where are you?" Cooper replied, his eyes moving left and right, trying to find Mike.

"Close by."

"They know I'm here, Mike. I can feel it."

"You're fine, James," Mike said. "In two minutes, I want you to walk to the bagel shop fifty meters to your left. You see it?"

James slowly turned his head to his left. There was indeed a bagel shop with a few tables and chairs set up restaurant-style. "Yeah, I see it."

"Buy a bagel and a coffee and sit at one of the tables. You're too close right now."

Shit! I knew it.

"So you think I'm burned?" Cooper said, his voice betraying his anxiety.

"I didn't say that, James. Just do what I say and you'll be fine."

Cooper swallowed hard. It was good to know he had Mike Walton close by. At least one of them seemed to know what was going on. "Okay."

Cooper mentally counted to one hundred before getting up. He did as Mike instructed and ordered a black coffee with a sesame bagel, cream cheese on the side. He was about to sit down at a table set exclusively for the use of the bagel-shop patrons when movement next to the Mercedes caught his eyes.

"Mike, someone's getting out of the vehicle," murmured Cooper into his mic. His heart was pounding and he felt sick to his stomach. His vulnerability and the thought of spending time in prison made him nauseous.

"Okay, James," Mike responded. His voice was reassuring and it had a calming effect on Cooper. "Use your smartphone to snap pictures of them if they come inside the terminal. Don't worry about zooming, your guys will be able to enhance the photos for us—"

"I know that, Mike," Cooper said, positioning his phone in a way that would allow him to photograph anyone coming through the terminal door.

"Of course you do. I'm sorry," Mike said. "One more thing, though. Make sure the flash isn't set at auto."

Cooper was about to reply that he knew that too, but checked anyway. *Holy crap!* The flash was indeed at auto. "Done," he said. "Thanks, Mike."

"Drink your coffee and eat your bagel, James," Mike said. "Act like you belong."

Cooper looked at his right hand. It was shaking. *I'm so much better in front of a computer screen.* He wondered how Jasmine Carson felt the moment just before she entered the room where she was ultimately killed.

"Did anyone enter the terminal?"

Cooper raised his eyes from his shaky hand and focused on the swivel door. "No," he answered, "but there are two people standing outside the vehicle."

"What are they doing, James?"

Cooper squinted. "One of them is smoking, I think," he said. For a moment, the lights of a passing car illuminated the couple.

"Mike, I believe Dr. Votyakov is one of the people standing outside the Mercedes."

. . . .

Mike Walton's brain went into overdrive. Why would Dr. Votyakov come to the airport to pick up Dr. Galkin? But at the same time, why not?

"You got that, Charles?" Mike said.

"We did," Mapother replied. "That doesn't change why you're there, Mike. Proceed as planned."

Capturing Dr. Lidiya Votyakov would be a game changer. There were ways he could make her talk. He'd need a secure environment to do so, though. And right now, his cover was wearing thin. It was one thing to do an exfiltration out of Russia with someone who wanted out; it was another to attempt it with somebody who didn't.

God, I wish Lisa was here instead of James.

"Charles, are you sure Dr. Galkin is privy to all the data related to Votyakov's research."

"Don't even think about it, Mike," Mapother replied. "It's too dangerous."

"What is too dangerous?" James Cooper interjected. "What are you guys talking about?"

"Shut up, James," Mike said. "You'll do as you're told."

"And so will you, Mike," Mapother said. "You won't attempt to abduct Votyakov. Is that clear?"

"Who said anything about abducting her? I want to put her down."

CHAPTER 29

IMSI Headquarters, NY

Charles Mapother looked in disbelief at Jonathan Sanchez. "Did he lose his mind?"

Sanchez shrugged. "I doubt it."

"How the hell does he think he can successfully kill Votyakov, who's protected by the FSB I must add, and capture Galkin without being caught?"

"Don't ask me, ask him," Sanchez replied.

"He's not Ethan Hunt, and we're not the IMF, for God's sake," Mapother said, slamming his fist on Anna Caprini's desk, the effect of which was to spill her coffee all over her lap and keyboard.

"What the hell, Charles?"

Mapother shook his head. "You're not supposed to have a coffee so close to your workstation," he yelled before walking out of the bubble.

. . . .

Jonathan Sanchez placed his hand on Caprini's shoulder. "Don't worry about it, Anna. I'll go talk to him. Are you okay?"

"It wasn't hot, if that's what you're asking," Caprini replied. "What got to him?"

"I have no idea."

"What are we gonna do about Mike?" she asked.

"Patch me to him," he said.

"You're good," she informed him half a second later. "Mike, this is Jonathan."

"Go for Mike," his friend replied.

"I don't need you to elaborate, but I need to know if you're confident about this," he asked.

"It's too good of an opportunity to pass up, Jonathan," Mike replied in a hushed tone. "In his briefing, Mapother told us she's probably the brain behind the scientific research that led to the discovery of the new pathogen agent they want to use against us. It's a no-brainer, buddy."

"It's not, Mike. Not if you can't get away."

"I can do this, Jonathan. Trust me."

If Dr. Galkin indeed had access to all the research data, and if Lisa was successful at convincing his wife to come with her so that Mike could get an actual shot at extracting Galkin out of Russia, then yes, it *could* be worth the risk. *But that's an awful lot of ifs.*

"If you tell me you can do it, I'm green lighting whatever you think is necessary to do in order to complete your task," Sanchez said, taking his first important real-life decision as the newly minted IMSI second-in-command.

"You have the authority?" Mike asked.

"I do," Sanchez lied, hoping his trust in Mike's capabilities wasn't misplaced.

· · · · · · · ·

Charles Mapother heard the knocks on his door. "Come in," he barked, knowing full well who it was. He had heard everything through the intercom linking his office to the bubble. He wasn't sure how he felt about Sanchez going over his head. Truth was, he had lost it in there. It had never happened before.

"I had to make a judgment call, Charles," Sanchez said, standing somewhat at attention in front of Mapother's desk.

"I know. You made a good call."

The IMSI director looked at the man he had chosen to succeed him. Sanchez was built like a tank. Even though he needed a cane to walk after what happened in Kosovo, he was in top shape. His fitness level was proof of his dedication to a healthy lifestyle. Not overly tall, his blond hair and green eyes didn't betray his Hispanic heritage. Mapother was aware that Sanchez had himself crafted his cane while he was in rehabilitation.

Mapother had brought Sanchez to the IMSI not only because he had been one of the best operators he had ever known, but also because of his high intellect and power of deduction. The bullet that had shattered his left leg and forced him out of the field had in no way lessened Sanchez's first-rate tactical instincts. Mapother's plan was to have Sanchez by his side for a few years and to teach him what it took to run an agency like the IMSI.

"What happened in there?" Sanchez asked.

Mapother sighed. He was tired. Since the loss of Sam Turner, he hadn't been the same, and he knew it. *Am I fit to run this organization?* Without Sam and the quick intervention of Mike, he'd be in the ground.

Mapother rose from behind his desk and fetched two bottles of water from his mini-fridge. He threw one to Sanchez who caught it with his free hand.

"I could tell you a lie and that I did that just to push you to make a timely decision," Mapother started, "but I don't think you'd believe me."

"You're right, I wouldn't," Sanchez replied with a smile.

"Good," Mapother said, opening his bottle of water. "But believe me when I say this won't happen again."

CHAPTER 30

Moscow, Russia

Mike Walton had no illusions about what would happen to him if he got caught. That is why he had asked James Cooper to leave the terminal and to pick up his car from the parking lot. Mike didn't know yet the exit he would take but he needed Cooper to be on standby and ready to go at a moment's notice.

He had told his friend Jonathan that he was confident he could pull it off but his plan was fragile. His number one objective remained the capture of Dr. Galkin, but if the opportunity to take care of Dr. Votyakov presented itself, he'd take it and wouldn't have time to ask for permission.

The Domodedovo airport was one big terminal and it was presently undergoing important renovations. Mike had read that the idea behind the overhaul was to add an extension to the current concourse. It seemed that most of the construction was being done at night as he could hear the specific sound of a jackhammer being used in the background. Mike was about to stop by a leather shop that had a good view of the door but a rude clerk stopped him in mid stride, speaking loudly in Russian.

Mike didn't understand what the woman was saying, but she showed him her watch and shook her head. The shop was closing. And, unfortunately for him, so were most of the other stores, at least those with a good vantage point on the Mercedes. Shopkeepers were sliding their doors closed while others were putting away their displays. That was going to complicate things a little. With nowhere to go, Mike felt like a sitting duck.

. . . .

Dr. Lidiya Vodyakov inhaled deeply and blew a stream of smoke out of the corner of her mouth. The light gray smoke stood out against the night. She hadn't been out of the car for three minutes and already her fingers were almost frozen.

Victor, standing next to her, hadn't move at all, except for his eyes that were in constant motion. Did Victor know the plan her Qasim had concocted? Was he aware that Russia, using Qasim's network, would wage biological warfare against the United States? She huffed one last time and flicked the butt into the street.

"How long?" she asked her bodyguard.

"Another half hour," Victor replied without looking at his watch.

"I need to go to the bathroom," she said. "Lead the way."

. . . .

Mike Walton saw the pair enter via the swivel door. The tall bodyguard was switched on. As soon as he set foot inside the terminal, he scanned his immediate surroundings and waited for his charge to walk in front of him. He followed about three steps behind while peeking behind him every twenty steps or so. He wasn't going to be an easy mark.

Dr. Galkin's flight wasn't due to land for another thirty minutes, and Mike wondered why they were here so soon. Surely the bodyguard had suggested they remain inside the Mercedes, by far the most secure place they could wait out the arrival of Dr. Galkin. Mike had no choice but to follow them from further away than he would have liked. The bodyguard's continued rear scans complicated Mike's job. If the bodyguard was half as good as Mike thought he was, he was mentally cataloguing everyone following his charge and would be suspicious of anyone approaching.

"James from Mike," he said.

"I'm listening."

"Votyakov's in the terminal. She has her bodyguard in tow."

"What do you want me to do?"

"For now, nothing. Where are you?"

"I'm in your car, engine running. I prepaid the exit ticket. I'm good to go."

"Lisa's handgun is in the glove box, James."

Cooper didn't answer right away. "Okay, I got it. As I said, I'm good to go," he finally said. Cooper sounded confident and focused. Gone was the shaky voice.

The bodyguard suddenly stopped and turned around. Mike was still fifty meters behind him but saw the universal sign of a public bathroom above the bodyguard's head.

Votyakov had to go to the bathroom. That made sense. With only two people between him and the bodyguard, Mike had no way out. Any evasive maneuvers would only make him even more suspicious. He had no choice. He had to walk in front of the bodyguard and he knew he couldn't do it again. It would be extremely hard to follow them again.

Unless I move now.

Mike dropped his pen behind him and turned around to pick it up, using the moment as an excuse to see how many people were behind him. Two businessmen with tiny carry-ons were walking toward the screening point. They were engrossed in a conversation and didn't pay any attention to him. With his pen back in his pocket, Mike continued to walk toward the men's bathroom located right next to the ladies'. He could feel the bodyguard tense as Mike approached him. Trying to look as non-threatening as he could, Mike nodded to the bodyguard as he walked past him. He didn't get any nod back. The bodyguard was taller than Mike had originally thought. The man was over six and a half feet tall and was larger than a side-by-side refrigerator. Conscious the bodyguard had his eyes glued to his back, Mike pushed the door of the bathroom and entered a small enclosure with a garbage bin. He pushed through another door and a powerful scent of industrial disinfectant hit him right away. A janitor, whose back was turned, was mopping the floor. A quick look under the stall doors confirmed no other passengers were there. When Mike looked up, the janitor had a silenced pistol pointed at his head.

CHAPTER 31

Moscow, Russia

Makhmud Geremeyev looked at the man standing in front of him. He was clearly surprised and his body language indicated he was terrified. Unfortunately for him, Geremeyev wasn't duped. A former member of Chechnya's Kadyrovites, a pro-Moscow paramilitary unit known for its involvement in the kidnapping, torture and murder business, Geremeyev knew a soldier when he saw one, and the man's eyes had betrayed him. Sent as extra security by the Sheik to ensure Dr. Votyakov's safety, Geremeyev hesitated for a fraction of a second before pulling the trigger as he pondered if the man was friend or foe. The man's actions gave him the answer he needed.

. . . .

The man was out of Mike's reach and he'd be shot dead before he could pull his own pistol from the holster in the small of his back. It was no good trying to grab the man's gun so he let himself fall to the floor while extending his right leg in an attempt to sweep the other man's legs from under him with a low, spinning kick. Mike's foot connected with his opponent's left ankle at the moment the man fired his pistol. The bullet went over Mike's head as the man fell hard on his side. Mike jumped on him with both hands reaching for the man's wrist. Another shot went off and the bullet lodged in the wall between the last stall and the hand dryer. Mike used his left elbow to smack the man's head several times against the tile floor. Mike tried to angle his body in a way that would allow him to hit the man in the throat but only managed to hit him in the chin. His second and third efforts had better results. Using his body weight, he kept the pressure on and thrust the tip of his elbow deep into the man's throat with all his might. The gargling sounds coming from the man's mouth told Mike his windpipe had collapsed and that he had only a few seconds to live.

But Mike didn't have the luxury of waiting out those precious seconds. He had no idea if the commotion had alerted Votyakov's bodyguard, so he let go of the dazzled man's throat and wrestled the gun away. He placed it under the man's chin and pulled the trigger. Brain matter splattered against the back wall of the bathroom. The whole encounter had lasted less than twelve seconds.

Mike got to his feet just as the bathroom door burst open. A middle-aged man stopped dead in his tracks. His eyes moved from the gun in Mike's hand to the bloody corpse on the floor. Mike took two quick strides and smacked the butt of the pistol on top of the man's head. Mike caught him as he fell and gently laid him on the floor. The man had no luggage so he was probably there to pick up someone. He dragged him next to the urinals. He hoped he hadn't killed the man, because if he had, this poor man would be the second innocent he'd killed that day.

Mike looked down at the pistol he was holding. It was a Russian-made PB silent pistol. The pistol used an integral suppressor, which, unlike most similar systems, consisted of two parts. It allowed the pistol to be carried and kept concealed without the front part of the suppressor attached. Mike ejected the eight-round magazine and confirmed it had five rounds remaining.

He had already spent too much time in the men's room and he could only hope Dr. Votyakov wasn't done with her business. Mike quietly pulled on the door leading back to the terminal and peeked outside. The bodyguard hadn't moved but he was speaking into a smartphone he was holding against his ear with his shoulder. He was still in the same position Mike had seen him in a minute ago. Mike remembered what the bodyguard had done earlier this morning when Lisa had slipped in front of him outside the terminal as Dr. Votyakov climbed into the waiting vehicle. He had rendered assistance to the fallen old lady, and Mike wanted to capitalize on the fact that the bodyguard was most probably a kind man.

"Excuse me, sir," Mike started in English, doing his best to look like a frightened tourist. "Please call the police. I think someone had a heart attack. Please help me."

The bodyguard turned toward him and placed his phone in his coat pocket. Mike knew he was being gauged. "Quick," Mike added, trying to press the issue. The bodyguard replied something in Russian but Mike shook his head. "I don't speak Russian, sir, but you need to help me."

With that said, Mike reentered the bathroom. The ball was in the bodyguard's court.

CHAPTER 32

Moscow, Russia

Victor Simonich understood English perfectly. His father, a Russian diplomat and brother to current Russian president Veniamin Simonich, had made sure of that. He wanted his son to speak as many languages as he could master. Having sent him to the best international schools, his dad had longed for him to become a diplomat and to join the Ministry of Foreign Affairs. But the FSB had a long reach, and they recruited young Victor with the promise of a life filled with excitement. And they hadn't lied. Victor had enjoyed every minute of his time with the FSB. He loved his country, and honestly believed in the work he was doing.

Five years ago, at the specific request of his uncle Veniamin Simonich, Victor was transferred to the Presidential Security Service. His family's ties gave him unprecedented access to his uncle, and Victor was honored to serve his family and his country at the same time. When his uncle first talked to him about the project with which he had tasked Dr. Votyakov, Victor was stunned. He feared the American retaliations that were sure to come and said so to his uncle. Fear turned into horror when Veniamin Simonich told him he'd partnered with the Sheik in order to accomplish his objective. The plan was to place the blame of the whole operation on the Sheik's network. His uncle would look like the champion who'd finally stopped the master terrorist and Russia would get away unscathed. Nevertheless, Victor had heard about the Sheik and the atrocities he'd waged across the globe. The man was an animal. How could Russia be associated with such a monster? Of course, he hadn't voiced his concerns to his uncle. Family or not, there would have been dire consequences to disagreeing with the Russian president.

Torn between his duty to his country and his conscience, Victor had decided to play it safe and to follow his uncle's orders by ensuring the safety of Dr. Votyakov during her visits to Moscow. There had been no other options, no one he could talk to. Until today.

Summoned to the Sheik's office inside the Kremlin Grand Palace, he had learned that Dr. Galkin—Dr. Votyakov's main associate—was a traitor. The fact that the Sheik had his own office inside a building such as the Kremlin Grand Palace sent shivers down Victor's spine and he wondered who the traitor really was. The Sheik hadn't divulged how he had found out about Dr. Galkin's treason but he had told Victor to be careful around him. He was to bring him directly to an address the Sheik had written on a piece of paper. Victor had no doubt about what was to happen to poor Dr. Galkin. He just wished he wouldn't have to watch. Victor had never felt so alone in his life. He was no scientist, but what he knew about Dr. Votyakov's research was enough to bring fear and regret into any man's heart. The new thread of Marburg virus Dr. Votyakov had created would make Ebola look like a mild fever. It would bring chaos and misery everywhere it went. How could his uncle approve of such a thing? How could he be so sure his own country wouldn't be affected?

Did they have a vaccine? Some sort of remedy? They had to. If not, it was madness. Was Dr. Galkin able to communicate the research data to anyone? To whom had he tried to pass information? Maybe there was a chance after all.

Victor was thinking about his options when the tourist he had seen enter the bathroom two minutes ago came out asking for help. The man looked confused and about to lose it. He had indeed seen an older gentleman enter the bathroom right after the panicked tourist. Dr. Votyakov had been in the ladies' room for less than four minutes. If she came out and he wasn't there, she'd think he was probably relieving himself and she'd wait for him.

Victor made his decision and followed the man inside the men's room.

. . . .

Mike Walton figured that if the bodyguard didn't enter within the next ten seconds, he'd have to go to plan B. Problem was, there was no plan B as yet. But he should not have worried because he heard the first door open. Visualizing what was about to happen, Mike held his breath as he waited for the bodyguard to open the second door. As soon as he did, Mike grabbed the taller man by his tie in an attempt to rush him in and to shoot him inside the bathroom. He jerked on the man's tie as hard as he could but the tie stayed in his hand and, for the briefest moment, the two men locked eyes. Having lost his balance, and with the clip-on tie in his left hand, Mike found himself at a disadvantage when the bodyguard chopped his wrist with the outside of his left hand. The blow was so powerful Mike felt as if he had touched an electric fence. The pistol flew out of his hand at the same moment the giant bodyguard's right hand shut up in an uppercut that knocked him out of his socks and two feet back. He almost passed out right there, but a little voice in his head told him he was about to die if he didn't get back in the fight. The bodyguard reached for the pistol and Mike saw no option but to rush him.

. . . .

Victor knew he was fighting for his life the moment his opponent hadn't gone down with his last punch. *Tough sonofabitch.* The uppercut had connected perfectly with the man's chin. He had dispatched more than one opponent with a less lethal blow. Still, the man had stepped back and it allowed Victor half a second to take in his surroundings as he fumbled for his gun. A middle-aged man lay dead or unconscious next to the urinals. Another one, dressed in a janitor's uniform, had his brain splattered on the wall. Victor recognized him as one of the Sheik's men.

Who the hell is this guy? Was he here to collect Dr. Galkin? In that case . . . But he couldn't finish his thought. The man rushed him like a bull. Victor stopped trying to unholster his firearm and grabbed the charging man by the shoulders while pivoting one hundred and eighty degrees on his left foot. Victor's blunt force added to the man's momentum helped him throw his opponent against the wall. The man grunted as his back slammed violently against the hand dryer. But that didn't stop him. It seemed to have the opposite effect.

. . . .

Mike was literally seeing stars. His eyes had become unfocused and the pain in his back was excruciating. He didn't know what he had hit but it had taken his breath away. His body was about to shut down and he knew it. His only chance was to go on the offensive and that's what he did. He had no idea if any of his punches caused any real damage but he kept pushing forward, battering the body-guard with a steady barrage of combinations to the head and body.

. . . .

Victor couldn't block them all. The attacks were coming so rapidly that he had to step back. He needed some distance in order to draw his weapon and finish this. But he didn't dare drop his guard, aware that a lucky punch could ultimately lead to his death. Just when he expected another barrage of punches to the head, his opponent kicked him in the groin. He involuntarily bent forward and didn't see the man's knee before it was too late. His head snapped back and his foot hit something. He tumbled backwards.

. . . .

Mike saw the bodyguard fall on his back as his foot hit one of the dead man's legs. Mike looked for his gun but couldn't immediately locate it. What he did find was the bodyguard's clip-on tie. In three strides, he had picked up the tie and positioned himself behind the fallen bodyguard. He wrapped the tie around the other man's neck and started to pull, using all of his remaining strength.

. . . .

Victor figured he must have lost consciousness because he sud-denly realized he was on his back with someone under him. Then he felt something soft slide around his neck.

My tie!

He just had time to slip two fingers of his right hand between the tie and his neck before the man started to choke him. He tried to elbow and head butt his way out, but the man knew what he was doing and kept himself glued to him, leaving Victor with no room to maneuver. Victor tried to grab something, his left hand seeking anything he could use as a weapon. Nothing. The only thing his fingers touched were the cold tiles of the bathroom floor. Darkness was closing in, his vision already blurred by the lack of oxygen reaching his brain. He had mere seconds to get out of this but didn't know what to do. Then he did. He had one last card to play.

. . . .

Mike held the choke and knew he had him. But at what cost? This was supposed to be a five-second takedown but it had lasted over thirty. Where was Dr. Votyakov? Was she still in the restroom? What if she was gone? No, she wouldn't be. She'd wait for her bodyguard.

A sound escaped from the bodyguard's lips. The man was trying to say something. Mike didn't care. He just had to hold on for a few more seconds. But the Russian did something Mike didn't expect. He removed the two fingers he'd been able to squeeze in between his neck and the tie and reached for his right pocket. That was a dumb move as it allowed Mike to tighten his hold even more. Mike half expected to see a knife appear, but a folded piece of paper came out instead. Then the Russian went limp and the piece of paper fell to the floor. Mike had a decision to make. If he held the choke for another twenty seconds, it would kill the man. If he let go now, the man would regain consciousness within seconds. Why in hell did he let go of the tie?

Shit!

Mike used the tie to quickly secure the bodyguard's hands behind his back. He then relieved him of his pistol and picked up the one he had dropped on the floor. He was about to snatch the piece of paper off the floor when the bodyguard said in heavily accented but grammatically perfect English, "It's the address where we're supposed to take Dr. Galkin. That's why you're here, yes? For Galkin?"

Mike aimed a pistol at the man's head but only got a smile in return.

"You use this in here, you'll never get out of here alive."

"You're right," Mike said, switching to the PB silent pistol. "Why?"

"My name is Victor Simonich. I'm with the FSB. I'm with the Presidential Security Service and my uncle Veniamin Simonich is the Russian president."

"I couldn't care less who your uncle is, shithead."

"We know Dr. Galkin is a traitor. I think we're bringing him here to be interrogated by the Sheik."

Mike was taken aback. The Sheik? Here in Moscow? And if the Russians knew Dr. Galkin had betrayed them, that meant they knew someone would try to get to his wife. Lisa! He had to warn her. She was probably walking into a trap.

"Don't look so surprised. The man you killed is one of his men," Victor said, pointing to the dead man on the floor with his chin. But Mike was barely listening. His mind was spinning at one hundred miles an hour.

So the Russians knew Dr. Galkin had tried to communicate with someone outside Russia. If the Sheik was working for the Russian government, he had to inform the IMSI immediately.

"Why are you telling me this?"

"I'm a patriot. I love my country. But what my uncle and the Sheik have in mind is madness. It will bring chaos and mayhem to our two countries."

God damn it! This was bigger than everyone had originally thought. "What are you proposing?"

"Let me go, and bring your team to the address written on the paper."

When Mike didn't reply right away, Victor continued, "What are you gonna do? Kill me? Kill Dr. Votyavov? Kill Galkin?"

"I could."

"Yeah, but you won't. You'll never know what the Sheik's plan is if you do."

Mike kneeled next to the Russian and dug the pistol into the man's neck. "Then tell me," he hissed.

"There's no need for that," Victor said. "I'm not afraid to die. Believe it or not, we want the same thing."

"And what is it that I want?"

"To stop a dangerous new pathogen from reaching your country, and maybe, just maybe, to catch the Sheik. But to do this, you need to let me go. Now. I've been here too long."

This is insane. Am I actually considering this? The Russian was right. He could still pursue his original plan, but to what end? If the Sheik was involved, it was an entirely new ball game. Dr. Galkin could only provide so much. He was most certainly not aware of the whole plan. *What do I have to lose except my life?*

"All right," Mike said. "Slowly get up and turn around. I'll untie you."

"Already done," Victor said. He slowly moved his arms from behind his back and showed Mike the tie before clipping it back on. "Just a small gesture to let you know that for now, we're on the same side. I need my gun back."

"Turn around," Mike said. "Now."

Once the Russian had his back to him, Mike ejected the magazine and cleared the pistol. Twenty seconds later, he had removed the firing pin and reassembled the gun.

"Here you go," he said. He tossed the pistol and the magazine back to the Russian once they were face to face again.

"I know you've removed my firing pin," Victor said, holstering his pistol. "I want it back."

Mike threw it on the ground as he positioned himself to cover the Russian with his own pistol. "Pick it up," he said.

Victor looked at him and shook his head but nevertheless picked his firing pin off the floor and put it in his coat pocket. The Russian spent ten seconds in front of the mirror trying to freshen up. He said to Mike, "Lock the door behind you." Then he left without another word.

CHAPTER 33

Moscow, Russia

Dr. Lidiya Votyakov needed another cigarette. Her makeup was a mess and she didn't have anything to fix it with. The loss of her son had shaken her to the bone. Qasim had promised he'd make the people responsible for her son's death pay. She'd do her part. Even if it cost her soul. She stormed out of the restroom determined to bring misery to her son's assassins.

Where was Victor? It wasn't like him to abandon his post. Did he go back to the car? She was about to walk back to the car herself when she saw him leaving the men's room. He looked ruffled and held a bloodied handkerchief under his nose.

"What happened to you?"

"Entered the restroom at the same time someone tried to come out. I walked right into the open door. My mistake."

"Your nose is bleeding."

"I'll be fine. We should go back to the car, Dr. Votyakov," her bodyguard said. "Dr. Galkin's flight won't be here for another twenty minutes."

"Are you sure you're all right, Victor?" she asked. She'd never seen him like this.

"Of course I am. Shall we?" Victor replied, gesturing toward the outside of the terminal.

Walking back toward the car, her mind slipped back to her mission. Producing the new Marburg thread in sufficient quantity wouldn't be a problem. She had everything she needed but she worried about the timeframe. The virus was fragile and couldn't be mass-produced rapidly. Dr. Galkin knew as much as she did about the virus and she planned on spending the night brainstorming about their options with him.

Once outside, she dug into her pocket for the pack of cigarettes she knew was there. She offered one to Victor but he waved her off. A flick from her lighter followed by a long drag sent the smoke into her lungs. It felt so good.

. . . .

Mike Walton waited two minutes before making his exit. He used the set of keys he had found on the Sheik's enforcer to lock the bathroom door behind him. It would buy him enough time to leave the airport. He called James Cooper and asked him to pick him up at the arrivals. Mike climbed into the passenger seat two minutes later.

"Where to?" Cooper asked.

"Just drive, James. I need to think."

Thinking wasn't the only thing he needed to do right now. He had to contact the IMSI to advise them of what had just happened inside the terminal. He also needed to find a way to reach Lisa, and to warn her about the trap she was probably walking into.

Mike looked down at his secured smartphone. The screen was cracked. "Look at this, James," he said, showing his phone to Cooper. "Should I be worried?"

Cooper took his eyes off the road and examined Mike's phone. "I won't know for sure until I test it. I have all the equipment in Support Two's van. I wouldn't make a secure call before then if I were you."

That was a problem. IMSI assets like Mike depended on their secure smartphone to communicate in the field. Their wireless earbuds and mics wouldn't work without it. If the security of their smartphone was compromised, so was the Bluetooth interaction between the different components.

"How can I reach IMSI headquarters?" Mike asked.

"You can use mine," offered Cooper. "But it doesn't have the same level of encryption as yours."

"How long before the conversation is picked up by the Russians?"

"I wouldn't talk for more than ninety seconds or so with this phone."

"They're that good?" Mike hadn't expected the Russians to be so switched on.

"We don't really know how good they are, I'm afraid," Cooper replied. "What we know is that since March 2015, and with the implementation of SORM-3, their capabilities have grown exponentially."

Mike was no expert in these sorts of things but he trusted Cooper. He unplugged Cooper's phone from its USB cable and was about to dial the IMSI's number when Cooper had an idea.

"Support Two has a local number. Use them to connect you through to the IMSI. Their encryption level is higher than my phone and the Russian government doesn't keep track of as many local calls as they do international ones. It should give you an extra minute of talk time."

When the phone finally rang at IMSI headquarters, Anna Caprini answered.

"Can you put either Jonathan or Charles on the line?"

"I'll have both in a moment," Caprini replied. Mike started the timer of his Tag Heuer. Fifteen seconds later, Jonathan Sanchez and Charles Mapother were on the other end. Mike explained to them what had happened at the airport.

"Holy shit," Sanchez said. "What do you want to do?"

"Do I have any choice?" Mike said. "I need to get to this address. In the meantime, I need you to find everything you can on Victor Simonich."

"We will," Sanchez confirmed.

"What about Lisa?" Mike asked. "Where is she?"

Charles Mapother replied to this one. "She boarded her flight to Koltsovo two hours ago. She'll be landing soon."

"You need to pull her out of there," Mike said, picturing his wife by herself against a bunch of Russian federal agents. "She won't last long if this is indeed a trap."

"We'll take care of her, Mike," Mapother said. "I promise."

CHAPTER 34

Moscow, Russia

Victor's phone vibrated in his pocket. A quick look around satisfied him that there were no immediate threats to Dr. Votyakov. He placed his phone against his ear. It was the Sheik.

"Change of plan, Victor," the Sheik said. "You're coming directly to me at the Grand Palace."

"What about the address you gave me?" Victor asked, thinking about the foreign agent he had fought with in the men's room. *Does he know?* Despite the blistering cold, perspiration had formed on his forehead. *Because if he does, even my uncle won't be able to save my ass.* But the Sheik's reply somewhat reassured him he wasn't a dead man yet.

"I've lost contact with one of my men. Bring Dr. Galkin to me, Victor."

The Sheik ended the call before Victor could reply.

"I'm freezing," Dr. Votyakov said, standing next to him.

"Why don't you stay in the car, Doctor? There's no need for you to waste your time inside the terminal. I'll get Dr. Galkin."

"But you've never met him, Victor. How will you—"

"I'm FSB, Dr. Votyakov. Trust me, I know what he looks like."

Dr. Votyakov nodded and climbed back into the Mercedes while Victor headed back inside the terminal. He rubbed his hands together in an attempt to warm them up. Victor forced himself to focus on the problem. Once Dr. Galkin was in the Sheik's hands, it would be all over. There was a way to keep Dr. Galkin out of the Sheik's reach. But it would require him to take a step he wasn't sure he was ready to take. It was a big risk, and he doubted it was worth the reward. But what was the alternative? If there was something he could do to save his country, didn't he have to try? Even at the cost of his own life?

. . . .

Victor could see that Dr. Galkin was someone who liked to travel light. With the exception of a small, rolling carry-on bag, his only other luggage was a medium-sized leather bag he carried over his shoulder.

"Dr. Galkin?" Victor asked, knowing that it was.

"Yes?"

"I'm Victor. I'm with Dr. Votyakov," he said as a way to introduce himself. "Please follow me."

He didn't offer to carry Dr. Galkin's bag. If the scientist was nervous, he concealed it well.

"We have a long drive to Moscow, Doctor," Victor said. "I suggest we stop by the restroom."

"Yes, of course," Dr. Galkin replied. "I was thinking that myself."

They were still fifty meters away from the restroom when Victor saw a middle-aged man coming out. Even at that distance, Victor could see that the man's head was bleeding badly. The man lost his balance and staggered to his left before he decided to sit on the floor. Luckily, most passengers had checked-in luggage so there weren't that many people from Galkin's flight walking with them. Still, some passengers had seen the distressed man and were now approaching him.

"Follow me, Dr. Galkin," Victor said, jogging toward the man. "This gentleman needs your assistance."

The foreign agent had locked the door as he had asked him to, but he had forgotten about the unconscious man, which actually helped Victor's plan. A couple of passengers were already kneeling next to the injured man. Victor flashed his FSB badge and asked the people to leave. One woman hesitated and offered to stay but Victor told her that if she did, she'd have to give a deposition at the FSB headquarters in downtown Moscow. She left promptly.

Victor helped the man to his feet. "Follow me, sir," he said.

"There's a dead man inside the restroom," the man said, clearly distraught.

"Show us," Victor said, looking back to make sure Dr. Galkin was still with him. He gestured Galkin to follow the man in. Once both men were in front of him, Victor took a second to lock the door behind him. When he turned back, Dr. Galkin was looking at him, eyebrows raised in a silent question.

"We don't want anyone to panic," Victor explained, gently pushing Galkin forward. The moment they entered the restroom, Victor shoved Galkin to the side and took three strides toward the injured man. Victor knocked him out with a powerful left hook to the chin. The man crumbled to the floor right next to the Sheik's man.

"What are you doing?" Dr. Galkin yelled, his eyes set on the exit door.

Victor pulled out his pistol and aimed it at Dr. Galkin's chest, though it couldn't fire as it was still missing its firing pin.

To his credit, Dr. Galkin didn't panic. "What do you want?"

Victor had only one shot at this, and he knew it. This was the point of no return.

"I'm sorry about this, Dr. Galkin. I really am," Victor started, locking eyes with Galkin and looking for any signs of deceit. "Did you know that Dr. Votyakov's working with the Sheik?"

Dr. Galkin's reaction wasn't immediate and Victor wondered if the scientist was about to try to bluff his way out of this. He hoped he didn't, because they had very little time before his partner called him to inquire about what they were doing.

"So you know about me?"

"Yes, I do. And so does the Sheik."

"What will you do about it, Victor?"

"I'm supposed to take you to the Sheik at the Grand Palace where you'll be—"

"The Sheik has an office at the Kremlin Grand Palace?" Dr. Galkin interrupted. "I can't believe we've sunk so low as to work with a piece of shit like him."

"Neither can I, Doctor."

Dr. Galkin looked at him, his confusion evident. "If you aren't with him, young man, whose side are you on?"

"I'm on Russia's side, Dr. Galkin. And always will be."

Dr. Galkin sighed. "So am I. Where does that leave us?"

"I need to know everything there is to know about the virus. More precisely, I need to know—"

"May I?" Dr. Galkin asked, pointing to the leather bag he was still carrying.

Victor nodded. Galkin unfastened his bag and laid it on the floor to look through its contents. He showed a blue flash drive to Victor. "On this you'll find everything you need to know about the virus. Very few people are privy to this information. I was hoping to give it to an American operative but I guess that's not going to happen."

"Who did you contact in the United States?" Victor asked.

Dr. Galkin pondered if he should answer the question or not. "I guess it doesn't really matter anymore. I'm already dead, am I not, Victor?"

Victor didn't lie. He nodded sadly. "It's your only way out, Doctor."

Dr. Galkin seemed to accept his fate in stride. "I contacted someone at the FBI named Charles Mapother. I didn't hear from him, but I've always known him to be quite resourceful. If he got my message, he'll find a way to help us."

"He already did. He killed this man," Victor said, pointing his gun toward the Sheik's soldier. "He was working for the Sheik."

"Mapother didn't do this," Dr. Galkin said. "He's only a few years younger than me."

"Then he sent someone."

"Listen to me carefully, Victor," Dr. Galkin said, his voice cracking. "A week ago, we didn't know we had the right thread. All this is still very new. If you destroy our Koltsovo complex, you'll destroy everything we have. Do you understand?"

"I do. Anything else?"

"Do what you must," Dr. Galkin said, clearly resigned to his fate.

"I'm sorry, Doctor."

"You've said that already. Go on." A single tear rolled down on his cheek. "I'm ready."

"You'll have to give me a moment," Victor said, feeling terrible. *Damn firing pin!*

"Just do it, for God's sake."

Victor fumbled with his firing pin and dropped it to the floor. He didn't dare look at the poor doctor who was patiently awaiting his execution. Victor was tempted to apologize again but didn't. He had just slammed his magazine back into his pistol when he sensed movement. When he looked up, Dr. Galkin seemed to be charging him, but rushed right past him and into the injured middle-aged man. Victor looked at both men as they fell to the ground with Dr. Galkin on top. *What the hell?* Victor racked the action and shot the middle-aged man right in the middle of his forehead. He kneeled down next to Dr. Galkin and rolled him over. A combat knife was protruding from his chest, and blood was already pouring out of Galkin's mouth. His left hand grabbed Victor's bicep.

"You . . . you need to stop this . . . this madness . . . my friend," Dr. Galkin said before his eyes rolled over.

Victor looked at the scene and knew he could turn all of this to his advantage. It seemed obvious that the poor middle-aged man had had enough and had perceived them as a threat. He had most probably taken the knife away from the Sheik's man. *I can't really blame him. I'm the one who attacked him first after all . . .*

It was time to play now and Victor called his partner. His colleague hadn't said hello before Victor started yelling, "We're under attack, exfil, exfil, exfil." Protocol dictated that the driver take the main charge to the closest secure location and Victor could imagine his partner taking off at full speed with the Mercedes.

Victor assumed that the shot he had fired had been heard and that the police were already on their way. He hurried out of the restroom and showed his FSB badge to the curious who had gathered outside. Victor couldn't believe they hadn't heard the shot. *Then what are they doing standing there with their phones?* It didn't make any sense to him. People were sometimes so stupid. *And I'm risking everything to save them? Maybe I'm the stupid one.*

CHAPTER 35

Moscow, Russia

Mike Walton asked Cooper to let him out five blocks away from the address Victor had given him.

"Are you sure, boss?" Cooper asked.

"Drop me here and go back to Support Two to get the equipment I need."

The sky was overcast and the streetlights weren't doing a good job at keeping the streets lit. Mike wasn't familiar with this neighborhood and wished he had his smartphone with him. With all the applications the IMSI had downloaded onto it, he would have learned everything he needed to know about this shitty place in a matter of minutes. The only thing he knew was that the address was located inside the Solntsevo District in northwest Moscow. And by the look of it, it wasn't the nicest or the safest place to be. But it was so cold that nobody dared venture outside if they didn't really have to. Tall apartment buildings with large exterior parking lots filled with rusted old cars seemed to be the norm.

Mike had asked James Cooper to drive past the address once before dropping him further down the street. The address was another tall apartment building located on a street corner. The piece of paper hadn't specified an apartment number and Mike couldn't find a place to keep an eye on the building. Staying by himself outside in the cold would become dangerous in a matter of minutes, and even though he couldn't see them, Mike was convinced people were already looking at him from the windows of their apartments. In this type of neighborhood, people didn't call the police when they became suspicious of someone. They trusted the criminals to take care of anyone not belonging.

Mike estimated that Cooper would be back within fifteen minutes with the equipment he had requested—a heat-sensing, thermal-imaging camera and a night-vision monocular. In the meantime, he'd try to keep himself from freezing to death by walking around the block one more time.

. . . .

Victor didn't wait for the police to arrive. His window of opportunity was closing rapidly and he had to act fast. He hurried down to the taxi stand and waited what seemed like a small eternity for one to finally show up.

"Where to?" the tired driver asked once Victor was in the backseat.

Victor gave him the address and was told they were three quarters of an hour away.

He would have given a year's salary in exchange for a bottle of vodka. Victor was puzzled by his own actions. Who was he to question the will of the Russian president? *My own goddamn uncle!* But it was too late to do anything but to listen to his conscience. And if he was being honest with himself, he knew the path he had chosen was the right one. Dr. Galkin had been a patriot too, and Victor wouldn't let the man's sacrifice be in vain. The question was: would Mapother's man show up?

His phone rang. He looked at its screen to see who the caller was. He didn't recognize the number. What to do? With Dr. Votyakov secured and already gone from the terminal, protocol dictated he should have stayed at the terminal until the arrival of the police. Whoever was on the other end of the call would know he had no good reason to leave the scene, especially with the bloodbath he had left behind. Victor turned off his phone and removed the battery and the SIM card before throwing it out of the window. He was now officially a rogue agent, wanted by his own government.

CHAPTER 36

Moscow, Russia

T he Sheik dialed the number again. It went directly to Victor's voicemail. *What's going on?* Victor hadn't checked in yet and it worried him. He knew Lidiya was safe and on her way to join him at the Grand Palace, but what about Dr. Galkin? And what about the man he had placed at the terminal? Things weren't looking up, and he hated being in the dark. He needed Dr. Galkin alive to know if he had any accomplices inside the Koltsovo facilities. It was at times like these that he really missed his former associate Omar Al-Nashwan. In anger, the Sheik threw his phone against the wall. Two armed men belonging to the Presidential Security Services entered his office to see what the commotion was about. The Sheik chastised them with his eyes and they left without a word.

The Sheik wasn't duped. Even though the Russian agents were tasked with his protection, he was aware that as soon as Veniamin Simonich thought he'd become more of a liability than an asset, their roles would change drastically. The Russian president's assurances of a beautiful dacha on the Black Sea didn't mean much, especially if the Sheik failed to deliver what he had promised. Following his failure to bring the United States' economy to its knees by attacking its strategic oil resources less than a year ago, another flop would discredit him for life. He needed a win to reclaim his rightful place at the top of the food chain. And the first step toward this victory was to talk to Dr. Galkin to assess the damage, if any, he had done.

But first, he needed to find out why he wasn't able to reach Victor. He walked out of his office and told the two agents posted outside his door where he was headed. One of them remained behind while the other escorted him. In order to keep the Sheik's mission a secret, Veniamin Simonich had authorized the creation of a small team of Russian intelligence officers, working together with his men inside the walls of the Kremlin Grand Palace. Access to the Russians' intel was a blessing. Following the raid on his mobile headquarters by Charles Mapother's men, the Sheik had lost a good part of his once massive yet efficient intelligence gathering apparatus. Weeks after the raid, some of his most senior operatives had started to disappear. Even smaller-scale operations were being undone before they had started. In order to stop the hemorrhage, the Sheik had cut his ties with Mouin Bashi, one of his most trusted lieutenants and the man in charge of his intelligence network. Truth is, he had abandoned him to the wolves that had been chasing him. His capture had allowed the Sheik to escape to Russia. Bashi's body was later found in a safe house in Zagreb. The Sheik was convinced it was Mapother's men who were once again the culprits. He couldn't wait to get his hands on Ray Powell. He'd get him to talk or he'd use him as bait to draw in Mapother's team. One way or the other, the ambassador would die, and he'd make sure it would be a painful death.

The office Veniamin Simonich had assigned his team was on the third floor of the building. It was a medium-sized room with no windows that had been fitted with all the latest technology available inside Russia. Only one door led in or out of the room and two more agents from the Presidential Security Services protected it. One of them opened the door to let him through.

"I need someone to tell me where is Victor Simonich," he said.

There were only two people working the night shift and they both turned to face the Sheik. They were both Russians, which meant his men had been sent home to their apartments outside the Kremlin. One of the Russians was an attractive female with short blond hair and deep blue eyes. She was the first to speak.

"What's his number?"

The Sheik gave it to her. "How long?" he asked.

"Not long."

The Sheik placed his hands on her shoulder. He squeezed gently and she shivered at his touch. She didn't do that out of pleasure but out of fear, and the Sheik loved it. His reputation was alive and well.

"I can't seem to find him, Sheik Al-Assad," she said.

He squeezed again, this time harder. He felt her stiffen. "Find him. Then call my team."

CHAPTER 37

Moscow, Russia

Mike Walton walked to the rendezvous point and spotted the Toyota Camry parked across the street. Hands in pockets, chin tucked in, he jogged to the vehicle and opened the door. The cold had bitten through his shoes and he couldn't feel his toes anymore. The same went for his hands. The light gloves he'd been wearing weren't enough to keep his fingers warm.

He couldn't remember the last time he had shivered out of control like this. His teeth were chattering and his ears were beyond frozen.

"I've got everything you've asked for," James Cooper said.

Mike nodded, his jaw refusing to move. Cooper turned the heater to the maximum. They spent the next four minutes in silence as Mike tried not to scream as his limbs started to thaw. He'd swear the tips of his fingers were on fire and that his socks were filled with needles and broken glass. His mind suddenly flashed back to the time he spent in the army as an infantry officer. His whole body shuddered at the memories. Being cold and wet had been part of his life for a long time. He had good grades in school and could have done anything with his life. His father had done everything in his power to discourage him from joining the army. But Mike had joined anyway and, despite being wet and cold all the time, he had enjoyed every minute of it. The brotherhood that came with being a paratrooper was something he held dear.

"I've found a spot from where we can see the building," Mike said, once he trusted himself to speak clearly.

Cooper followed Mike's directions and they were able to squeeze between two beaters.

"Did you see anything while I was away?" Cooper asked.

"No, and I stopped caring about three minutes after you left," Mike said, rubbing his hands together as Cooper turned off the engine.

"Yeah, I know it's cold."

"Cold? It's freaking colder than the Arctic Circle," Mike replied. "Climate change hasn't reached Moscow yet, that's for sure"

"Careful what you say about climate change, Mike, you should know—"

"All right, James, I'm not in the mood to hear your rhetoric about climate change right now," Mike said, louder than he intended. A quick look at Cooper told him he had taken the rebuke personally.

"I know how you feel about the environment, James, and you're right. It's something we need to take seriously," Mike said, knowing this was what Cooper needed to hear. "Can we focus on the mission now?"

"Aren't you from Canada?"

Mike raised his eyebrows. "What does that have to do with what we're doing here?"

"I just thought you'd be used to being cold."

"Not this kind of cold," Mike grunted, before adding, "All right, show me what you've got."

Cooper reached for the backpack he had placed on the back seat. Inside were all the items Mike had requested, plus a few extras, including spare batteries, a new smartphone and a lock-pick gun.

"It's secured," Cooper said as Mike slipped the new phone into his pocket. "We've programed it the exact same way as your previous one."

Mike reached under the passenger seat and retrieved the computer he had used earlier to track Victor's movements. He powered it on and waited for the welcome screen to appear. He entered his username and password and clicked on the app that was linked to the tracker his wife had placed on the Russian agent. While the app loaded, his thoughts went to Lisa. Was the IMSI successful at warning her? He should never have allowed her to leave for Koltsovo without him. They were a team. *Damn it!*

"They're coming our way," Cooper said.

"What?" Mike said.

Cooper pointed to the computer's screen. "This thing doesn't lie."

Cooper was right. The tracker was still active and it was moving toward their location. Mike dug into the backpack until he found what he was looking for. "Good of you to think about this, James," he said, pulling out a pair of infrared, night-vision binoculars and a set of night-vision goggles.

"Glad to be of assistance," Cooper replied with a smile.

Mike adjusted the binoculars to his eyes and the integrated range finder told him they were three hundred and fifty meters away from the building they were watching.

"You keep watch around the car while I stay on target, okay?"

"Sure thing," Cooper replied.

. . . .

Victor Simonich's heart was beating faster than he cared to admit. Chances were that the intel unit his uncle had placed under the Sheik's direction was already trying to locate him. If he were the Sheik, he'd also send men to the Solntsevo District to investigate any breach in operational security. Victor looked at his watch—an old Poljot his father had given him for his twenty-first birthday— and realized he would have only a few minutes to make contact with one of Mapother's men before he'd have to leave. He hoped to see the man he had fought earlier in the bathroom. The man had looked sharp and knowledgeable. He had tricked him into entering the men's room and had nearly choked him to death. And Victor wasn't fooled easily.

As the taxi driver made the last turn toward their destination, Victor removed his pistol from its holster and placed it in his coat pocket. He didn't want to use it, but he had a feeling things wouldn't go as well as he hoped.

. . . .

Mike Walton didn't like it one bit. The angle wasn't right, and his field of vision wasn't as good as he had originally thought. They could see the building's door but not much else, and Mike wanted to be in a position to observe the surrounding area. That meant that he had to get out of the vehicle and be exposed to the inclement weather once again.

"Where are they?" he asked, keeping his sight on the building's entrance door.

"About five miles away. They'll be here shortly."

If he wanted to change location, now was the time to do it.

"Stay here," he said, his decision made.

Cooper looked at him quizzically. "Where are you going?"

"I need a better spot," Mike said, putting the binoculars down. "You see this apartment building on our left?"

Cooper twisted in his seat and cranked his neck to look where Mike was pointing. "Yeah?"

"That's where I'm heading." Mike put his gear together. "From the roof, I'll have a better chance at spotting surveillance and counter-surveillance."

Cooper was shaking his head. "Better you than me, my friend. You'll freeze your ass up there."

I know that, James . . . From the backpack, Mike took a pair of ear buds and synced them with his new phone.

"Put this in your ear, James," Mike said, giving the Support Two team leader an ear bud. "Sync it with your phone and we'll test our comms once I'm outside. Got it?"

"Got it."

As soon as Mike opened the door, the cold hit him like a brick. "Shit."

He closed the door behind him and headed straight to the tallest building on his left. He crossed the street and nearly lost his footing on a patch of black ice. He managed not to lose his balance but not without straining his back.

"James from Mike, radio check," he said, once he was at the building's door.

"You're five by five."

"Copy."

Mike unzipped his backpack to get the lock-pick gun but tried to open the door to confirm it was indeed locked. It wasn't.

"I'm in."

"Door was unlocked?"

"You're a genius, James," Mike replied as he entered the foyer. There were only two elevators for what Mike estimated to be a three-hundred-and-fifty-unit building. If he needed to get out of there in a hurry, he'd have to pray one of them was available. If not, he'd be caught without an exit route. He searched for a staircase and found one a bit further down the hallway. He tried the door. Unlocked.

Good.

Next to the door was a fire escape plan. Mike pulled it off the wall and stuffed it in his pocket. He went back to the foyer and pressed the button to call one of the elevators.

"Any movement outside?"

"Nothing, Mike, but the windows are fogging up," Cooper said. "In another three minutes or so, I'll be completely blind."

Shit! Why didn't I think of that? Get your mind right, Mike!

"Understood, I'm heading up. Will let you know when you can move out."

A ding announced the arrival of the elevator and Mike's hand moved to the small of his back where he had concealed the PB silent pistol. The elevator doors slid open and he half expected to see someone walk out, but it was empty. He walked inside and pressed the button that would take him to the top floor. The elevator was slow and noisy. Mike glanced at his watch to see how long it took to reach his destination.

"I'm in the elevator, James. Acknowledge reception," Mike said, testing if their comms were good even inside the elevator shaft. When Cooper didn't reply, he had his answer.

The doors finally reopened. It had taken him just over two minutes. He had used the time wisely, studying the fire escape route. He knew which way to go. He stepped outside the elevator and headed towards the staircase that would lead him to the roof, one floor up.

"I'll be in position in sixty seconds," he told Cooper over their comms system.

"About time. I can't see shit."

At the end of the corridor, a gray door stood between the hallway and the staircase. Mike turned the handle but it wouldn't twist without a key inserted in.

"They're less than a mile away, Mike," Cooper warned him.

Damn it! He pulled the lock-pick gun out of his backpack and started working on the door. Much faster than the traditional method of lock picking, which used trial-and-error methods to find the correct alignment of the locking pins, a lock-pick gun uses the laws of physics and transfer of energy to push all of the driver's pins out of the lock system while keeping the bottom ones from sliding in.

Fifteen seconds later, Mike was rushing up the staircase two at a time. He pushed the last door open and landed on the roof of the building. Except for the light glow the moon provided, it was pitch black. He adjusted his night-vision goggles over his tuque and walked to the edge of the building. The wind had picked up and it felt at least minus thirty with the wind chill. At this temperature, he wasn't sure how long his batteries would last. There weren't many pieces of equipment built to sustain this kind of punishment.

"Two hundred meters," came in Cooper through his earpiece.

"Be more precise, James," Mike replied impatiently. Mucus flowed from his nose before freezing almost instantly on his upper lip.

"From the north. You should see him."

The night-vision goggles had helped him reached his position safely, but they were useless at finding his target at such a distance. He replaced them in his backpack and used a thermal rifle scope to scan the neighboring area. There was nobody in the adjacent streets. It was dead quiet. Way too quiet for his liking. Where were the Russians?

. . . .

Victor asked the driver to drop him off two apartment buildings away from his real destination. He left a generous tip for the driver and stepped out of the cab. He dug his hands into his pockets as much to feel his pistol as to keep them warm. If Mapother's men were as competent as he hoped they were, he was probably already under surveillance. He walked at a brisk pace, feeling his legs rattle as the cold cut through his clothes.

A quick peek revealed no one behind him. He looked at the tall white buildings surrounding him. *If I wanted to make sure I wasn't walking into a trap, that's where I'd be. On the roof. And I'd stay there until I was damned sure I knew what I was up against.*

But there was no time to play games. If the Sheik had indeed sent a team to this location, time was of the essence. He needed to do something that would provoke Mapother's team into action. He shook his head in despair. He had no idea what to do until he walked past a Toyota Camry with frosted windows. *Someone's been there for a while.*

It was time to gamble a little.

. . . .

It doesn't make any sense. Mike Walton had spotted his target as he disembarked from what looked like a taxicab. At this distance, he couldn't be one hundred percent certain, but the car didn't have the shape of a Mercedes. A single man had climbed out and walked on the sidewalk, hands in his pockets. Why was the Russian bodyguard by himself? Wasn't he supposed to bring Dr. Galkin with him? What had happened? Victor had looked sincere, and Mike couldn't believe he had been played so easily. Even worse, Victor was now approaching the Toyota Camry. Mike prayed he didn't notice the frosted windows, but he knew that was asking for a miracle.

"James, our target is approaching—"

"I know," Cooper replied. "I've been tracking him on the—"

"Close the goddamn screen," Mike warned, but it was too late. Victor had made his move.

. . . .

Victor didn't waste any time. If he was going to do something so drastic, he couldn't hesitate. Not one second. And, once committed, there was no going back. Unfortunately for him, the moment his foot hit the slippery road, he lost his balance and he fell hard on his shoulder. The force of the impact caused him to drop his pistol at the same moment the vehicle's occupant opened the driver-side door.

Victor was on his feet in an instant but the man already had a small pistol aimed at him.

"Get up," the man said in English.

Victor tried to look furtively for his pistol but it was nowhere in sight. He thought he caught a glimpse of it under the Toyota but he couldn't be sure. It was too dark to tell. He slowly got up, making sure his hands were held high to his side.

"On your knees," the man yelled. Victor could see the man was shaking, and it wasn't from the cold. The man was an amateur.

"You told me to get up," Victor replied. "I'm up."

The man looked confused, as if he was waiting for directives. *That's it! That's exactly what's going on.* Victor figured somebody else was watching him and was providing instructions to the man standing in front of him. That was why the driver had been able to exit the vehicle with such speed. Someone had warned him. Victor estimated the distance between him and the man at less than six feet. Hoping the man on watch didn't have a sniper rifle trained on him, Victor took a second to make sure his feet had traction. Once he was sure he wouldn't die because of a patch of ice, he leaped forward and down at the man's knees. His left shoulder made contact first and Victor half expected to be shot in the back. But it didn't happen. The man fell backward and yelped in pain as his head hit the frozen asphalt with a thump.

Victor was on his knees before his opponent could regain his senses and easily robbed him of his pistol. Victor forced the man to his feet. He placed himself in a defensive position, using the man as a shield by holding him tightly against him while burying the newly acquired pistol into the man's back.

"Is there anyone else in the vehicle?" Victor asked.

The man tried to speak but Victor was choking him. He relaxed his grip slightly. "No."

"What's your name?"

"What?"

"What's your name?" Victor repeated, pushing the barrel of the pistol hard against the man's kidney.

"James," the man replied, his voice barely audible. "My name's James."

"James, I will say this only once so you'd better listen . . ."

. . . .

Mike Walton was on the move the moment he saw Victor step behind the Camry. He briefly considered taking the stairs but figured that if the elevator was still on the top floor it would be quicker. The doors slid open almost instantly and Mike stepped in, thanking God for this small miracle. Just as the doors were closing, Mike heard Cooper grunt. *What the hell?*

Whatever had just happened, there was nothing he could do. He had to wait. Even though he was still half frozen from his time on the rooftop, a fine moisture had started to form in his back. Worse, he started to hyperventilate. He recognized the symptoms for what they were. A panic attack.

Fuck! Not now.

His heart rate was going through the roof and he was losing control. He forced himself to concentrate on his breathing but to no avail. He put a knee down in fear he'd lose consciousness in the elevator. The walls closed in on him and he closed his eyes. He lost his balance and fell to his side.

He had no idea how long he stayed there, but when he opened his eyes, an elderly lady was looking at him, her right arm between the elevator doors in an attempt to keep them opened. If the sight of his pistol in his right hand worried her, she didn't show it. She was yelling at him in Russian. He slowly got up, using the handlebar inside the elevator to help him. He nodded his thanks to the lady and walked across the foyer to the door that would lead him outside. The cold wind slapped him in the face. He took two deep breaths, but what he saw next nearly sent him spiraling out of control again.

· · · · · · · ·

Victor barely recognized the man who'd had the better of him less than two hours ago. He looked confused, out of a breath and completely out of his element. These two were certainly not the type of individuals he needed as allies against the Sheik. Was there a way for him to backtrack? To go back on his decision? What if he killed them both? The Sheik would certainly understand. His uncle would.

Just as he was about to send a couple of rounds into James's spinal cord, the other man's demeanor changed drastically. He was suddenly less than twenty meters away, and his pistol was up and on target. He wasn't shaking as James had been.

"Let him go and we'll talk, Victor," the man said. "Or I'll fucking kill you right here."

The man was still walking toward him, closing the distance. He had no doubt the man could shoot, but the low visibility would make him a hard target to hit while he was using James as a shield.

"Stop," Victor warned. "You'll never be able to—"

Victor never heard the shot. The round hit him high on the left shoulder and the force of the impact swung him over to his side. James had used the distraction to get out of his grasp and to recover the pistol he had lost to him minutes ago. Victor knew he was a dead man if he moved. He slowly turned back toward his opponent, who still had his gun aimed squarely at his chest.

"Talk," the man said.

Victor felt the back of his shirt becoming soaked with blood. The bullet must have gone right through. "We don't have much time," Victor replied. "The Sheik has already sent a team to this location. They're on their way."

"Where is Dr. Galkin?"

"He's dead."

. . . .

Mike Walton didn't want to believe Victor but something was telling him he was speaking the truth. Why would he lie? To save his life, that's why.

"Your doing?"

"Yes. I had to."

Goddamn it. He's telling the truth. "Why? And before you answer me with some bullshit, Victor, know that I'll shoot you in the gut if I feel you aren't being completely honest with me."

"Why isn't important—"

"I decide what's important," Mike warned him. If there was indeed a team coming to their location, he needed to know if Victor was on his side or not.

The Russian bodyguard raised his hands by his side. Mike could see that caused him much pain. "Okay, okay," Victor pleaded. "I've gambled everything to warn you. You have to trust me on this when I say I had no choice."

"You're wasting my time—"

"The Sheik was going to torture him, and he was going to kill him. Me killing him was a blessing. Plus, he gave me this," Victor said reaching inside his pocket.

"Careful," Mike cautioned him.

Victor showed him a USB key. "Before he died, Galkin told me that on this," Victor said, shaking the USB key, "there's everything we need to know to understand the virus Dr. Votyakov and he created."

Was the Russian agent telling the truth? There was only one way to find out. "Do you know how to access the apartment you were supposed to bring Dr. Galkin to?"

Victor nodded.

"James," Mike said. "Take the USB key to your guys and once you're sure it doesn't contain any viruses, send it to the boss."

Mike covered Cooper as he moved close to Victor to collect the USB key. "Ask them to cancel Lisa's assignment. We won't need Galkin's wife after all."

"What about you, Mike?" Cooper asked.

Mike chastised him with his eyes for saying his name out loud but doubted Cooper even realized it. "Victor and I will wait for the Sheik's men to show up. Now go."

CHAPTER 38

Koltsovo, Russia

L isa Walton's plane landed without incident. The coffee the flight attendants had served during the flight was so acidic it was undrinkable. The IMSI-issued go-pills were her only salvation against the fatigue that had taken over her mind and body. Lisa had made sure to hydrate herself properly on the flight, hoping it would keep the migraines she knew were coming at bay a little longer.

She had kept an eye on the two SVR or FSB agents—she wasn't sure for whom they were working now that she knew they weren't protecting the Russian TV star—and they hadn't looked at her once.

The car Support Two had rented for her—a late model Volkswagen Polo—was ready and already paid for at the Europcar counter outside the terminal. Lisa made the twenty-five-mile drive between the Novosibirsk International Airport and Kosoltvo in just under an hour. She had removed the battery from her smartphone the moment her flight had taken off. Knowing that Russian intelligence—especially in a semi-military city like Koltsovo, where one of Russia's largest virology centers was located—might track all cellphone activations at the airport, she waited until she reached the city before turning it on again.

There were three new emails from the IMSI server, all of them urgent if she was to believe the red flags next to them. Lisa parked the Volkswagen on a quiet street on the outskirts of the city and punched in her twelve-digit password. She waited for the phone to confirm it was secured before downloading the full messages. The first was from Jonathan Sanchez and it contained the contact information and the address of Dr. Galkin's wife, Sophia Galkin. The next one was Charles Mapother asking her to contact the IMSI as soon as she landed. The last message was from Mike. She listened to this one twice. *He wants me to abort the mission. What the heck?*

She dialed IMSI headquarters. Anna Caprini picked up.

"We've got you just outside Koltsovo. Everything okay?"

"I've got your messages. I'm on my way to pick up Dr. Galkin's wife."

"Wait a sec, I'll put you through Mapother," Caprini replied.

Lisa turned off the engine and observed her surroundings. It reminded her of a quiet university town. The streets were clean and well lit. Her GPS showed her to be about six miles away from the Biopreparat facilities in Koltsovo. She figured she was in one of the neighborhoods where the Biopreparat employees lived. There were a lot of small apartment buildings but they were well kept. She had also noticed a few parks and playgrounds.

"Where are you?" Mapother asked.

"Good evening to you too, Charles," Lisa replied, surprised at Mapother's severe tone.

"Lisa, we need you to abort the mission. Dr. Galkin's dead."

What? Oh shit! Was Mike all right?

Mapother continued before she could voice her concerns, "Mike's okay, Lisa, but we need you back in Moscow now."

Her mind was spinning. "What about Dr. Galkin's wife?"

"We don't need her anymore."

"So we'll leave Sophia behind?"

"Damn it, Lisa! Just do as you're told."

This wasn't right! From what she understood, Dr. Galkin had sacrificed his career—and now his life—to give them intelligence he thought they needed to counter Russia's apocalyptic ambitions. The least they could do was to help the woman he had left behind.

"If they're on to her, she'll be tortured for days, Charles. You know how the Sheik operates," Lisa said, "because I sure do."

"Listen to me—"

"No, I'm done with this, you cold-hearted sonofabitch," Lisa said. "I'm not leaving anyone behind. Not again," she said louder than she really wanted to.

. . . .

Jonathan Sanchez looked at Charles Mapother. The IMSI director was clearly pissed at being hung up on by one of his assets.

"What the hell's wrong with her?" he asked.

"Shouldn't we try to call her back?" Caprini asked. The three of them were in Mapother's office where they had listened in on the conversation.

"What do you think, Jonathan?" Mapother asked.

"Give her a few minutes, Charles. She's upset and can't think straight," he replied.

"Lisa's a trained asset, Jonathan," Mapother replied, hitting his desk with his fist. "These things shouldn't happen. Never. My assets do as they're told, goddam it!"

Sanchez understood Mapother's anger. He treated his assets in the field like his children and had always backed them no matter what. The only thing he asked in exchange for his unconditional support was for them to obey his orders. And now Lisa had gone haywire. Mapother was in uncharted territory and Sanchez doubted he knew what to do.

"As I said, Charles, give her a few minutes. She'll come around."

"How can you be so sure?" Caprini asked.

"I'm not," he conceded. "But I know that if you try to call her back right away, she'll hang up again and we'll lose her for good."

There was one thing he knew that nobody else in the room did. Right after the terrorist attack that had wiped out her entire family, he had visited Lisa at the hospital. She had no idea who he was at the time and she'd been convinced she had lost Mike too. He had introduced himself as a friend of Mike and had offered her a way to get back at the Sheik. She had jumped at it and had proven herself not only during the IMSI asset training but also in the field. But there was something Sanchez had never shared with Mapother or the psychologists at the IMSI. When he had first made contact with Lisa in her hospital room, she'd been in the bathroom and just about to slit her wrists with a broken piece of glass from the mirror she had shattered. Sanchez had seen with his own eyes how desperate Lisa had been at that moment. But he had also seen the sheer dedication she exhibited when offered the chance to get her revenge on the man responsible for her losses. Sanchez knew the sweet taste of vengeance had pushed Lisa through training and kept her alive in the field. Still, a doubt had always lingered in the back of his mind about what she'd do if she had to choose between obeying orders or pushing through with a mission that would allow her a chance to get close to the Sheik. Deep down, the answer had always been there but he'd chosen to ignore it. And now it was biting him in the ass. If Mapother knew what Sanchez had seen at the hospital, he would have never allowed her to become a field asset. *Too fragile*, he would have said. The problem was that if he hadn't convinced Lisa to join the IMSI, Mike would have refused too. And they needed Mike. Badly. Someone with Mike's skill set who had a personal vendetta against the man the IMSI had been tasked to take down was a dream come true. And they had nearly succeeded, first in Spain and then in Croatia. Only luck had saved the Sheik, but the IMSI had nevertheless delivered a solid blow to his network. Sanchez was confident that this time around, with the help of Zima, the IMSI would finally put an end to the Sheik.

"I'm done waiting," Mapother announced. "Put me through to her, Anna."

Anna walked back to her desk in the bubble. Seconds later, Sanchez could hear Lisa's phone ringing as Mapother had put his on speaker.

Come on, Lisa, pick up the damn phone. When the call went to voicemail after a half-dozen rings, they tried again. This time, it went straight to voicemail.

Mapother looked at him. "Now what?"

. . . .

Lisa Walton left the battery in her phone, knowing it would allow the IMSI to track her. She reckoned it would be easier to ask for forgiveness than to ask permission to go after Dr. Galkin's wife. Charles Mapother was upset—maybe even hysterical—at her right now, but he'd come through for her when she needed his assistance to exfil once she had Dr. Galkin's wife in tow. How could he even think about leaving her behind? He was a better man than that.

Using the car navigation system, she found her way to Dr. Galkin's apartment building. She made one pass and had to trust the navigation system to be precise. The light in front of the building wasn't on, preventing her from confirming the address. If it was indeed the correct address, it was a five-story, pleasant-looking edifice in which all the units had a balcony facing the street. There was only one entrance, but she couldn't see if a key was needed to get in. It was well past midnight, and she hadn't seen anyone in the street except one man walking his dog. She parked the Volkswagen three streets north of Dr. Galkin's apartment. Aware that the Russians—or the Sheik for that matter—might already have sent someone to pick up Sophia, she hoped she wasn't too late. She would have welcomed the luxury of properly monitoring the area for longer, but it was impossible. Every second counted.

Before opening the door, she made sure the interior lights were disabled. Never having driven this car before, it took her a moment to find the switch. She climbed out of the car and walked straight to Sophia's building, while doing her best to avoid the patches of light offered by the streetlamps.

The weather was brutal. A strong northerly wind had picked up since she had left the airport and she longed for warmer clothes. She shivered from the cold and tears formed in her eyes. She turned up the collar of her coat to protect her neck. The message had said that Sophia's apartment was on the second floor. *Number 202.*

She tried the main door of the building. Unlocked. Another door separated the vestibule from the small lobby. She needed someone to buzz her in. There was an old-school panel on the wall on which all the tenant names were written next to their apartment number. She picked up the handset attached to the panel and dialed the number two-zero-two. Nothing. She tried star-two-zero-two. She heard a click and it started to ring.

The door clicked open. She replaced the handset, wondering why someone would let a stranger walk into the building at this hour without first checking who they were.

Lisa wished she had a gun with her. Was someone waiting for her? If that was the case and she had just walked into a trap, it was too late to do anything about it.

She called the elevator. The doors slid open.

· · · · · · · ·

Jonathan Sanchez looked at the screen in front of him. He could hear Charles Mapother breathing behind him. "She did that on purpose, didn't she?" he asked.

Sanchez nodded. "Of course she did. She ain't stupid, our Lisa."

"Is that the address?"

"It is. She's in."

"When can we get eyes on target?" Mapother asked.

"Everybody's trying to find a solution but there are no street cams in Koltsovo we can hack into."

"So we're blind."

Sanchez knew how Mapother hated it when he had no control over an operation. He didn't show it, but Sanchez was good at analyzing people's behavior, and for him it was obvious that Mapother was stressed out. Sanchez had noticed a big change in Mapother's demeanor since the attempt on his life.

"I need to contact DNI Phillips about what's going on, Jonathan. Please let everyone know that I want all hands on deck to help Lisa. I need an exfil plan in case she succeeds at convincing Sophia Galkin to leave with her."

"Will do," replied Sanchez.

CHAPTER 39

Koltsovo, Russia

A faint odor of coffee and burnt toast reached Lisa's nose as soon as she stepped out of the elevator. She made a right into the hallway but turned around when she realized she wasn't heading in the right direction. Apartment 202 was at the end of the hallway. As she approached the apartment, its door opened and an older lady stuck her head out, saying something in Russian.

Lisa waved at her. *It's like she's expecting me. How could this be?* The woman waved back but her demeanor changed when Lisa reached her door. She once again said something in Russian but this time her door was almost shut.

"Can I come in?" Lisa asked in English.

"Who are you? You're not with the government," the lady replied in heavily accented English.

"No, I'm not. I'm a friend of your husband. You're Sophia, right?" The lady nodded. "Can I come in?" Lisa repeated.

Sophia stepped away and opened the door to let Lisa in.

"Tea?"

"We have very little time, Sophia," Lisa said, following Galkin's wife to the kitchen. "Your husband needs you. He asked me to come and get you."

"My husband took a plane to Moscow earlier today," Sophia replied, adding water to a teapot. "Why would he need me in Moscow? He knows I hate it there. And who are you again?"

Lisa guessed that Sophia was in her mid sixties. She looked in great shape and her eyes betrayed her above-average intelligence. "Why did you let me in, Sophia?"

"Someone from my husband's office called me an hour ago to let me know someone needed to talk to me urgently. I thought you were that person."

Lisa looked at Sophia, trying to detect any signs of treachery. She didn't see any. "They want to kill you, Sophia," she said. "You have to trust me." That got Sophia's attention.

"What's the code?"

"What code?"

"My husband didn't really send you. I don't know who you are, but you're lying."

Lisa's eyes locked onto Sophia's. "No, I'm not lying. I swear."

"My husband and I have a code. If something happens to one of us, and we need to pass on a message to the other using a messenger, we use a code. We always did. And you don't know the code," Sophia said, her tone becoming more and more aggressive as she spoke. Lisa tried to gently approach her but the woman stepped back and reached for the knife block sitting on the counter.

By the time Lisa reached her, Sophia was holding a small carving knife.

"You don't want to do this, Sophia," Lisa pleaded. She didn't want to hurt the woman but the situation was slipping out of her control. Mapother hadn't mentioned a code in his mission brief. Surely he would have been aware such a code existed. *Unless . . . Unless there's no code and Sophia is just wasting time.*

When the door of the apartment burst opened, Lisa's first instinct was to protect Sophia. But when she heard the familiar sound of a grenade striking the tile floor she hit the ground while opening her mouth and placing her hands over her ears. She had no way of knowing what kind of grenade it was, but chances were it was a stun grenade. Even though she was right, the force of the blast still shocked her.

Time was up. They needed to get out of there. Now. She turned toward Sophia just in time to see a flash of steel but not in time to move completely out of the way. Lisa partially blocked the knife but it slashed through her coat and into her forearm. Lisa used her left hand to strike the older lady on the throat before using her elbow to strike down on her wrist. The knife fell to ground. Lisa had no idea how deep the cut was but she didn't yet feel the intense pain a knife cut usually delivered. It would be coming soon, though. Of that she was sure. But, for now, she was still able to use both her arms. Lisa grabbed a larger knife from the knife block just as two men entered the kitchen. Lisa threw the knife at the first assailant, forcing him back into the hallway, and she picked up the one Sophia had dropped. She put in her pocket.

The patio door leading to the balcony was only twenty feet away. Could she make it? A jump from the second floor wouldn't kill her, right? *No, but you might break a leg. Maybe she should have listened to Mike and Charles and not come here.*

It was too late for second guesses now. She jumped over the counter and sprinted to the patio door. She had just unlocked it when she heard the first shot. The bullet passed inches from her head and the second was even closer. Its impact shattered the patio door. The fact that they weren't using silencers told her they weren't afraid to get caught. These men were either above the law or didn't fear it.

"You move, you die," one of the men said in English. He walked toward her, his gun steady in his hands.

Lisa recognized him as one of the men she had seen at the airport. His partner—a man she had never seen before—was covering him from the kitchen while speaking to Sophia, who was now standing up and holding her neck with both her hands. Her eyes drilled into Lisa. Pure hatred emanated from them.

She was expecting me. It was indeed a trap. And I walked right into it.

"Get on your knees," ordered the man. "Slowly."

Lisa obeyed, her heart rate exploding. She tried to remain focused in case an opportunity presented itself, but the men were well trained. Plus, her right forearm was now killing her. Warm blood slid down to her hand and red droplets splashed onto the beige carpet of the living room. The second man moved to his left to get a better angle on her.[4]

"Now, from your knees, turn around and face the balcony."

Is this it? I'm so fucked.

"Cross your legs and interlock your fingers," the man continued, once she was facing the balcony.

Maybe she had a chance after all. She had practiced this exact scenario countless times while in training. The man giving the command would holster his pistol while his partner covered him. He would then grab her hands one by one to handcuff her. If that was what was going on here, she would have a small window of opportunity when she could strike back. Of course, it was a huge gamble and the odds were stacked against her. Still, men tended to dismiss what a woman could do in these situations much more than if they were dealing with another man.

Lisa felt the man's presence behind her and waited for the sound that would tell her he had holstered his firearm. It came a second later. She closed her eyes and took a deep breath. As soon as she felt his hand on her wrist, she pounced. She was on her feet in an instant and pivoted one hundred and eighty degrees to her right while her right hand clutched the man's forearm. She took one step to her right to shield herself from the remaining shooter, while her left hand dug into her pocket for the small carving knife. She kicked the man hard on the shin to gain the extra half second she needed to pull the knife out. The man yelled in pain and she used this distraction to plunge the knife deep into the man's neck. His eyes opened wide and both his hands shot up in an attempt to remove the knife embedded in his throat.

Lisa spun around the man, knowing it would be easier to get to his gun. Unfortunately for her, the man's strength was leaving him quickly and he fell backwards just as she was about to pull his pistol from its holster. Lisa let herself fall with him, knowing that if she remained standing she'd be a sitting duck for the other shooter. The man's weight was crushing her and she hurried to get her hand around his pistol. The other shooter was yelling in Russian and she saw him squeeze the trigger twice. The man on top of her jerked as the rounds hit him in the chest. She finally managed to get the gun out with her left hand and she fired. Her first round went high and the second shooter ducked behind the counter. She fired three more rounds to keep him pinned down. She pushed the man off her and screamed in pain, feeling the cut on her left forearm open wide. Her shooting hand was her right one, and she wasn't as good shooting one handed, especially from her left hand.

Surprising her, the second attacker dove out of cover while shooting. His first three rounds went wide but the fourth hit her just above her left knee. She returned fire again and again, not understanding while they weren't hitting each other. They were less than twenty feet apart yet none of their bullets were hitting their marks, or so it seemed. Finally, one of hers ricocheted of the tile floor and entered the man's brain through his left eye.

Fuck! She looked for an exit wound in her leg but there wasn't one. The bullet had remained lodged. The pain was like nothing she had ever experienced. Her whole leg was like dead weight. She couldn't move it. She tried to step toward the balcony but she collapsed. Sounds behind her warned her she wasn't out of danger yet.

Sophia. In the heat of the moment, she had completely forgotten about Dr. Galkin's wife. She was reaching for the dead shooter's gun.

"Don't, Sophia," she said, her voice only a whisper. But the other lady wasn't listening. Or maybe she hadn't even heard her. And it didn't matter because Lisa fired her pistol the moment Sophia pointed the gun at her. She kept firing even after Sophia had crumpled onto the floor. Once the magazine was spent, Lisa let go of her pistol. Why was she so tired so suddenly? She hadn't lost so much blood, had she?

She could hear shouts coming from the hallway. The cavalry was coming, but it wasn't to save her. She reached for her smartphone, tucked under her coat, and dialed the IMSI's number.

Anna Caprini answered. "Where are you?"

"I'm done. I'm all shot up," Lisa replied, tears filling her eyes. Her hand moved to her stomach. It was sticky and warm. She'd been shot more than once after all. Why wasn't she feeling the pain?

"Hang in there, Lisa," Mapother said, coming on the line. "We'll get you out of there."

"They set us up using Galkin's wife as bait," she said, out of breath, her whole body shaking. "They're coming for me—"

"We'll track you down, Lisa—"

"I'm so sorry, Charles, I should have listened to you," she said, her strength vanishing quickly. Fatigue was taking over. "Goodbye, and thank you for everything."

She had one more call to make before dialing the number that would erase all the data from her phone. Her fingers, red with blood, had difficulty dialing the correct numbers. She fumbled with the phone, the voices of the advancing troops adding an edge to the craziness of the whole situation.

They had now entered the apartment. She could feel the floor shake underneath her as they ran through the apartment looking for her. There were a lot of them. More than she could ever handle. She wouldn't have the time to speak with Mike after all, so she held down the number five and star keys together for two seconds. That would automatically take care of her phone.

Her thoughts turned to Mike. Was he safe? And would he be okay without her? She was so worried for him. He had already lost so much. Tears ran freely down her cheeks. She was ready. She was ready to see her parents again. And Melissa.

Oh, Melissa. Mommy's coming to see you.

CHAPTER 40

Moscow, Russia

Mike Walton breathed a sigh of relief. The Russian was built like a tank and the gunshot wound he had sustained wasn't as bad as Mike had originally feared Before leaving, James Cooper had left them the small emergency kit that was inside the vehicle. The Russian had hastily applied a sterile bandage and an antiseptic cream while in the elevator. Mike's plan was to head back to the same rooftop. That would give them the vantage point they needed to spot anyone attempting to reach the address Victor had given him.

"Why aren't we going to the apartment?" Victor asked, putting his jacket back on. He winced.

"I was hoping you'd know better than to ask a stupid question like that, Victor."

Mike needed an ally. He dared hope that Victor would be this person, but he needed to confirm his story before trusting him even a little.

"I'm just trying to figure out what your plan is. Is Mike your real name?"

Mike didn't bother to reply. Once out of the elevator, he gave Victor the directions to the rooftop.

"Door's locked," Victor said.

"Step back," Mike ordered. "Move away from me and stay where I can see you."

Mike took out the lock-pick gun from his bag and was about to start working when Victor said, "I know how to use one of these. Let me."

Mike let the Russian take his place but kept his gun trained on him as he worked.

"Done," Victor said almost immediately.

"Let's go," Mike said. "Lead the way. You know where we're going."

Despite his injury, the Russian climbed the stairs two by two.

It hadn't got any warmer on the rooftop and Mike hoped they wouldn't have too long to wait.

"This neighborhood doesn't get much traffic at night," Victor said. "We should be able to spot them from far away."

"If they aren't already there," Mike said.

"They're not."

"If you're the real deal, Victor, what's in it for you?" Mike asked. He had been wondering why someone in Victor's position would want to help him.

"Do you love your country, Mike?" the Russian agent asked.

"Why do you think I'm here? It's certainly not for the damned weather, is it?" Mike said, his teeth chattering again.

Victor chuckled. "It isn't that bad once you get used to it."

"So it's out of love that you're betraying your country?" Mike said, focusing with his binoculars on someone exiting the building across the street. He didn't know if it was because he was half frozen, or if his brain had simply ceased to function properly, but he realized the cruelty of his words too late. He never saw the Russian coming. Victor knocked the binocs out of his hands and punched him hard on his right ear. Mike's knees buckled and he struggled to stay on his feet but Victor's attack had stunned him and he was unable to stop the powerful kick to his groin. Mike doubled over, his breath knocked out of him. He heard himself moan as he writhed on the frozen rooftop.

"I'm no traitor," Mike heard Victor say just before he was kicked in the stomach.

A sharp pain reverberated through his body. He knew he had to get up but he didn't seem to be able to. The next strike could finish him, so he curled up and brought his arms around his head while doing his best to catch his breath.

But the next blow never came. Instead, Victor said, "I think they're here. Get up."

Mike painfully got to his knees.

"Come on, I didn't hit you that hard," Victor added.

Victor was squatted near the fringe of the rooftop with the infrared binoculars in his hands.

"You sucker punched me," Mike said.

"Stop complaining. You nearly killed me with my own clip-on tie. And as if this wasn't enough, you shot me."

"Maybe I should have killed you," Mike said, holding his side. Mike was man enough to know that if the Russian had wanted him dead, he'd be dead already.

The Russian glanced at him. "Are we good now?"

"Yeah, we're good."

"Take a look," Victor said, handing him the binocs.

Mike brought the binocs to his eyes. An SUV had stopped in front of the building they were watching and four men got out while one remained in the driver seat.

"What do you want to do?" Victor asked.

Mike scanned the surrounding rooftops and streets. "What are they gonna do once they realized there's nobody up there?"

"What would you do?"

"I wouldn't stick around for long," Mike replied. "Are you sure they're working for the Sheik?"

"Yes. These guys aren't Russians."

Mike couldn't spot anyone else in the vicinity. The vehicle was idling in the street in front of the building's main entrance. "I need one alive," Mike said.

"How do you want to do this?"

"We need to take out the driver first," Mike said. "Then we take them out in the lobby as they exit the elevator."

Victor nodded. "What about the one you want to talk to?"

Mike thought about it for a second. "If the Sheik wanted to originally bring Dr. Galkin here, I'm sure he bugged the room and there are probably cameras all over the apartment. I don't believe he ever intended on coming here himself."

"So we won't go up to the apartment," Victor said.

"We'll take the SUV."

"All right," Victor said. "We should go."

Mike returned the binocs to his backpack. "I didn't mean to say what I said, Victor," Mike said. "I know why you're doing this."

Victor nodded. "I can't go in there empty-handed."

Mike handed him the PB silent pistol. "There are three rounds left in the magazine plus one in the pipe."

Victor expertly checked the magazine and confirmed there was a round in the chamber. "Thanks."

"No, Victor, thank you," Mike said as they headed to the elevator.

CHAPTER 41

IMSI headquarters, New York

Charles Mapother was dumbfounded. He couldn't believe the conversation he'd just had with Lisa was for real. His asset was in big trouble and he had no idea how to help her. Jonathan Sanchez looked as stunned as he was. Mapother had lost assets before, but not this way. It had been a terrible idea to send her alone and he only had himself to blame for it. The loss of Lisa was a horrible blow that could have been prevented if he had been more conscious of her capabilities. *She just wasn't ready and, deep down, you knew it. But you let her go anyhow. This one's on you, Charles.*

"Mike's on the line," came Anna Caprini's voice.

Oh shit. What am I gonna say to him?

"Mike?" he said, picking up.

"I'm with Victor Simonich. We're taking aggressive measures—" Mike started before Mapother interrupted him mid-sentence.

"What did you just say?"

"Charles, we don't have much time. Victor is with us."

Mapother's brain was in overdrive. He looked at Sanchez who simply shrugged.

"Go on," he finally said.

"Victor thinks the men we'll hit are part of the Sheik's network in Russia," Mike said. "We'll do our best to keep one alive and we'll convince him to speak with us. How's Lisa?"

Charles Mapother wondered if he should tell Mike about Lisa, but that would throw him off his game and Mapother didn't want that. Still, he felt bad lying to Mike. "She's fine."

"Okay. Good," Mike replied. "Got to go."

"One more thing," Mapother said, glad Mike didn't dwell on the subject. "Call me if you're indeed able to capture one of the Sheik's men."

"Something I should know?" Mike asked. He sounded strained and Mapother decided it wasn't the best time to talk to him about Zima's troubles in Syria.

"Not for now," Mapother said, ending the conversation.

Sanchez sat down in one of the armchairs facing Mapother's desk. "You made the right call, Charles," he said.

Mapother nodded. "I know. He needs to focus on the task at hand. But everything is going to shit."

"Not everything," Anna Caprini said, marching into his office. "We've started to analyze the info Support Two downloaded from the USB key Dr. Galkin passed on to Victor Simonich."

"And?"

Caprini handed him a red folder. "This is what we've got so far but there's more to come. It's incredible."

Mapother opened the file and started reading. *My God!* This was bigger than they ever thought. "We can't deal with this on our own," he said a minute later. He passed the file to Sanchez. "Call back DNI Phillips, Anna. I need to talk with him again."

. . . .

Director of National Intelligence Richard Phillips was in the bathroom when his personal cell phone chirped. Not many people had his personal number.

"Can it wait?" he said for greeting.

"No, Richard. It can't."

Charles Mapother.

The director of the International Market Stabilization Institute rarely called, and when he did, it was never to do small talk. He had spoken to Mapother less than an hour ago when the director had informed him of the developments in Russia. The conversation had given the DNI cramps, hence the reason he had spent the last ten minutes in the bathroom. The United States military was already stretched thin, and a new cold war with Russia wasn't something anyone wanted. Phillips had decided he wouldn't bother

POTUS—the President of the United States—with the intelligence Mapother had disclosed regarding a potential biological attack until the IMSI could at least confirm their initial findings.

"Shoot."

"Sir, I'm afraid I have bad news."

Phillips's stomach knotted in a ball. "What is it?" With Charles Mapother one could always expect the worst.

"Our asset in Koltsovo has been neutralized, I'm afraid," Mapother said.

Phillips allowed himself to relax. Losing men in the field was part of the game. He cared for everyone ready to put their lives on the line to keep others safe but the loss of one asset wasn't that big a deal. Unless neutralized meant compromised? *That* would be an issue and something Phillips was truly afraid of. Not only would exposure of the IMSI drastically diminish their efficiency, it could cause upheaval within the government and the intelligence community. Even though the IMSI had been a superb ally in the war on terror, especially in the fight against the Sheik, they were operating outside official channels and had nothing to do with the United States government. Officially.

Unofficially, things were a bit different. DNI Phillips had used them a few times to do things he knew couldn't be sanctioned by the government. The Croatian operation came immediately to mind. Plus, his friend and sitting US president Robert Muller had given the go ahead to the establishment of the IMSI. If it wasn't bad enough to acquiesce to the creation of a privately funded, direct-action agency, the whole thing had become a nightmare when the IMSI had itself discovered that one of its financial benefactors had been in bed with the Sheik. Since then, Phillips had weekly discussions with Robert Muller about how best to distance themselves from the IMSI. Nothing was off the table, including disbanding the whole shebang. Of course, Mapother knew nothing of this, and wouldn't hear about it until a final decision was made. With the attempt on Mapother's life, Phillips had thought it was the perfect time to pull the plug. That was until they came in contact with the Russian threat. Now everything had changed. Again.

"Is the asset dead?" Phillips asked. Truth was, he was feeling guilty as hell about hoping it was the case.

"We can't confirm death at this point, Richard. And don't sound so fucking happy about this," Mapother said, his tone glacial.

"I'm not, Charles," Phillips replied, making sure to keep his tone in check. "But I'm sure you know as well as I do what capturing one of your *assets* could mean to this administration, yes?"

"I won't even bother to reply to your stupid remark, Richard," Mapother said. "I was under the impression you actually cared about the men and women serving this country. Was I wrong?"

"You know damn well how I feel about them?" Phillips replied, yelling into his phone. *How dare Mapother say something like this to him? Hadn't he proved his loyalty already?*

"Just wanted to make sure where you stood," Mapother said. "Because there's something else we need to discuss."

Goddamn it. What now?

"We've looked at some info we were able to put our hands on and it doesn't look good, Richard," Mapother started. "From what we've got, I can pretty much tell you that the Russians were successful at creating a new thread of the Marburg virus."

Phillips sighed. *I'll definitely have to go to the president with this.*

"This isn't some kind of speculation, is it?" he asked. "You actually have proof of this?"

"I wouldn't call you if I didn't," Mapother replied. "The intelligence was passed to us by someone I've dealt with in the past."

"What's next?"

"I have another asset in Moscow. His job is to determine how far along the Russians are in the process of producing this new virus and what is the Sheik's involvement."

"Too bad you weren't able to kill him in Croatia," Phillips said.

"I'll let you know once I have more info," Mapother added before hanging up.

Phillips finished his business and got up from the toilet, only to find himself falling back on his seat again. His legs had cramped from sitting on the toilet for too long. Again.

CHAPTER 42

Moscow, Russia

M ike Walton used his infrared binoculars to scan for any other threats in the vicinity while Victor kept an eye on the SUV.

"It's all quiet," Mike said. "If someone's lurking, I can't see them."

"I don't think they positioned anyone else," Victor replied, keeping his voice down. "We would have seen another vehicle. This one was full and everyone is accounted for."

If they acted quickly and managed to surprise the Sheik's men, Mike was confident they could overtake them all without much problem. The wild card was Victor. Mike was still not one hundred percent sure about him. But he needed his help.

"Ready?"

The Russian nodded.

Mike emerged from the relative safety of the shadows and headed toward the SUV. If Victor had bluffed his way, Mike would find out now. He'd be shot in the back. Half expecting a bullet in the back of the head, Mike continued along the sidewalk. His senses were alert and he embraced the adrenaline rush that came every time he put himself in danger. There were no safety nets on these kinds of operations and Mike compared them to parachuting in the dark. A simple slip or mistake could trigger a whole chain of events that would result in his death.

His plan for taking out the driver was simple enough. He would approach the SUV from behind and lightly touch the side windows to see if they were bulletproof. If they weren't, he would fire at the driver from the outside. If they were, he'd continue walking to the end of the street and Victor would take over. Twenty feet away from the vehicle, Mike could see that the SUV was a G-Class Mercedes and that it was probably armored. Mike had seen these exact vehicles while training with the Germans for a protection mission back when he was working for the Royal Canadian Mounted Police. He didn't even have to touch the windows to know they were reinforced. A large caliber round would go through but his pistol would do no more than chip the window.

Hands deep in his pockets, Mike walked past the Mercedes without glancing at it or attempting to look inside. The tinted windows would have prevented him from seeing anything anyway.

The ball was now in Victor's camp and Mike would know soon enough if he had been right to trust the Russian with his life.

· · · · · · · ·

Victor Simonich swore under his breath. How many other things would go wrong before the day was over? When he woke up this morning, he would never have believed anyone telling him how this day would shape up. Nevertheless, he was proud of what he was doing. When he saw Mike walk by the SUV without firing his weapon, Victor knew it was his turn to act.

He approached the SUV with confidence and hoped the driver wouldn't notice he had no car. The only thing he needed the driver to do was open the door of his vehicle. Victor would take care of the rest but he needed to hurry. The rest of the Sheik's men would come down any moment now.

Victor knocked on the window, his badge out. "Police," he said.

The deeply tinted windows forbade him a look at the driver. "Turn off the engine," Victor ordered in Russian. The driver didn't obey, but responded by opening his window a couple of inches.

"We're on official government business. Just run our license plate, you'll see," the driver said, closing his window. *This is taking too long. I'm running out of time.*

"I already did and it came back stolen," Victor replied, taking his gun out and aiming it at the window. "I need to see some ID."

The window stopped its ascent and the man swore in Arabic. "Nonsense," he said in Russian, but the window was coming back down.

Victor fired his PB silent pistol the moment the window was lowered enough for him to see the man's eyes. But the driver must have felt something was wrong because he ducked and Victor's first bullet missed. The driver fired back at Victor, hitting him high on the left shoulder. The Mercedes probably had the "one touch down" button option because the window kept going down while both men continued firing at each other at close range. Victor was hit again and he fell to the pavement, two new holes in his body. His rounds had also found their mark as the driver slumped to his side. Victor's last round had mushroomed into his brain.

As he lay on the street, his eyes to the black skies, Victor swore he saw a bright shooting star pass just over him. He briefly wondered why he had never seen one before. Then darkness took over.

· · · · · · · ·

Mike Walton knew there was trouble the moment he heard gunfire. Victor's PB silent pistol might not have been completely noiseless but it didn't produce the noise level he had just heard. His own pistol out in front of him, Mike sprinted to the Mercedes just in time to see Victor collapse on the street like a marionette whose strings had been cut.

Fuck.

He was fifty feet from the SUV when he noticed movement at the building's entrance. Four armed men were coming out, running toward the Mercedes. Mike automatically dropped to his knees to establish a better, more-stable firing position. Lying flat on the sidewalk would have made him a smaller target, but firing a pistol from a prone position was much more difficult and precision was often less than spectacular.

Mike pulled the trigger as fast as he could while maintaining proper sight alignment. He started working on the man closest to the Mercedes and worked his way to his left. He fired ten rounds in less than three seconds. Caught by surprise, the three men Mike fired at first fell almost together. The fourth one went down too but returned fired. His shots went high and right. Mike rolled to his left and fired again, this time taking half a second to do so. His round hit the man in head. He hoped he hadn't killed the first three men to go

175

down. He did a tactical magazine change and cautiously approached the downed men while making sure he kept the SUV in his line of sight in case Victor had failed to neutralize the driver.[5]

Two of the men were still moving. Clearly in pain, one of them saw him and looked for the firearm he had dropped at his side. Blood came from two bullet wounds in his legs. He used his arms to thrust himself forward, toward the Mercedes.

The wailing of police sirens pierced the night and their proximity told Mike he had, at best, a minute or two before they were on scene. Betting the man who was crawling to the SUV was in good enough shape to answer his questions, Mike fired at point blank range into the head of the other surviving member of the Sheik's team before he grabbed onto the injured man. The man rolled onto his back and yelled something in Russian.

Mike shoved the barrel of his pistol into the man's mouth, breaking two teeth in the process. "You speak English?"

The man nodded with enthusiasm. Satisfied he had picked the right man, Mike slammed the butt of his pistol into the man's forehead, knocking him unconscious. He then advanced toward the SUV, pretty sure that if the driver hadn't engaged him by now, Victor had taken care of him.

Shit! Victor. I can't leave him here.

The sirens were now dangerously close. As he moved to the driver's side of the SUV, he saw Victor twitch on the pavement. A large puddle a dark blood poured out from under him.

Mike kneeled next to Victor. The man was still alive.

"Shit, Victor, I'm sorry," Mike said, desperately trying to find the entry wounds.

"Don't let it be . . . for nothing," the Russian replied, his voice barely audible. But Victor still had enough strength to push Mike's hands away from him. "Don't let all of this fool you . . . my American friend. Russia . . . is a great . . . country. Proud."

"I know."

"Go. Now . . ."

"Fuck," Mike said out loud as the last sign of life vanished from Victor's eyes, leaving them fixed, blank and empty.

Mike jumped to his feet and rushed to the SUV. He reached inside and unlocked the doors. He grabbed the dead driver and threw him on the ground next to Victor. He then hurried back to the man he had knocked unconscious and dragged him inside the Mercedes and placed him on the back seat.

Mike climbed into the driver's seat and drove away with only seconds to spare before the first police vehicle turned onto the street. It took five minutes to reach the highway and another two minutes until he was satisfied he wasn't being followed. Mike wasn't naïve enough to believe he was safe, though. He glanced at the unconscious man on the backseat and wondered if he hadn't hit him too hard.

It would be a shame to have gone through all this only to accidentally kill the man that could lead him to the Sheik. Before he could attest to the man's health, he needed to contact Support Two.

"Are you okay?" Cooper asked. "The police have sent numerous units to the Solntsevo District."

"I need help, James, and I need it now."

"Anything," Cooper replied.

"Do we have a safe house in Moscow?"

"We don't. But I can have an ad hoc one in thirty minutes."

Shit! "A hotel room? That won't do."

"That's the best we can do on such short notice. We aren't in—"

"Stop with the excuses, James," Mike roared. "I know we're in Russia but I need a place where I can interrogate someone and I need it now."

"What about the embassy?"

"I'll call you back when you stop talking nonsense," Mike said before he terminated the call.

Did the CIA or any other federal agencies have one they could share? That would cost Mapother a lot of IOUs, but what if he could arrange one? It was worth a try.

"Holy shit, Mike!" Mapother exclaimed once the call went through. "What did you do?"

"What I had to, Charles, and now isn't the time to debrief. I need help."

Mapother's tone changed immediately. "Whatever you need."

"I hope you mean that because what I need is a real safe house in Moscow."

"What else?" Mapother replied.

"You have one?" Mike asked. Didn't Support Two just tell him there weren't any?

"Kind of. What else?"

"That's it for now. But I'll need Support Two to take care of the vehicle I borrowed from the Sheik."

There was a long silence on the other end and Mike thought the line had been cut.

"I just sent the pertinent info regarding the safe house to your smartphone."

"Thanks. How did you—"

"It doesn't matter how I got it, Mike, I got it. And one last thing?"

"I'm listening." Mike looked in his rearview mirror for any sign he had picked up a tail.

"The intelligence Support Two forwarded to us is invaluable but we need to corroborate it before it can be dispatched to the rest of the community. It's just too big."

"Understood. I'll get you what you need. And much more."

CHAPTER 43

Moscow, Russia

S heik Qasim Al-Assad pressed the button that would send his text message to Lidiya Votyakov. When news of the attack had reached him, he had felt the clutch of fear for the first time in a very long time. He still needed to find out exactly why he had felt this way. Was it because Lidiya still meant something to him? Or was it because without her, there was no way he'd be able to achieve the results the Russian president expected of him?

"Sheik Al-Assad?" said the female Russian agent working the operation center.

"What is it?" the Sheik replied, walking to her workstation.

"Your team isn't responding," she said. "And we're receiving numerous reports of shots fired on location."

The Sheik had dispatched two teams. The first one, a team of two, was in Koltsovo conducting surveillance on Dr. Galkin's wife. Only the Sheik, and other persons the Russian president had chosen, knew that Sophia Galkin had stopped loving her husband decades ago, but she had stayed with him because he was a good man. A loyal man. But everything changed when he confessed to her that he had contacted an American acquaintance regarding his work at Biopreparat. He had told her to be ready to leave at an instant's notice. The Russian president had not been very clear about why she had betrayed her husband, but the next morning, Sophia Galkin had contacted her brother, an FSB agent working in Moscow. The Sheik suspected that the opposition didn't know about the differences between Dr. Galkin and his wife, and that if a deal had been reached they'd tried to get Sophia out of Russia.

The second team, a team of five, was in the Solntsevo District. Their orders were to verify that the address where he had originally planned to conduct the interview with Dr. Galkin hadn't been breached. The fact that shots were fired didn't worry him. It simply confirmed that somehow the opposition had found out about the safe house he kept in the Solntsevo District. What troubled him was that they didn't respond. These five men were the best he had in Moscow.

"The police are now on location, Sheik Al-Assad," the Russian agent said.

With Dr. Galkin dead and Victor Simonich not answering his phone, the Sheik didn't like the direction the whole operation was suddenly taking. They were still far from ready to launch a full-scale biological attack on the United States. They had a few doses ready, but that wouldn't be enough to consider moving forward with the original plan. And with the threat of discovery, he was afraid the Russian president would cut his losses. *And cut me loose.*

"The police say that there are several bodies."

"Any signs of our SUV? It's a G-Class Mercedes."

"There's no mention of that yet," the male Russian agent replied from the other side of the room. He was holding a police radio to his ear. "Everybody's dead. There are no survivors."

"I want to know what happened," the Sheik yelled. *This can't be happening.* He needed to find out who the opposition was and what they knew about Biopreparat's discovery. Whoever they were, they couldn't leave Russia. He had to think about a way to hide what had just happened from the Russian president.

"Sheik Al-Assad, we're getting a live report from Koltsovo," said the female agent. "A team of FSB agents found your men dead in Sophia Galkin's apartment."

The Sheik felt as if he had just been punched in the stomach. Since the terrible loss suffered at Benalmadena, only bad news seemed to find its way to him. Why was he so cursed? Two years ago he was on top; now he was fighting for survival. And it had all started with Charles Mapother. How could he turn the tables on the man who had wreaked havoc on his organization? Could he use Ray Powell somehow?

"They found a woman," she added. "And she's still alive. Looks like she's been shot numerous time."

"Who is she?" the Sheik asked.

It took a moment for the female agent to reply. "There's no ID on her. The agents are taking a picture. We'll get it in a minute."

The Sheik paced the room. This could be the breakthrough he was looking for. If he could catch one of his foes alive, he'd find a way to get the answers he needed.

"This is from the Solntsevo District, Sheik Al-Assad," said the male agent. "Victor Simonich is amongst the dead. His body was found next to one of your men."

The Sheik wondered how the Russian president would react to the loss of his nephew. Not well, he guessed. *But I might be able to use his anger to push forward even with our latest setbacks.*

"Here's the picture, sir," the female agent said. "It's coming online now."

The Sheik focused on the face that was slowly appearing on one of the flat screens above the agent's desk. *This isn't possible. It can't be.* The Sheik started to shake in anger. He couldn't believe what he was seeing. *Dr. Lisa Harrison Powell. Wife of Mike Powell and daughter-in-law of Canadian ambassador Ray Powell.* Didn't she die at the Ottawa Train Station? The newspapers had covered her death and her husband's. *Unless* . . . Didn't Omar Al-Nashwan mention Mike Powell just before he passed? *Charles Mapother, Mike Powell, and now Dr. Lisa Harrison Powell.* They were all working together, and the Sheik was now certain they were the ones who had killed his associates in Croatia.

Then it came to him. He would indeed use Ray Powell. And he would use his daughter-in-law too.

"Get me my son," he ordered the female agent.

"Which one?" she asked.

How dare she insult him like this? Doesn't she know? The Sheik lost it as anger took over his mind and body. Every muscle tightened and he felt like a bomb about to explode. All the frustration and setbacks of the last few months erupted. He sprang out of his chair and pounced on the female agent. He ripped off her headset and smashed her head multiple times on her desk. He then swung her around and punched her three times in the teeth with all his might. As he looked at her distorted and bloody face, he felt a huge impulse to bite off her nose. And that was exactly what he did. Movement

181

behind him made him turn around. The other agent had risen from his seat and was watching in horror. The Sheik spat the nose at his feet and yelled at him to sit back down if he didn't want to be next. The moans of the female agent behind him brought him back to reality. He looked at his hands, then at her. *What have I done? And why does it feel so good?*

The taste of blood in his mouth made him feel almighty. He snatched a pencil from the agent's workstation and stabbed the defenseless woman in the neck. The pencil broke, barely breaking skin. The agent screamed. The Sheik grabbed the wireless keyboard with two hands and smashed it against her head again and again until her whole face was just a bloody mess. He looked at the male agent to gauge his reaction. The man was immobile, and clearly scared about what would happen to him. The Sheik wiped the blood off his face with his sleeve. "Get me my son, would you?"

CHAPTER 44

Al-Mazzeh Military Airport, Syria

Igor Votyakov didn't hear his phone ringing. The noise of the Antonov An-2's single engine was so loud that Igor needed to shout at his men to be understood. But, as a precaution, he always set his phone to both vibrate and sound when he wasn't tactical.

"Yes," he yelled into his phone.

"It's me," his father said. Even with the kind of commotion coming from the plane's engine, Igor had no problem identifying the caller. The rich, deep voice of the Sheik couldn't be mistaken.

"We're about to take off," he said, climbing into the cabin of the Antonov. At least inside he could hear what his father had to say. The roar of the engine persisted through the lightly insulated cabin but it wasn't as bad as outside.

"Any issues?"

"None since we last talked. Local authorities have actually been very helpful. The Syrian president's visit to Moscow certainly helped smooth things out," Igor said. He could feel the plane's forward momentum as it started to roll on the tarmac. He looked outside and estimated he had about three minutes before they were airborne.

"I'll be joining you in Mykonos, Igor," his father said.

"Is that wise?"

"I don't have much choice, I'm afraid."

"What happened?" he asked his father, his eyes settling on Ray Powell. The ambassador's hands were tied behind his back but it was only a precaution. An hour ago he had been sedated, and chances were he wouldn't wake up until they were at the Mykonos safe house.

"Things got a little out of hand here in Moscow. I'll see you soon," his dad said before hanging up.

Igor swore loud enough that his men looked at him. "The Sheik is coming to Mykonos," he said. "You'll do whatever he says, unless I tell you otherwise."

His men nodded. They would obey him no matter what. He had gained their trust fighting alongside them against the insurgents in the North Caucasus and on a secret, long-range reconnaissance mission in Syria. But why was his father coming to Mykonos? With most of the world's intelligence agencies looking for him, Igor couldn't comprehend his father's reasoning. He never had. There were two people in the world he could call to help him understand, his mother and Veniamin Simonich, the president of the Russian Federation. But he had only one of them on speed dial.

"Mr. President, this is Igor. Were you aware my father was planning on coming to Mykonos?"

CHAPTER 45

Damascus, Syria

Zima Bernbaum had used almost all the money she had left trying to get back to the Canadian embassy in Beirut. After the second checkpoint, she had very little cash. The bribes needed to pass through were getting more expensive by the hour and Zima had no idea why until one of the militia told her driver the Russians had started bombings their positions.

Zima was sure he was wrong. *They wouldn't dare.* Russia wouldn't dare bomb anything other than ISIS targets. She knew the Syrian president and his Russian counterpart Veniamin Simonich were close but not *that* close. If the Russians had really begun a bombing campaign against everyone opposing the Syrian president, Zima guessed that the Syrian conflict was about to enter a new dynamic. She doubted the Central Intelligence Agency would sit idly by while Russian warplanes killed people they had helped train—like the militia she had just given a bribe to.

With no money left, she wouldn't be able to get through the next checkpoint, but she offered the driver her last twenty to borrow his cell. She called the unsecured IMSI number, the one regular folks called when they were looking to hire the IMSI to conduct a foreign-market analysis.

"International Market Stabilization Institute, Karen speaking,"

"Hello, Karen, my name's Shawna Blanchard," said Zima. Shawna Blanchard was the name all female assets were told to give to whoever answered the phone. In theory, the person at the other end would know who to transfer the call to.

"Please hold," Karen said.

The cab driver turned in his seat and looked at her. "How long? I'll need more than twenty dollars if you're calling long distance."

Zima heard a few clicks then Anna Caprini came on the line. "We're secured here. What about you?"

"I'm calling from a borrowed cell phone inside Syria," Zima said while gesturing to her driver she wouldn't be long.

"Glad to hear your voice. What can we do to help?"

. . . .

Jonathan Sanchez hurried to the bubble where Anna Caprini was on the phone with Zima. His leg was killing him but he'd be damned if he didn't get there in time to speak with her. The last communication they'd had with her had ended abruptly. Since then, Sanchez had tried to convince himself that Zima was all right, but with every hour without news, and with reports coming in of a shootout where the meet between the Canadian emissaries and the Syrian troops was supposed to take place, he was losing faith.

Zima was a fantastic woman and he wouldn't be completely honest if he didn't admit a certain attraction to her. The last person he had fallen for had died on the Benalmadena raid. There wasn't a day he didn't think about Jasmine Carson, but she was gone, and he had to move on. Nevertheless, the painful thought of losing Zima made him shiver with fear. And the worst thing about all this was that she had no idea how he felt about her. *You're acting like a god-damn teenage boy, buddy. You'd better wake up and start thinking like a leader here, or you'll lose her too.*

Anna Caprini was scribbling notes on a piece of paper.

"Are we tracking this call?" he mouthed to Caprini.

She nodded. "We know exactly where you are, and I can also confirm what you've just said. Russia has indeed started bombing ISIS and non-ISIS positions inside Syria," Caprini said before adding, "You're now on speaker phone with me and Jonathan."

"We were worried about you," Sanchez said. "Glad you're okay."

"Thanks. The last few hours weren't easy, and there are a lot of things I need to pass on," Zima said. The line was unexpectedly clear and Sanchez thought Zima's voice breathed relief.

"We'll get you out as soon as we can. Stand by for a minute." Sanchez was glad they had worked on an exfil plan the moment they had felt things going to shit. He brought up a map of Syria on one of the screens and zoomed in on Zima's location on another one. "About ten miles north of your position there's a makeshift helipad."

Sanchez's grasp of Arabic was basic but he knew enough to hear Zima ask for some sort of map from her driver. "What are the coordinates?" she asked seconds later.

Sanchez gave them to her. "We can have a chopper on location in about four to six hours. Can you hold up until then?"

"Stand by."

· · · · · · · ·

Zima Bernbaum unfolded the map and searched for the coordinates Sanchez had given her. "I don't see a helipad on the map," she said.

"Trust me, it's there."

Zima wished Sanchez could give her more info, but the fact they were communicating via an unsecured line prevented that. "I can make my way there but there are a lot of unknowns right now. I might not be able to go through another checkpoint," Zima said, studying the map.

"You'll find a way. You need to," Sanchez said. Zima had never heard Sanchez sound so sincere. Did he care for her?

"What should I expect?" she asked.

"You'll know when you see it," Sanchez said. "Just make sure you have eyes on the location."

The cab driver was getting more and more agitated and she hoped it wouldn't become an issue. "I'll be there. Four hours."

· · · · · · · ·

Sanchez left the bubble and walked as fast as his leg allowed him. He knocked on Mapother's door and it opened automatically. The IMSI director was on the phone and he signaled Sanchez to take a seat.

"I understand completely, Richard, but I have a feeling we'll need to move within the next twenty-four to thirty-six hours," Mapother said.

As Mapother continued his conversation with the DNI, Sanchez's mind wandered to Syria. He pictured Zima stuck in a stinky cab with militia and government troops fighting. He hoped she'd find a way to hunker down until help arrived. Zima was well trained, and she had experienced life on the run before. Her dark skin would help her blend in and her wit would keep her alive. *She'll be fine,* Sanchez concluded, but felt a pinch in his heart.

"You have an update?" Mapother asked, snapping Sanchez out of his reverie.

"Zima contacted us," he said. "She's stuck in Syria."

"What the hell happened?"

"She couldn't talk much, Charles," Sanchez explained. "She was using an unsecured cell phone but she gave us her coordinates."

Mapother opened the laptop on his desk and turned it toward Sanchez. "Show me."

Sanchez loaded the same maps he and Anna Caprini had looked at in the bubble. "She's right here."

Mapother studied the map and scrolled through the area using the mouse pad. "Did you activate Operation Sunglasses?"

"That's why I'm here. I don't see any other solution."

"Neither do I," replied Mapother. "She could get out on her own, but it would take much longer. Time we don't have."

Sanchez nodded. He had come to the same conclusion.

"I'll make the call," Mapother said.

I'm glad you agree, Charles, because I would have made the call even if you'd disagreed.

CHAPTER 46

IMSI headquarters, New York

Charles Mapother dialed the number he'd been given a month ago by Meir Yatom, the head of the Special Operations Division of the Israeli Mossad. He didn't know who would answer but he had been promised that whoever it was had the power to grant Mapother a wish.

Six weeks ago, during a follow-up operation Mapother had authorized after their success in Benalmadena, Mike and Lisa had found themselves in Croatia chasing the Sheik's top lieutenants. During the course of their mission, they had not only blown a gaping hole in the Sheik's network, but they had also prevented an attack on the Israeli embassy in Zagreb, Croatia. Immensely grateful, Meir Yatom had promised unrestricted assistance if Mapother ever needed it. Mapother had put the info in a file and called it Operation Sunglasses. Never did he expect he'd need the help so soon.

"I guess this isn't a courtesy call, Charles?" It was Meir Yatom. He had given Mapother his private number.

"I'm afraid not. We're in a bind and I'm calling in the favor."

"I already told you. Anything." Yatom's voice was raspy and he always sounded as though he was out of breath. Mapother imagined him smoking cigarette after cigarette in a windowless room somewhere on the Mossad campus.

"I have an asset stuck in Syria. I need to get her out. Time is of the essence."

"I see," Yatom said. "It wouldn't have anything to do with big the shootout in central Damascus earlier today, would it?"

Mapother, a veteran of the FBI who had worked freelance for the CIA for many years, never understood how the Mossad always managed to stay connected to pretty much everything going on in every conflict around the planet. "Would that change anything?" he asked.

"Of course not. Where's your asset?"

Mapother gave him the details and had Yatom promise he'd send a helicopter to the location in exactly four hours.

"Understand this, Charles. My debt is paid. In full," Yatom said. "This number won't work anymore. Goodbye."

CHAPTER 47

Mykonos, Greece

It was Igor Votyakov's first time at his father's house in Mykonos. Perched atop a small hill less than one mile northeast of the Mykonos ferry port, the splendid villa offered its occupants a commanding view of the Aegean Sea. Its floor-to-ceiling bulletproof windows provided all the sunlight and security someone stuck inside could hope for. Specifically built for the divorced wife of a Russian oil executive, the Sheik had bought it from her half a decade ago. It was one of his father's last strongholds. But for how long would it remain so?

His dad's adversaries were attacking from all flanks and Igor actually felt sorry for him. *Not that he deserves any pity.* His father's quest to avenge his family had consumed his heart and soul. And if this wasn't enough, it had also transformed a decent man into someone no one could love. Not even his own sons. But that wasn't entirely true, was it? His brother Zakhar had always wanted to please their father. He would have done anything for Qasim's affection. And he did. And it cost him his life.

Some said the love between a father and his son was unconditional, but Igor knew better. His father's unscrupulous behavior had forced him to kill his older brother, and for that Igor would never forgive him. He'd continue to do his father's bidding as ordered but Russia's support was coming to an end. The moment his father's actions weren't in Russia's best interests, he would have no hesitation. He would take his father down like the dog he was.

The flight from Syria hadn't been the smoothest but it could have been worse. They had stopped in Cyprus to refuel. They had to stop a second time at a minor airfield north of the small Turkish town of Bodrum. The flight from Bodrum to Mykonos lasted just over an hour. Russian officials from the embassy in Athens were waiting for them in three minivans. Igor didn't know what kind of bullshit they had told the Hellenic police but he suspected a large quantity of money had changed hands. However the diplomat had obtained the favor, Igor didn't care. The important thing was that no officials even bothered to look at their passports. By the time they reached the villa, Igor and his men were exhausted. One of the diplomats—by now Igor was pretty sure the man was with the SVR—gave him the address of the small hotel where they stayed and told him that he was only one phone call away in case there was any trouble. Igor didn't expect any. At least not for now.

Exhausted or not, his men were pros and none of them would complain until they had taken care of business. What they had to do before anyone even thought about shutting eyes was create an appropriate defensive position. The villa was outfitted with imposing security arrangements that included powerful floodlights and a closed-circuit security system. Igor posted one of his men in the control room where he would have access to all the video footage. He assigned another man to patrol duty as the villa was close to four thousand square feet of interior space and he didn't want to be caught off guard if somebody was able to sneak in. His two remaining men would get some rest in one of the villa's four bedrooms. Igor took a few minutes to work on a rotation schedule and used a magnet to attach his orders to the fridge. Next he headed to the control room to check on his man.

"You've got everything you need?"

"Yes, sir," the soldier replied.

"Can you show me the room where our guest is staying?"

The soldier touched a few keys on the touchscreen and Igor was rewarded with a perfect view of the ambassador. "I think I'll pay him a visit."

. . . .

Ray Powell had regained consciousness minutes ago. Still, he hadn't opened his eyes and had forced himself to remain immobile. He found it easier to focus with his eyes closed. The first thing he did was assess his health. Pressure to his wrists and ankles told him they were bound. The softness behind his head and back indicated he was on a mattress, and an expensive one at that. For a while there were no sounds, but a faint odor of coffee told him he wasn't alone. The fact that somebody might be watching him crossed his mind and he was glad he hadn't moved. His rationale was that if they didn't know he was awake, they wouldn't do anything. He wanted to believe this.

His body ached from head to toe. He had no idea how long he had been unconscious, but the steady growling of his stomach implied it had been at least twenty-four hours. His mouth was dry, and he longed for a glass of water.

A sound to his left startled him and he involuntarily gasped, knowing he had just betrayed the fact that he was awake. He opened his eyes in time to see the same man who had choked him in Syria empty a medium-sized drum of ice-cold water over him. Powell was sure he was going into shock or having a heart attack. The effect didn't last long but the man definitely had his attention.

Powell looked at him. Just over six feet tall, with broad shoulders, dark skin and eyes that didn't miss a beat, the man was built like an Olympic swimmer.

"Welcome to Mykonos, Ambassador."

"Who are you?"

"Your file says you were with the Royal Canadian Mounted Police, Ambassador," the man said, walking to the windows on the other side of the bed. He opened the first curtain and sunlight entered the room, filtered by a palm tree just outside the window. "I was wondering if a little cold shower would bring back memories from your time at Depot?"

Powell didn't reply. It wasn't a secret that before accepting the Canadian ambassadorship to Algeria he'd had a career with the RCMP. Depot was the training division of the RCMP. Every member of the Canadian federal police force had to go through Depot to become a fully fledged Mountie. That wasn't a secret either.

"No answer?" the man asked, a smile creeping onto his face. "That's fine. I understand. Why volunteer information to someone you don't know? I don't blame you."

The man moved to the second window and opened its curtain. "Magnificent view, Mr. Ambassador. You'll love it,."

"What do you want?" Powell asked, shivering. His wet clothes were plastered against his body, bringing his discomfort to another level.

The man laughed. "No small talk for you, I see."

A knife magically materialized in the man's right hand. "Fuck you!" yelled Powell, struggling against the tie wraps. They were cutting through the skin around his wrists, but he didn't care.

"You should be careful how you speak to a man armed with a knife, Mr. Ambassador," said the man, tilting his head. "I'm actually quite good with one."

The man's voice was calm and in some way serene, and that scared Powell to death. The man was a sociopath or he wanted Powell to think he was. *Psychological warfare.*

With one quick movement of the blade, and before Powell had time to react, the man cut through the tie wraps around his ankles.

"If you know me as well as you want me to think, you're well aware I don't give a shit what happens to me." Powell tried to bluff.

The smirk on the man's face told Powell he wasn't buying.

"You don't know me, Mr. Ambassador, so let me introduce myself. My name is Igor Votyakov."

The name Votyakov did ring a bell but Powell didn't remember where he had heard it before. "What do you want?"

"Me? Nothing. Absolutely nothing," Igor replied, placing the tip of his knife under Powell's chin. "But someone else is coming here to see you, and I know that this person won't be as pleasant as I am."

"I've been rotting in jail for the last two and a half years. I have no value. None whatsoever," Powell said, feeling the knife would break skin if he moved an inch.

"Don't sell yourself short, Ray," Victor said. "I can call you Ray, right?"

What did this guy want? What he had said was true. He'd been out of the loop for more than two years. What could he possibly know that could push someone to mount a full-scale assault only to capture him again? *Again? Holy crap! Was the Sheik behind this?* That would make a lot of sense.

Powell looked into the man's eyes and said, "We're waiting for the Sheik, aren't we?"

Igor chuckled, and then replaced his knife in its sheath. "I told you not to sell yourself short, Ray."

CHAPTER 48

Syria

As tired as she was, Zima Bernbaum couldn't sleep even if she'd wanted to. The throbbing in her right arm had intensified. She needed antibiotics and a doctor. With no pain killers or clean bandages, her hand would need amputation if it didn't receive proper medical attention within the next twenty-four hours. Zima could have run away with the cab driver's cell phone but she was in no shape to fight him off. Plus, it would have attracted unwanted attention. Instead, she had thanked him for his services and had walked the ten miles to the location Jonathan Sanchez had given her. At least the man had let her keep the map.

If the excruciating pain in her hand wasn't enough, the weather had taken a turn for the worse and a cold front had swept over the area. Zima would give a week's salary to have clothing appropriate for the near-freezing temperature she was now experiencing. *Make it a month's salary.* Twice fighter jets screamed overhead. Flashes of light lit the sky to the north as they dropped their ordnance, pounding everything below. *Where the hell did Jonathan send me? No way a helicopter will land anywhere close to here.* She glanced at her watch. It had taken her just under four hours to cover the distance. The map indicated she was in Deir Qanun, a small village about six miles east of the Lebanese border. There were no street-lights, for which she was grateful. A weapon would have been nice, though. The buildings around her were decrepit and no light came from the windows. With the exception of a couple of dogs barking at each other, the village was dead. Or so it seemed. She continued walking toward the end of the narrow street. The map showed an open field at the end of it.

Zima shivered. She didn't like being stuck in Syria. Was leaving her job at the Canadian Security Intelligence Service the right choice? She was starting to doubt it. Being cold, hungry and in pain wasn't helping. Her right index was gone, and there was a good chance she'd lose her hand if help didn't materialize soon. Zima studied the map, hoping to find a sheltered spot where she could observe the field without dying from exposure to the cold. But the moon wasn't bright enough. She was in the process of folding the map when she felt a presence behind her. She froze instantly.

"Raise your hands slowly over your head and interlock your fingers. Do it now," someone whispered in Arabic. The voice was clearly masculine and belonged to someone used to being in control. "Do not turn around."

If he wanted me dead, I'd be dead. So just do as you're told and wait for an opportunity. It never crossed her mind to feign ignorance. She obeyed.

"I've been watching you for the last ten minutes. I know you're by yourself," the man said, keeping his voice low. "So there's no reason for you to lie. I'm sure you've realized that if I wanted to kill you, you'd be dead already and we wouldn't be chatting. I've risked a lot to be here, so I'll ask you this once, and only once. If I don't like your answer, or if I think you're lying, my voice will be the last thing you'll ever hear. Nod if you understand."

Zima nodded. The man was a professional. He wasn't too close behind her. She'd have no chance of disarming him before he shot her.

"What's your name?"

"Zima," she replied without hesitation.

"Good," replied the man. "I'm glad you said that. "Who's Charles Mapother?"

Oh shit. How could she answer the question without giving away too much?

"I hope he's the man who sent you here," Zima said. "That's all I'll tell you, so if that isn't enough, just shoot me and be done with it."

"Turn around," the man ordered.

Had she passed? The man standing in front of her was well over six feet tall with a medium build. He was dressed in dark clothes and wore night-vision goggles.

"Name's Eitan," the man said. "Follow me, and stay close. The streets aren't as empty as they look."

"You're here for me," Zima said, feeling as if a huge weight had been lifted from her shoulders.

"The chopper is about six hundred meters this way," Eitan said in English, pointing toward the field. "We landed thirty minutes ago and I know government troops are heading our way. And I wouldn't be surprised if ISIS had a few men here as well. Those bastards are everywhere."

Zima was now able to identify Eitan's accent. "You're Israeli," she said.

"Just keep your mouth shut and watch our six, will you?" he said, transitioning from his pistol to something that looked like an MP-5. "Let's go."

Eitan was walking rapidly, the barrel of his weapon flashing left and right, looking for threats she couldn't see. She checked behind her and rammed into Eitan who had stopped walking.

"Watch your step, goddam it," he hissed. "Two men approaching our position. Fifty meters. We can't cross."

They were at a crossroad. Half-destroyed buildings occupied the four corners. They looked uninhabited but you never knew where snipers could hide. Zima felt like a sitting duck and wished they could get moving.

"Thirty meters," Eitan said.

The man was in full control. *He's done this before.* "Give me your pistol," she said. Their backs were against the wall of a building.

"Just sit tight and stay quiet," he said. "I've got this."

Zima couldn't believe this. She was dealing with a freaking misogynist. She shook her head. *What an asshole.*

Two seconds later, she watched him pivot and get on one knee. While half his body remained behind cover, he peeked around the corner and fired four rounds. Two double taps. "We're clear. Let's move."

They dashed across the street. They were almost halfway when she heard the all-too-familiar sound of AK-47 assault rifles opening up on full-auto from their left. Rounds flew over them. Tracers brightened the night as Eitan screamed for her to continue toward the field.

As soon as they reached cover, Eitan stopped running and signaled her to keep going. She didn't listen and took position next to him. "Give me your fucking pistol," she yelled over the sound of his weapon. Eitan continued firing, pumping round after round at targets she couldn't see. When his weapon clicked empty, he took cover behind the wall and changed magazines.

"Start the engines," she heard him say through his comm system. "We're being engaged by at least half a dozen troops."

"Your pistol?" she repeated, as he was about to re-engage.

"No way," he said. "You're my mission. Go to the chopper now."

Zima was done listening to him. As he turned to fire, she grabbed the pistol from his leg holster. He either didn't care or was too busy engaging his targets because he didn't say anything. She waited by his side and tried to take his place when it was time for him to reload again. But he wouldn't let her. He grabbed her shoulders and slammed her back against the concrete wall where they had taken cover. "I'm here to buy you some time. Don't be a fool. I'll follow you."

Without another word, Zima sprinted toward the field, cursing the man's machismo. She could hear the engines of the helicopter powering up and she hoped Eitan had advised whoever was in the helicopter that there was a friendly approaching. She'd know soon enough.

The firefight behind her reached a new crescendo. Eitan was now firing on full-auto, as if he was being overrun and aiming didn't matter anymore. She wanted to go back, but to what end? Her foot hit a rock and she fell forward, the pistol flying out of her hand. A powerful pair of hands lifted her off the ground. A man dressed like Eitan was standing by her side. He fired a few shots toward the village before pushing her toward the helicopter. The wind of the rotor made the ground shake under her feet as she climbed in. She recognized it as a modified Bell 206.

The man squeezed himself in and ordered the pilot to take off. "What about Eitan?" she asked as the helicopter lifted off the ground. The soldier ripped off his night-vision goggles and shook his head. "You'd better be worth it. Eitan was one of the best we had."

A profound sadness enveloped her. She had caused this. *Oh my God, this loss is on me. Again.* If only Eitan had let her help. *Why do men always feel they have to protect me?* As the wind rushed through the open doors of the helicopter, she fought the tears she knew were coming as her mind raced back to Edmonton. Six months ago, she had helped stop a terror attack that would have devastated the Canadian gas industry and the United States' strategic oil supply. Shane, a Royal Canadian Mounted Police swat member, had given his life so she could live. She had sworn that wouldn't happen again. She had joined the IMSI because she had thought she could make a bigger difference. *And now this.* Another white knight had fallen because of her. Whatever she did, it was never good enough.

"Welcome to Israel," the soldier next to her said ten minutes later. He handed her four pills and a bottle of water. "Painkillers. For your hand."

"Thanks," Zima said, popping all four pills into her mouth.

"We'll be in Haifa in no time."

"I don't know what else to say."

"There's nothing to say," the soldier said. "We all do our part. We did ours. Now you do yours."

CHAPTER 49

Moscow, Russia

Mike Walton's phone chirped. He picked it up from the passenger's seat.

"The navigation system tells me I'm two minutes away," he said. "Anything I should know?"

"The safe house isn't really a safe house, Mike," Mapother said. "The place belongs to my brother."

Holy shit! "Please tell me your brother isn't there," Mike said. He had never met Mapother's brother, a man named Frank.

"Don't worry, he isn't," Mapother replied. "The building has a secured underground garage with a private elevator leading directly to my brother's penthouse."

Mapother gave him the codes for the garage and elevator before adding, "Try to keep the place clean, Mike."

"I'll let you know as soon as I learn something useful," Mike said.

The condo tower was located in Tverskaya, one of Moscow's most sought-after neighborhoods. Tverskaya Street was the equivalent of New York City's 5th Avenue, where luxurious hotels, high-end fashion stores and expensive restaurants lined up the illuminated sidewalks. Not the best place to conduct an enhanced interrogation, but at least Mike would be able to hide the SUV. Mike turned into the ramp leading to the underground parking lot and punched in the code for the automatic door. Once in, he looked for the parking spot assigned to the penthouse and squeezed the G-Class between a yellow Ferrari Italia and a superb Jaguar F-Type.

I guess this is where Russia's one percent lives.

Mike knew Mapother's father had hit it big with his international import-export business. When he died, he left his empire to his two sons, Charles and Frank. Charles decided to join the FBI but Frank, already a vice president of the company, stepped into his father's shoes and brought the business to new heights. Charles Mapother sold his shares to his brother and never looked back. Mike didn't think Frank would approve of what was about to happen in his posh apartment but he didn't have all the facts.

Mike opened the door, careful not to bump it against the Jaguar's side, and looked for surveillance cameras. There were at least two. He would ask Support Two to take care of them and their feeds. He walked to the rear passenger side door and looked through the window to make sure his prisoner was still unconscious. He had moaned a lot during the trip but Mike hadn't seen him open his eyes. Mike feared he had hit him too hard and caused some kind of brain injury. He couldn't care less if the man died, but first he had to talk. He opened the door and dragged the man out of the vehicle by his belt. Just as he was about to pull the man out, the Russian kicked him just above the knee and Mike was pushed back against the half-closed SUV door. The door banged against the side of the Ferrari, leaving a deep dent. The kick didn't have much force behind it and Mike blocked the second one by grabbing the Russian's ankle. He twisted it until he heard the Russian yell in pain. Mike held the position for a moment then decided to continue with the rotation. He felt the creak of the cartilage, pushed to breaking point.

The Russian screamed for him to stop but Mike pushed through until the ankle popped. The man felt silent. *Oh shit!* Mike dragged him out of the SUV and checked for a pulse. The Russian still had one. He had simply passed out from the pain. Mike closed the door of the SUV, picked up the Russian and placed him over his shoulders. He couldn't help but wonder how much it would cost to fix the Ferrari.

There were six elevators in the foyer but only one with an electronic keypad. Mike entered the eight-digit number Mapother had given him. The low hum of the elevator mechanism told him the code had worked. The doors slid open and Mike entered the tight space. With the Russian on his shoulders, the space felt cramped, and he thought about the time he and Lisa got stuck in a similar-sized elevator during a leisure trip in Rome. It had taken over two hours for the fire brigade to pull them out. The Russian had peed in his pants—he could tell by the warm, smelly liquid sponging his coat and wetting his skin—but Mike managed a smile at the thought of what he and Lisa had used the time for while stuck in the elevator. Next time he spoke to Mapother or Sanchez, he'd ask for a more specific update on his wife's whereabouts.

The doors opened to a luxurious foyer. A marble-tiled hallway led to a spacious living room with a killer view of the Kremlin. Mike reckoned he was probably one of the most wanted men in Russia, and the fact that he was so close to the Kremlin sent a chill down his spine. He dropped the Russian on the swanky carpet and went to the kitchen to look for something to secure his prisoner. He found a roll of electrical tape and went back to the living room, only to find the Russian crawling toward the entrance.

"Where are you going?"

Seeing Mike, the man panicked and tried to stand up, but his bad legs wouldn't cooperate. Blood gushed out of his wounds at a faster pace. He placed his back against the wall and dug for something inside his jean's pocket. A switchblade.

Mike wasn't impressed but was a bit disappointed with his own performance. In his rush to get out of the Solntsevo District, he hadn't searched the Russian. He should have known better. That was the first thing you learned as a police officer: you always search a suspect right after his arrest.

"That's really what you want to do?" he asked the Russian.

Determination had replaced the earlier fear Mike had seen in the man's eyes. *Does he really think he can take me on?* Then he understood what was happening and his hand moved to the small of his back. The last thing he wanted was to use his pistol. It wasn't suppressed, and the sound would bring in a lot of unwanted attention. Still, he had no option as the Russian tried to stab himself in the throat. Mike fired, hitting the man in the bicep. The round went through, missing the bones. The man dropped the knife and swore loudly in Russian. Mike holstered his pistol and picked up the knife. He looked at his watch. Being so close to the Kremlin, if anyone had heard the shot, police would be there in a heartbeat.

"You're fucked," the Russian said through his broken teeth.

Mike kicked him in the face, breaking the man's jaw, and watched the Russian slide off the wall and onto his back. Mike sat on top of the man, using his legs to keep the Russian's arms pinned down.

Mike plunged the knife into the man's side while placing his free hand on his mouth. Not a fatal wound, but a damned painful one if he was to trust the distorted face the Russian made as the blade cut through his skin. The man tried to bit his hand but Mike removed it in time and buried his thumb deep into the Russian's left eye as retribution.

"You're dying," Mike said. "I win, you lose."

"Fuck you—"

Mike grabbed the man's hair and bashed his head twice on the tile floor. "Where's the Sheik?"

The Russian tried to spit in his face but Mike bitch-slapped him before he could do so. He did it again before repeating his last question. "Where's the Sheik?"

"Why would I tell you?"

Mike slowly pulled the blade out of the man's side. The Russian screamed and this time Mike let him. "Where's the Sheik?" he asked again, twisting the knife.

"The Kremlin," the Russian said. "He's inside the Kremlin. He works with Simonich."

"The Russian president?"

The man nodded. His eyes were rolling back. Mike let go of the knife and slapped the man again. "I want you to say it. Is the Sheik working with Vienamin Simonich?"

"Yes," the Russian said weakly. "The Sheik is working for Vienamin Simonich."

"Why?"

The Russian smiled. "You don't know?"

Mike twisted the knife. The man screamed.

"Why are they working together?"

The man shook his head. "Kill me now. I'll never tell you."

It was Mike's turn to smile. "You'll die, trust me. There's no way out for you, I'm afraid. The only question you should ask yourself is how painful you want it to be."

Mike moved his hand toward the knife and felt the man jerk under him as he anticipated the pain. "Stop, stop," the Russian pleaded.

"Tell me why the Sheik is working with Simonich," Mike asked.

"It's . . . It's because of the new . . . virus. The Sheik has a plan to bring it to the United States."

"What kind of virus is it?"

Fear returned to the man's eyes. He truly didn't know the answer. "I . . . I . . ."

"I believe you," Mike said. "When and how is the Sheik supposed to bring the virus to America?"

"I have no idea. The Sheik doesn't share this kind of information with us."

Mike inched the knife deeper. The Russian yelled. "How and when," Mike hissed.

The man started to shake uncontrollably. He was dying. Blood was coming out of his ears now. Mike had probably caused some kind of internal bleeding while bashing the man's head on the floor. "You'll . . . never . . . see it coming," the Russian said as his eyes rolled back for the last time.

Mike wouldn't get anything else out of the Russian. In one fluid movement, he removed the knife from the man's side and thrust it hard into his neck, severing the jugular.

He wished he could have videotaped the interview but an audio recording would have to do. The IMSI wanted something they could take to DNI Phillips, not evidence that needed to stand up in court.

"Support Two from Mike."

"We're here, Mike," responded Support Two team leader James Cooper. "We got all of it."

"Any chatter regarding shots fired at this address?" asked Mike. Support Two was always listening to the police and security agencies' frequencies.

"Nothing yet. There's no other apartment on your floor. Maybe you got lucky."

"What about the camera feeds? I've seen at least two in the underground garage and another one in the—"

"We've got them all, Mike," Cooper replied before adding, "While you were busy, Mapother called to let us know where you could find the keys to his brother's cars."

. . . .

Mike took a couple of minutes to change from his blood-soaked clothes into some he found in the master bedroom. Mapother's brother had expensive tastes. Luckily for Mike, Frank Mapother's Italian shirts were the right size and he picked a white one to go with the black leather jacket. The designer jeans were a bit too large but the Ferragamo belt ensured they wouldn't go down. The car keys were right where Mapother had said they would be. The Ferrari was too flamboyant so he picked the Jaguar F-Type.

"Still nothing regarding a shootout at this location?" Mike asked Support Two.

"There's a shootout but it's at the other end of the city. We've also taken care of the video feed."

"What about the penthouse?" Mike wondered how they'd get the body out. He had also left his old clothes in a garbage bag next to the body.

"We're not sure about that yet," James Cooper replied. "We'll figure it out."

Mike certainly didn't want to get Charles Mapother's brother Frank in trouble but they'd had no choice. He wished they hadn't had to use his penthouse but it seemed like a good idea at the time.

He unlocked the F-Type and the door handles popped out of the door panel. The inside was just like the cockpit of a fighter jet. The start engine began to flash in a heartbeat-like pulse pattern. Mike pressed the brake pedal while he pushed the start-engine button. The F-Type's five-hundred-fifty-horsepower V8 roared to life. Mike's pulse quickened. *Holy shit! Maybe the Ferrari would have been subtler after all.*

The garage door opened automatically when the F-Type's front bumper broke the infrared beam. Mike accelerated north on Tverskaya Street and laughed out loud at the crackling sound of the F-Type sport exhaust.

"Mike, Support Two," came in James Cooper.

"Go ahead for Mike."

"I'll patch you through to the director."

Mike heard a click and then Mapother said, "We've just finished listening to your . . . hum . . . conversation with the Sheik's man."

"I wish I had more, Charles," Mike said, "but he didn't cooperate much."

"Still, it's enough for me to take to Phillips."

"Good," Mike replied. "What about Lisa? Where is she?"

When Mapother didn't answer right away, Mike knew something was terribly wrong. Mapother always knew where his assets were.

"Charles," he said, his heart sinking fast. "Is she all right?"

"We lost contact with her earlier today—"

"What the fuck are you talking about? What do you mean you lost contact?"

"Calm down, Mike," Mapother said. "We'll find her."

Mike parallel parked the Jaguar on a side street. He didn't trust himself to drive. Enraged at Mapother, he slammed his fist on the steering wheel. "Fuck," he yelled at no one.

"Something happened in Koltsovo," Mapother continued. "We don't know what exactly, but Lisa was injured."

Mike shook his head, not believing what was happening. *Not again.* He started hyperventilating and he felt a huge pressure on his chest. Another panic attack was coming and he was powerless to do anything to prevent it. He looked at his hands; they were trembling like never before. He needed some air. His hand was on the door handle when Mapother said, "What's going on, Mike?"

He couldn't find the right words. Nothing came out of his mouth. He felt as if his soul was slowly disconnecting from his body. He imagined Lisa tied to a chair with the Sheik pouring gasoline over her naked body. Mike yelled as his mind showed him the Sheik about to drop a match on his wife. He tried to stop it but couldn't move. His feet were encased in a solid, unbreakable lump of cement. Mike could see in slow motion the match leave the Sheik's hand and fall on Lisa's lap. She screamed at the top of her lungs as fire engulfed her body.

It took a moment for Mike to realize it wasn't really happening and that Mapother was talking to him.

"Talk to us, Mike. We're here. Just talk to us and let us know what's going on."

Mike was drenched with sweat. He took in his surroundings. He was in Moscow. "I'm . . . I'm fine," he finally said. "I think I had a panic attack."

He cracked the window open and cold air immediately rushed into the small passenger compartment of the F-Type. He forced himself to take five deep breaths. Feeling better, Mike said, "I'm fine."

"Okay, Mike. We'll talk about this later," Mapother said. Mike could tell he was concerned. Truth was, he was worried too. His panic attacks were getting out of control and were starting to impede his work. "What we need to do now is to bring you back stateside."

"I'm not leaving without her, Charles," Mike said. "You'd better understand this."

He heard Mapother sigh. "We don't know where she is, Mike."

"Then find her, for Christ's sake!"

"Listen to me, Mike," Mapother said. "This isn't a suggestion. It's a goddam order. If you want us to find Lisa, you'd better do as you're told, because right now I'm wasting time with you instead of focusing on finding your wife."

Mapother's words rang true. Plus, his cover as Luc Walker was blown and he was driving a car belonging to the man who owned the penthouse where he had left a dead body. It was only a matter of time before he got caught. "If I do this," Mike said, "you'll let me help with Lisa's search?"

"Yes."

Mapother wouldn't lie to his face, but would he on the phone? It didn't matter; the IMSI director had a point. His being in Russia was a distraction. "What's the plan?"

"The IMSI's jet is presently on its way to Kiev where it will refuel. Your job is to get to the Yuzhny Airport," Mapother said. "It's about four miles southwest of Oryol. It should take you between four and five hours to get there."

"Who's flying?"

"William Talbot and Martin St-Onge."

Good. Talbot and St-Onge had been of tremendous help not only in saving Lisa's life in France, but also in Croatia.

"They'll be in Oryol just long enough to pick up Vincent Marquis, a rich French oil executive."

Mike didn't like leaving anyone behind. Especially his wife. But for now, he'd go with Mapother's plan. If his wife was still alive, the IMSI analysts would find her. And Mike would go get her.

CHAPTER 50

Haifa, Israel

Zima Bernbaum couldn't help but admire the beautiful sunrise over the city of Haifa. She'd had the chance to visit Israel, the country where she was born, many times over the years. Surprisingly, she'd never set foot in Haifa, the third largest city in Israel. Built on the slopes of Mount Carmel, Haifa was one of the Middle East's more picturesque cities.

She felt the helicopter veer left and start its descent toward the Haifa naval base. "What now?" she asked the soldier next to her.

"Someone will be waiting for you," he replied, his eyes still closed.

The helicopter landed without incident and she unclipped her seatbelt. She looked at the soldier who had risked his life for hers and she thanked him one last time. "Here they are," he said.

Zima turned around and saw two more soldiers dressed identically trotting toward the chopper. "Where are you going?"

"Eitan's alive. We have a fix on his position. We're going to get him back," the soldier said, while the two other soldiers strapped themselves in their seats. Zima was relieved but the sensation only lasted a second. Three more operators were going to risk everything to get one of their own back. She wished the men good luck and the helicopter took off as soon as she had cleared the rotor, its blades kicking up clouds of dust. She watched the helicopter disappear over the horizon. To her right, a black minivan flashed its lights. She walked to the waiting vehicle. The driver's side window slid down and a man told her to climb in. The interior of the minivan smelled like the inside of a cigar lounge. An odor Zima had always liked, until now. It just didn't fit with her mood. The driver—sixties, full face, friendly green eyes, brown tie loosened at the neck—extended his hand.

"I'm Meir Yatom," the man said. "I'm a friend of Charles Mapother."

Zima shook his hand with her left. "Thank you."

"I owed Charles a favor. You're my payment."

"I see," Zima replied.

"You were supposed to be driven to Tel Aviv and placed on the next flight to New York, but something came up," Yatom said.

"I need medical care for my hand," she said, showing him the dirty dressing covering her right hand."

"You'll get it where we're going. The best."

"Are you with the Israeli military?" Zima asked.

"You don't believe that," Yatom replied. "Do we really need to go through this?"

"I guess we don't."

"I believe a relationship shouldn't start with two friends telling lies to each other," the Israeli said. "I don't want to put you in a situation where you'll have to lie to me, so please do the same for me. Can you do that for me?"

Zima didn't know how much the Israeli knew about the IMSI. She wasn't ready to volunteer any information without Mapother's approval, so it was best to do as Yatom had suggested.

"Of course. I'm sorry," she said.

"As long as we understand each other."

"You said that something came up, Mr. Yatom—"

"Please call me Meir," Yatom replied with a smile. "A beautiful lady like you shouldn't have to call anyone by their last name. You get a free pass."

"Does that mean I won't be flying back to the States, Meir?" she continued.

"In the end, the decision will be yours. Shall we?" Yatom said as he accelerated away from the helipad.

"Does Charles know this?"

"Of course. Water?" Yatom asked, offering her a bottle.

She thanked him and twisted the cap off the bottle before taking a long pull.

. . . .

Zima woke up with a jolt. Yatom was gently squeezing her shoulder. "We've arrived," he said.

She hadn't realized she was so tired. She had so many questions she wanted to ask. How could she have fallen asleep? She looked at the empty bottle of water at her feet.

"You drugged me," she said. "Why?"

"So I wouldn't have to lie to you, my friend," Yatom said. "Now come."

Zima took in her surroundings. They were in an underground parking garage. For how long had she slept? She had no idea if she was still in Haifa or if they had reached Tel Aviv. There weren't many cars parked yet, and Zima suspected it was still early in the morning. Yatom hadn't wanted her to see where they were or how they got there. That probably meant that she was either at the Mossad headquarters or a Mossad office somewhere in Israel. But she was definitely in a Mossad compound.

She followed Yatom along a hallway located on the same level as the parking garage. Yatom knocked on the first door to his left. A nurse—or maybe she was a doctor—opened the door.

"Please have a seat, Zima," she said, inviting her in. "I'll take care of your hand."

. . . .

The nurse worked well and fast. During the forty-five minutes she had spent with her, Zima must have thanked her ten times. It was weird to have a hand with only four fingers. It didn't feel right. But, then again, many soldiers had lost much more and they were now thriving in civilian life. She'd be okay. She was thankful for Yatom's help. Without him, she would have lost more than a finger.

Yatom picked her up from the infirmary not long after the nurse had applied a new dressing. She thanked the nurse one more time before following Yatom out of the room. They walked along an underground hallway before stopping in front of another door with no marking. Seconds later, the door opened and Yatom signaled Zima to walk in front of him. The room smelled the same as the minivan's interior. Six people worked in front of terminals and none of them turned to welcome her.

"Do you speak Hebrew?" Yatom asked in his native tongue.

"I do," Zima replied in the same language. Her parents had taught her from an early age and she'd had the chance to keep it current while working for the Canadian Security Intelligence Service.

Yatom asked one of the employees to explain to Zima what had transpired. A light-skinned black woman in her early twenties, with short black hair, stood up and walked to another computer. "Hey, I'm Chaya," she said to Zima as she sat down.

"Zima," she replied, observing the young lady as she typed her username and password on her keyboard.

The flat screen came to life and a video of the whole Damascus shootout began to play. Zima clenched her fists as she watched the firefight between the Canadians, the Syrians and an unknown enemy. *Oh my God! The Syrian driver was a turncoat. He started the whole thing.*

"How did you get this?" she asked. The computer monitor was now zooming in on her as she tried to speak to the downed soldier.

"We got this via—" started Chaya.

"It doesn't matter," Yatom cut in. "What matters is that we got it."

"Can I get a copy?"

"You'll get your copy once we're done with it, and our technicians can guarantee you won't be able to identify our source," Yatom said.

"Fair enough." Mapother would love to see this and so would her ex-employer. The folks at the Canadian Security Intelligence Service would pay a lot of money to get their hands on this video.

"There's more," Yatom said. "It has come to our attention that a small Antonov plane carrying former Canadian ambassador Ray Powell took off from the Al-Mazzeh military airport shortly after the shootout."

Zima was completely taken aback by this sudden revelation. "You're sure the ambassador is still alive?"

"No. We can't confirm if he's dead or alive at this moment," Yatom said. "What we know, though, is that the Antonov made two refueling stops. The first was in Cyprus, and the second in Turkey. From there, they headed to Mykonos, Greece."

"Meir," Zima said, "how certain are you?"

"If I wasn't one hundred percent sure, I wouldn't tell you."

Unbelievable. She had to contact Charles Mapother. Now.

CHAPTER 51

IMSI headquarters, New York

In order for Charles Mapother to get what he wanted from Director of National Intelligence Richard Phillips, he had to give him something. And he did. A favor. Still, the DNI wasn't happy.

"The deal when we started all of this was for you to take care of your own shit, Charles," Phillips said.

"We do, and we often take care of yours too," Mapother said, not liking the hostility he was getting from the DNI.

"This administration has granted you unlimited access to our intelligence-gathering apparatus," Phillips said. "What else do you want? And have no doubt, if this ever gets out, we're talking impeachment—"

"You've known this all along, Richard," Mapother said. "Why the cold feet now?"

"You're supposed to be able to operate on your own."

"How many times did I ask for your help?" Mapother replied.

DNI Richard Phillips didn't speak for a moment. When he did, his voice was calmer. "What can the United States government do to help?"

"One of my assets acquired intelligence that you'll find interesting," Mapother started.

"Is that so?"

Mapother ignored the DNI's sarcastic tone. "I even think you'll feel compelled to brief the president the moment you've read through it. My office is sending everything to our joint account as we speak."

"You have proof that the Russians are working with the Sheik?" The DNI clearly sounded surprised.

"Nothing you could bring in front of a judge, but more than enough to stop the Russians dead in their tracks for fear of heavy retaliations from the United States and its allies," Mapother explained.

"So it's true then," Phillips said. "They're ready to start a war."

"I don't think so, Richard," Mapother said. "They're using the Sheik's network to separate themselves from any pitfalls."

"And if their plan fails, they'll deny any involvement or only admit to some rogue elements within their government," finished DNI Phillips. "What do you need from me?"

"My asset left a mess behind him obtaining this information," Mapother said. "I'll need a cleaning crew at my brother's penthouse on Tverskaya Street in Moscow."

"Frank knows about this?" the DNI asked.

"Of course not," Mapother replied. "And I'd like to keep it that way."

"Done. Anything else?"

"Let me know what the president says."

Mapother hung up at the same time Jonathan Sanchez barged into his office holding his cell phone up in the air. "It's Zima. She has intel on Mike's father's whereabouts."

Mapother wondered where this intel had originated. The Israelis? They weren't known to share with others. *Unless they want something.* He placed the phone on his desk and turned on the speaker option so Sanchez could listen in on the conversation.

"Zima?" he asked.

"I'm with your friend Meir, Charles," Zima started. "He says he knows where Ray Powell is."

"Can I speak to him?"

A moment later, Meir Yatom was on the other end. "Who would have thought we'd speak again so soon?"

With the Russian situation not exactly under control, Mapother had no time for small talk so he cut to the chase. "You really know where Ray Powell is?"

"He's in Mykonos. And yes, I'm sure."

That was terrific news. "What are you planning to do with this?"

"It depends," Yatom replied.

Mapother was losing patience. The Israeli spy might have saved one of his assets but Yatom's games irritated Mapother no end. "What do you want, Meir?"

"I'm curious to know why you're so interested in Ray Powell?"

There was no chance in hell he'd admit to Yatom that Powell was the father of one of his assets, so he lied. "We're doing a favor for the Canadians."

He knew Yatom didn't believe him but he hoped the message was clear. He wasn't going to say why.

"I see," Yatom replied. His tone indicated he wasn't impressed with Mapother's answer. "Zima will be on the next flight to New York. Goodbye, Charles."

The line went dead.

"He hung up," Sanchez said.

Mapother looked at Sanchez. "You're very good at stating the obvious, Jonathan. Bravo."

. . . .

"What the hell?" Zima asked. She couldn't understand why Yatom had just hung up on Mapother. They needed to work together.

"If your boss doesn't want to share the reasons why he's so interested in Powell, I'm done with this case."

"But—"

Yatom raised his hands, signaling her to stop talking. "Don't lie to me, Zima," he said. "We've been honest to each other so far. Don't ruin it by feeding me some bullshit about doing this for the Canadians."

"I'm a former Canadian Security Intelligence Service officer, Meir," she said. "Did you know that?"

The Israeli spy smiled. "Of course. I also know you left the CSIS months ago to work for Mapother. Why?"

For the second time that day, Zima's thoughts took her back to Edmonton. She remembered Shane, the fearless Royal Canadian Mounted Police swat member who had jumped on her just before the bomb meant for her exploded. His body had absorbed most of the blast and a piece of metal had ripped through his body armor and embedded itself in his back. Without him, she'd be dead. That's why she had joined Charles Mapother and the rest of the IMSI. She wanted payback, just as Mike and Lisa did for the loss of their family.

"Revenge," she said, her voice only a whisper. "I want revenge for what happened in Edmonton."

216

Yatom nodded. Zima thought he was about to say something but Chaya called him to her workstation.

"Sir, the team is in position."

"Put it on the screen."

A large flat-screen television was turned on and Zima recognized the voice of the soldier who had sat next to her in the helicopter. "Do we have authority to execute, sir?"

"You have the authority, Ari." Yatom replied.

His name's Ari. The flat screen showed the feed coming from the cam attached to Ari's helmet. Zima was mesmerized by what she was seeing. Ari kicked open a wooden door and moved inside a house, his weapon swinging left and right as he passed through one room after the other. *He knows exactly where he's going. He isn't wasting time. How did they get such good intel on Eitan's whereabouts?* Suddenly a shadow appeared in front of him and Ari fired his silenced weapon. The man fell backwards. Ari continued to move forward but stopped short of the door which the man he had just killed had come through. He looked at his two colleagues. One was right behind him while the other had his back turned so he could protect their rear.

Even though Ari's weapon had a silencer, Zima was certain the opposition had heard the shot. Not believing for one instant that there was only one hostile inside the house, Zima was sure the three-man Israeli commando team would face fierce resistance. Whoever was inside the room had now had the time to barricade themselves.

"They're waiting for them," Zima said to Yatom. "You have to stop them, Meir, they stand no chance."

"One of their team members is inside this room," Yatom replied, his eyes glued to the flat screen. "Ari will get Eitan out or die trying. That's how we do things in this unit."

Zima couldn't swallow. Her mouth was dry. She wanted to hide. She didn't want to see what was going to happen but she couldn't take her eyes off the screen either.

A moment later—less than twelve seconds after they'd breached the front door—Ari threw something inside the room. A deafening sound came from the speakers as the stun grenade exploded. Ari entered the room—Zima could swear she had just seen Eitan tied to a chair in the middle of the room—and turned right, firing two shots into the forehead of a man wearing a white robe. His AK-47 clattered on the floor next to him. Sounds of gunfire echoed in the small room where Zima was standing. The hostiles were returning fire. Ari's helmet cam showed him pivoting left and firing one more round into the torso of a man holding a pair of pliers.

"Clear," Ari said.

"Clear," replied another operator Zima couldn't see.

"Zachary?" Ari asked. Zima sensed tension in the team leader's voice. She understood why a second later, when the video feed showed one of the Israelis clutching his leg. Ari ordered his colleague to take care of their injured teammate and turned to face Eitan.

Zima had been right; Eitan was tied to a chair bolted to the floor. She couldn't tell if he was injured.

"You have hostiles coming up the alley. They'll be on you in less than two minutes," Chaya said. One of her screens showed the live feed of a reconnaissance drone Ari's team had deployed prior to their assault.

"Copy that," Ari replied while he cut Eitan loose. "Can you fight?"

Zima watched as Eitan stood up and massaged his wrists before picking up an AK-47 from one of the dead hostiles.

Zima smiled when Eitan inquired about her. "How's our lady friend?"

"She's listening in," Ari replied.

Zima's eyes watered when she saw Eitan wave at her through Ari's helmet cam.

"See you soon."

"All right, enough of this, Romeo. Help Zack while I cover your ass back to the chopper. Let's go!"

For the next ten minutes, Zima was able to appreciate the professionalism of the Israeli team. With the help of Chaya, the assault team was able to leave the house in which Eitan had been held hostage without engaging the dozen enemy combatants approaching their position. Just as they were about to board the helicopter that would bring them home, Zima heard a distant explosion.

"What was that?" she asked Yatom.

"A little gift Ari left behind for anyone trying to pursue his team."

Ari must have turned off his camera because the feed disappeared from the flat screen on the wall. "I'm glad Eitan's okay," Zima said, relieved. She didn't think her heart could take another blow like the one it got in Edmonton.

"Are you ready?" Yatom asked, heading toward the door. "One of our drivers will take you to Ben Gurion."

Zima took a deep breath. These guys were the real deal. She didn't care what Mapother would say, even if the price was to lose her position with the IMSI. She owed that much to Mike and Lisa.

"Ray Powell is the father of someone working for Charles Mapother," she said.

Meir Yatom smiled at her. "So he's family?"

"Yes, he is."

"Why didn't you say so before?" Yatom said. "Call back Mapother. I'll talk with him."

CHAPTER 52

Moscow, Russia

Sheik Qasim Al-Assad couldn't remember the last time he'd been put in such position. He felt as though the game of chess he had been playing for the last year was coming to an end. And the fact that there was a chance he wouldn't be on the winning side disturbed him. Charles Mapother's organization had blown a major hole in his terror network. The loss of his right-hand man Omar Al-Nashwan had started it all. He was beginning to think that killing his long-time associate—and Omar's father—Steve Shamrock might not have been his best move. The plan had been to distance himself from any fallout in the United States. He didn't think whoever was behind the raid on his yacht had the resources to go after the upper echelon of his network. But they had. And they did. Worse, he had barely escaped one of Mapother's killer teams in Croatia. Was Dr. Lisa Harrison Powell part of that killer team?

As he walked toward the Russian president's office, he wondered if Vienamin Simonich would have offered him refuge if he had known the real state of his network. *Probably not.* But it didn't matter anymore. He was in and he intended on carrying his revenge all the way to New York. He had a plan he hoped the Russian president would love. Because if he didn't, the Sheik wasn't sure he would get out of the Kremlin alive.

. . . .

The Sheik didn't have to wait long. That was a good sign. Or so he thought. Simonich's assistant motioned him to enter the presidential office. Standing next to Simonich were two members of

220

his protection detail. *That* wasn't good. With the exception of their first gathering, the Russian president had never had security by his side while meeting with him. The Sheik pondered why Simonich felt compelled to have his bodyguards with him. Was it because he feared the Sheik's reaction to what he was about to say? He'd know soon enough.

"Please have a seat, Sheik Al-Assad," Simonich said, pointing to one of the armchairs in front of his desk. "Would you like anything to drink? A peach juice, maybe?"

Even though he enjoyed a drink once in a while, the Sheik liked to let people believe he was following the Quran. "Thank you, Mr. President," the Sheik replied. "That would be great."

"If you don't mind, I'll have a drink myself," Simonich said. Not waiting for the Sheik's drink to arrive, he poured himself a healthy—or unhealthy, depending on one's view—measure of vodka. He emptied his glass in three gulps before looking at the Sheik. "You sure you don't want a taste?"

The Sheik shook his head. He needed to keep his head clear.

Vienamin Simonich sneered. "I'll have one more, then."

You can have the whole bottle for all I care. By the time Simonich's assistant arrived with his peach juice, the Russian president was done with his second drink and was pouring iced water into the same glass. He raised his glass to the Sheik. "To your health, Sheik Al-Assad."

"And to yours," he replied.

The president grinned. "Mine isn't in danger."

He had expected Simonich to say something like that but he was disappointed nonetheless. The president was having cold feet. He was folding his master plan too early.

"My friend—" he started but Simonich interrupted him.

"We're not friends, Qasim."

The Sheik felt his temper rising. Maybe the president was right to have his goons with him, because right now he wanted to tear the Russian's head apart.

"I've given you great latitude, Qasim," continued Simonich, "but the whole plan is now falling apart before it even began."

"Plans fall apart all the time, Mr. President," the Sheik said. "We can still succeed."

"Maybe. Maybe not," Simonich replied, rising from behind his desk. He looked at the Sheik with disdain. "I'm not sure you're the man for the job."

The Sheik could see the bodyguards getting edgy. Were they under orders to shoot him the moment the meeting was over? "If you'd only listen to me for a minute, Mr. President," he said, "I'll convince you otherwise."

"How dare you? How dare you kill someone belonging to me?" roared the Russian president, drumming his chest with his right hand. His face had turned red and the Sheik could see the veins in Simonich's neck pulsing, ready to burst. *So that is what this is all about.*

The Sheik had to admit he had lost it earlier in the control room. He wasn't in charge anymore. That much was clear. Killing the Russian analyst hadn't been his brightest idea. "I'll make amends," he said. "I shouldn't have done that."

Simonich's eyes scrutinized him, looking for any signs of deceit. The Sheik made sure there were none. He had no intention of dying in Russia.

"You're still committed?" Simonich asked.

The Sheik nodded, thinking about his son Igor. "Of course," he said as he reached for his peach juice.

"Then you'll do something to prove it," Simonich said. The Sheik didn't like the smile that was creeping onto the president's lips. "I want you to kill Lidiya Votyakov."

The Sheik nearly choked on his juice and coughed violently. Was this man crazy? Lidiya?

"Are you okay, Qasim?" Simonich asked, pushing a box of tissues in his direction. "Have I said something that offended you? I'm not asking you to do anything you haven't done before."

The Sheik looked at Simonich. "Why?"

"It's either that or my friend Bogdan shoots you right here, right now," Simonich said. The bodyguard to his left had his pistol pointed at the Sheik's chest. "Your choice."

How could this be happening? A year ago he was one of the most feared men in the world. Truth was, he didn't have to look too far to find the reason behind his fall from grace. *Charles Mapother and Mike Walton, Ray Powell's son.* If he had to kill the mother of his children to have a chance to lay his hands on Ray Powell, he'd do it. Without any hesitation. His heart started to beat faster at the thought of what he'd have Ray Powell undergo before his demise. Using the former ambassador and his daughter-in-law to carry the virus to the United States was a sure bet. He hoped the Russians were able to keep Dr. Powell alive. Using only the ambassador as a pathogen hauler could work too, but for personal reasons he'd love to see Dr. Powell endure the same fate.

Still, he didn't want to give in to Simonich's demand too easily. "Isn't she useful to your program?"

"Dr. Votyakov isn't the only one who contributed to this project," Simonich said, signaling his bodyguard to put his gun away. "Drs. Votyakov and Galkin took meticulous notes and I've received confirmation that we have everything we need to mass produce the virus."

"So why are you putting a stop to the project? We should be pushing forward."

Simonich waved his finger at him, as if he was reprimanding a child. The Sheik did his best to ignore the insult but wasn't sure for how long he could restrain himself from jumping over Simonich's desk to pierce his eyes with one of the pencils.

"Thanks to you, Qasim, we've lost the element of deniability. I can't guarantee the future of my country if our enemies are aware of our plan to infect their population with a new Marburg virus. They'll retaliate with their nuclear arsenal and they'll even have the support of the international community."

The Sheik couldn't fault that reasoning.

"So you don't need Lidiya anymore. You want her dead in case the international community decides to look deeper. You'll be able to tell them you took care of an internal problem. A simple rogue element within the Russian scientific community."

"We're dealing with this situation the same way we're dealing with the problem regarding our Anti-Doping Agency and the Athletics Federation," Simonich said, "but in a more permanent manner."

The Sheik knew what the president was talking about. It was in every newspaper worldwide. The article outlined endemic doping in Russian athletics, a stunning state cover-up and widespread inaction from the International Association of Athletics Federations. Heads would roll. But not in the same fashion.

"Give me a chance to make it right," the Sheik said. "It won't be spectacular, but I believe I can not only eliminate the people responsible for the debacle we find ourselves in, but I have a shot at killing the president of the United States."

Vienamin Simonich's reaction wasn't what the Sheik expected. The Russian president threw his glass of water across the room. Bogdan had his gun out again.

"Are you stupid? Are you really that dumb? Didn't you listen to anything I've just said?" the Russian president spat. Simonich seized the pistol from his bodyguard's hands and pointed it at the Sheik's head. The other bodyguard also had his gun out. Simonich walked around his desk and placed the barrel of his pistol against the Sheik's forehead.

"I should kill you—" he started, but the Sheik didn't let him finish. He'd had enough. He was the bully. Not the other way around. He sprang out of the armchair and grabbed the barrel of the pistol with his left hand, while hitting the inside of Simonich's wrist with his right fist. The effect was immediate. The pistol came loose and the Sheik twisted the barrel counter-clockwise and out of Simonich's hand. Terror filled the president's eyes as he realized his mistake. The bodyguard who still had his pistol brought his weapon up, but the Sheik was faster and double-tapped him in the chest. The man crumpled to the floor as the bullets slammed into his bulletproof vest.

"I shot him in the vest," hissed the Sheik. Bogdan had moved between him and the president. The Sheik removed the magazine and opened the slide of the pistol before tossing both on the floor. "I mean you no harm, Mr. President."

A second later, members of the Presidential Security Detail rushed into the room with their pistols drawn. They started yelling at the Sheik to get on his knees. The Sheik didn't move. His eyes were locked with Simonich's, who had pushed Bogdan aside.

Without breaking eye contact, Simonich ordered his men to leave his office. He asked Bogdan to help his colleague to his feet and to leave him alone with the Sheik. Bogdan protested but was cut short by Simonich.

Once they were alone, Simonich grabbed the vodka bottle and looked for his glass. It was at the other end of the room, broken in pieces. He smiled at the Sheik and took a long pull from the bottle. He offered it to the Sheik. *Why not?* A drink was definitely in order. The vodka burned his throat but he forced himself not to grimace. He handed the bottle back to Simonich.

"What is it that you want to tell me?" he asked, putting the vodka bottle back in his drawer.

"My son has Ray Powell secured in one of my safe houses."

"I know," Simonich replied. That surprised the Sheik, but only for an instant. He did not doubt his son's loyalty to him, but it was easy to understand that someone in Igor's unit might be reporting back directly to the Russian president or one of his close associates.

"Let me head back to Koltsovo, Mr. President," the Sheik said. "I'll take two samples of the new Marburg virus thread and bring them with me to Mykonos."

"Why would I allow you to do such a thing?"

"Didn't I just prove to you my loyalty, Mr. President?" the Sheik asked. "Here's what I want to do . . ."

For the next five minutes, the Sheik laid out his plan to the Russian president. Simonich's body language changed gradually and the Sheik felt he had regained some sort of control. This assumption was short-lived.

"Okay, go ahead with your plan, Qasim. You have my blessing," Simonich said. "But before you go, stop by to say goodbye to Dr. Votyakov, will you?"

CHAPTER 53

Ararat Park Hyatt Hotel, Moscow

D r. Lidiya Votyakov eased herself into the warm water of the hot tub. She instantly relaxed as the tension drained from her muscles. It had been two long days and she was exhausted. She wondered what had happened to Victor. She hoped he was okay. He had grown on her, even though he didn't say much.

For the last several hours, she couldn't escape the visions of her dead son. Qasim's promise to kill the people responsible for his death didn't bring her much comfort. As tears threatened again, she closed her eyes against them. She squeezed tightly, trying to hold them in. She had no time for self-pity. There was much work left to be done. She was scheduled to fly back to Koltsovo in the morning. Two more minutes and she'd go back to her room. President Simonich had kindly booked a suite at one of Moscow's most expensive and luxurious hotels. The Ararat Park Hyatt was located near the Bolshoi Theatre and the Kremlin, making it a prized place to stay among rich Russians and business travelers. The hotel was home to the Quantum Spa and Health Club, one of the best spas in Moscow.

Dr. Votyakov opened her eyes and was surprised to see that her bodyguard was nowhere in sight. Thinking he was probably in the bathroom, she decided to wait for him before exiting the hot tub. Her towel was twenty feet away and she hated being cold.

She closed her eyes again and forced herself to relax. Everything was going to be fine. She had some of the best scientists working for her, and Qasim would take care of the tactical side of the operation.

She felt the water move and opened her eyes. Qasim was standing on the first step of the hot tub holding a bottle of bubbly with two glasses, only wearing his bathing suit. She noticed the strength still emanating from him. A tad thicker around the waist, but he was still an attractive man. She had lost touch with him during recent years and wondered if everything they said about him was true. She had known him as an intelligent and charming man. She knew what had pushed him over the edge but it was hard to believe he had killed so many people. He'd always been most kind to her. And right now, she needed someone to help her cope with her reality.

She caught his eyes on her and she became self-conscious. Not that she wasn't pretty, but she hadn't kept in shape as he had. "Are you joining me?" she asked.

Qasim lowered himself into the water and sat next to her. "Champagne?" he asked.

She nodded. Maybe a drink or two would help put her mind at ease.

. . . .

The Sheik poured two glasses of Champagne. "To Zakhar," he said.

She touched his glass with hers. "To our son."

They drank in silence. "Have you seen my bodyguard?" Votyakov asked.

"I asked him to wait in the car. I told you you were planning to eat in the room tonight," he said with a smile.

She looked at him and her eyes sparkled. *She still loves me. And I have no idea why.*

"I'm flying back to Koltsovo tomorrow," she told him.

"Then we have the night," he said, his hand caressing the inside of her thigh. To his eyes, she was still beautiful and had kept the brilliant mind that his heart had fallen for so many years ago.

She moaned when his hand slid under her bathing suit, but she placed her hand on his, stopping him from going further. "Not here, Qasim," she whispered in her ears, her lips tickling his neck. "Why don't we go up? I have a suite."

Her vulnerability was intoxicating. He breathed in her scent. A tantalizing fusion of subtle, flowery soap and sweat—mixed with cigarettes and alcohol—reminded the Sheik of their first kiss. "There's nothing I'd like more," he replied, his tongue licking the back of her ear.

. . . .

Dr. Lidiya Votyakov inserted her keycard inside the lock mechanism. The green light blinked twice and she turned the door handle. She could feel Qasim behind her, his breathing becoming deeper. Her pulse was racing when she entered the foyer of her suite. She slipped the keycard into her bathrobe and continued walking toward the bedroom. She hadn't had sex for over a year, but she couldn't allow herself to get sucked into feeling secure and safe with Qasim. He wasn't that kind of man. Yet, tonight, he was exactly what she needed. Reaching the bedroom, she wondered if she should turn on the lights. Was she comfortable enough with her own body? It had been so long. She knew he wanted her. The bulge in his swimming trunks was proof of that. He had tried to hide it with a towel during their ride in the elevator but she'd seen it. And it turned her on. She undid her bathrobe, letting it fall off her shoulders to the marble floor beneath her.

. . . .

Sheik Qasim Al-Assad couldn't remember the last time he had felt so at a loss. If he was to trust the newspapers, he had done some pretty horrific things in the past but he felt no remorse. None whatsoever. He had been at war. He still was. And that's how he should look at the current situation too. *Am I getting soft?* While they were riding up the elevator, he actually thought about having sex with Lidiya before killing her. And that excited him. He had let her see his erection just to discourage any doubts about his real intentions. But once they had reached her floor, he decided not to disrespect her. He'd kill her quickly.

He followed Lidiya into her room. When her robe fell, she turned toward him, completely naked. The fact that she hadn't turned on the lights made it easier for him. He gently placed his left hand behind her neck and pulled her close to him. Their lips touched and he took a second to savor the moment. His right hand shook a little when he plunged the long, slender blade of the stiletto into her heart, piercing it. Her body tensed. She gasped. Then nothing. Her eyes became lifeless and her body went limp.

The Sheik laid her down on the bed. He turned on the lights and watched his reflection in the mirror. *I'm a sociopath.* He had just killed the only women he had ever loved, and he'd enjoyed it. The tremor in his hand while he had pushed the stiletto into her heart had come from the excitement of the kill, nothing else.

He used the room's phone to call the number Simonich had given him.

"It's done. Her room," he said, before hanging up.

CHAPTER 54

Oryol, Russia

Mike Walton knew he'd have to sleep soon. At least for a few hours. Go-pills were good but only to a certain extent. He had seen a lot of his fellow infantrymen get hurt because they had relied too much on those pills. Problems occurred when the brain told the rest of the body it wasn't tired when in fact it was.

It had taken him just under five hours to reach the airport. He located the private aviation terminal quickly and parked the F-Type a few spots away from the main entrance. Traveling via corporate jet had huge advantages. No questions were asked if you didn't have any luggage and you weren't being subject to search. Of course, the pilots would need to clear customs before Mike could board the plane but they wouldn't have brought anything remotely suspicious in any case.

The door of the small terminal slid open and he walked in. The private aviation terminal looked no different than what Mike was accustomed to. The lounge combined style with practical functionality, making the transition between aircraft and ground transportation much easier than in bigger and busier terminals.

"Mr. Marquis?" said the blond receptionist stationed behind the solid wood counter that served as her desk.

"C'est moi," Mike replied. "On vous a communiqué les informations concernant mon vol?" Born and raised in Canada, he spoke fluent French. Of course, he had a terrible accent but he doubted the pretty Russian in front of him would notice. From the look on her face, she probably didn't speak a word of French.

"Um . . . I'm sorry, Mr. Marquis—"

"No problem, we'll speak in English, yes?"

She nodded eagerly. "Yes, thank you," she said. "Your plane has landed thirty minutes ago."

"Perfect," Mike replied. He couldn't wait to get out of Russia. They needed to regroup and formulate a plan to find Lisa. They'd need to find a solution soon because if the United States government confronted the Russians with the intelligence he'd gotten from Dr. Galkin and the prisoner he had interrogated in Mapother's brother's apartment, there was a good chance the Russian borders would become much harder to cross. "Can I board?"

"Not yet I'm afraid, Mr. Marquis," the blonde said, her demeanor indicating she was genuinely sorry for the delay. "The customs officers are searching the aircraft."

Damn! He couldn't catch a break.

"Something wrong?"

The receptionist looked uncomfortable, shifting her weight from one foot to the other.

"What is it?"

She looked around, as if she wanted to make sure no one was eavesdropping. "I think they're looking for something very specific."

"I'm sure they're not," Mike replied, shaking his head vigorously. "There's probably a tax my pilots weren't aware of, that's all."

"Of course, that's what I meant," the receptionist said.

"Can I meet them on the tarmac?" he asked, dropping three twenty-euro bills on the counter.

The receptionist expertly pocketed the banknotes and smiled at him. "Of course, Mr. Marquis, I'm glad you understand."

Mike headed toward the exit leading directly to the tarmac. Just as the receptionist had said, a Federal Customs Service car was parked next to the IMSI's Gulfstream. There was someone in the backseat of the car. Mike approached the car and couldn't believe what he was seeing.

William Talbot, one of the two pilots, was in the backseat with his hands behind his back. *Why did they handcuff him?* Mike tried to open the door but it was locked. And where was Martin St-Onge, the other pilot? The stairs leading to the cabin of the Gulfstream were lowered. He signaled Talbot to sit tight. It didn't make any sense. Mike couldn't understand why the pilots hadn't paid off the

customs agents. He knew they kept large amounts of different cur-
rencies in a locked safe hidden in the cockpit.

Mike cautiously climbed the steps. He could hear Martin
St-Onge arguing with someone in English. He peeked inside the
cabin. Two uniformed Federal Customs Service agents were shout-
ing at the IMSI pilot.

"What's going on here?" Mike asked in French, entering the
cabin. Martin St-Onge, a former Canadian Royal Air Force pilot
spoke fluent French. He looked relieved to see Mike.

"We have no money left to pay them," St-Onge replied in the
same language. Mike was glad to see he had remained calm, even
though his partner had been arrested. "Talbot has been—"

Mike raised his hand. "I know."

"Who are you?" barked one of the officers, his hand moving
toward his pistol. Both officers were about six feet tall and looked
in good shape. They were probably former members of the Russian
military.

"I'm Vincent Marquis and this gentleman is one my pilots. Why
is the other gentleman under arrest?"

"He isn't under arrest. For now, he's only being detained," the
officer replied.

"Why?" Mike pushed on.

The two officers looked at him as if he was stupid. "I see," Mike
said when he got no reply. "I'm sure we can come to an arrange-
ment. Why don't you go back into the cockpit, Martin? I'll take care
of business with these two officers," Mike said in English, before
adding in French. "Start the engine and make sure we can leave as
soon as I tell you so."

St-Onge nodded and headed back to the cockpit.

"I'm so sorry about the misunderstanding." Mike started shaking his head as if he was disappointed in his employees' behavior.
"These guys are new and they don't understand the complexity of
the Russian tax system."

Mike thought he detected a change of attitude in the officers.
But it was short-lived. The next thing that came out of his mouth
seemed to agitate them even more. "Unfortunately, we don't have
the necessary funds to properly settle the departure tax," Mike said.

"Then we have a problem," the same officer said. "I'm afraid all of you will have to be detained." He moved his left hand behind his back to retrieve a pair of handcuffs.

Not good. "What about this?" Mike said, showing the keys to the F-Type.

"What is it?"

"My brand new Jaguar F-Type is parked right outside this terminal," Mike said, pointing at the private aviation terminal. "What if I leave it in your care?"

Mike's attempt at defusing the situation was an epic failure. Instead of soothing the officers, his offer enraged them. The two officers looked at each other and Mike knew trouble was coming. One of the Russians stepped back and unholstered his pistol while the other ordered him to turn around and place his hands behind his back.

Mike made sure to look terrified. He started shaking while obeying the officer's order. Now facing the cockpit, he saw Martin St-Onge move to cover behind the bulkhead separating the cockpit from the cabin. The moment he felt the handcuff clicked around his left wrist, Mike jerked his hand back and pivoted one hundred and eighty degrees. In one swift movement, he elbowed the arresting officer right under the chin while pulling him closer with his right arm. In the tight space of the aircraft, he knew the other officer couldn't fire at him without hitting his partner. The latter's knees buckled beneath him and he fell forward. Mike let himself fall to the ground with the officer as he reached for the other man's pistol, still in its holster. The other Russian agent tried to position himself so he could engage the man who had just put down his partner, but Martin St-Onge had the draw on him.

"Don't move," he yelled.

The expression on the Russian's face was one of pure confusion. His eyes moved from his downed colleague to the pilot pointing a pistol at him. Before the Russian could regain control, Mike pulled the pistol out and aimed it at him. "Drop your weapon," Mike said. "We can still work this out."

The agent on top of him stirred. He was going to regain his senses in a matter of seconds. They needed to end this before that happened. "Drop it," Mike said, this time louder. He placed the pistol's muzzle against the man's head. "Your choice."

Mike could see the man was thinking about his next move, wondering how to get out of this jam. He finally put his gun on the floor. "Good choice," Mike said. He crawled from under the Russian agent and got up.

"Plastic cuffs," he said to St-Onge.

"Got them," the pilot replied, placing them in Mike's outstretched hand.

Mike zip-tied the man's wrists and ankles while St-Onge held the attention of the other Russian officer.

"Your turn," Mike said.

The Russian didn't move. He was scared shitless. "Do as you're told and nothing will happen to you or your family," Mike said, his last words paying dividends.

Mike gave him the same treatment. The other officer was now fully awake. He cursed loudly in Russian. Mike helped him to his feet and forced him to sit in the armchair opposite the sofa where his colleague was now sitting. Once that was done, he frisked the officer and retrieved a handcuff key and the key for the car. "I'll be back," he said to St-Onge.

Mike hurried down the stairs and unlocked the car. William Talbot didn't seem surprised to see him. "Are the Russians dead?"

"Do I really have such a bad rep?" Mike replied, smiling.

"Nice to see you, brother," Talbot said as Mike helped him out of his handcuffs.

"Martin's keeping an eye on our two Russian friends," Mike said. "We need to get out of here ASAP."

"Roger that," Talbot said, climbing the stairs two by two. "I need two minutes. We've already filed the flight plan."

Mike turned his attention to St-Onge and the two Russian federal agents. "I got this," he said. "Go help William."

"Let us go," one of the Russians said. "You'll never get out of Russian airspace with us onboard."

"I doubt that," Mike replied. "I don't think anyone knows you're here, but even if they do, do you really think they'd shoot us down?"

I certainly hope not. But this is Simonich's Russia after all . . . Everything's possible.

CHAPTER 55

Koltsovo, Russia

Lisa Walton was in agony. Her head was throbbing and she had no idea where she was. She remembered being taken away from the Galkin's residence on a stretcher. She had drifted in and out of consciousness until someone all dressed in white had administered some kind of painkiller. Were her eyes even open? It was so dark, she couldn't say. Her mouth was dry and she could feel how dirty her teeth were by their texture when she passed her tongue over them.

She tried to move her right arm but it required too much effort. She thought she heard someone breathing next to her. *Or is it me?* She had the impression that an eighteen-wheeler had decided to stop on top of her stomach. Every breath she took was more painful than the last. Her left leg was on fire, and so was her forearm. But she didn't mind. That meant she wasn't paralyzed.

"Welcome back, Dr. Harrison Powell," someone murmured mere inches from her ears. She froze in horror. The voice sent a cold shiver down her spine. Was it really the voice that scared her? Or what it had said? *Dr. Harrison Powell.*

As her eyes became accustomed to the obscurity, she saw a dark figure move past her.

"At last we meet," the voice said.

Lisa tried to speak, but her mouth was too dry. "Oh, I'm sorry," the voice said, "you must be thirsty. Let me help you."

The next thing she knew, a warm jet of putrid liquid hit her eyes and mouth and found its way into her nose. The taste was repulsive and it took her a moment to realize what it was. *Urine.* She held her breath and moved her head to the side but that only resulted in getting a good amount of urine in her ear. As the urine made its way into her throat, she started coughing. The cough shook her whole body and she feared she was going to lose consciousness from the jolts of pain reverberating throughout her body.

Suddenly the lights were turned on and she angled her head to face the man who had just peed on her. She gasped in horror as she recognized him.

The Sheik.

. . . .

The Sheik couldn't have been happier with the reaction he got from Dr. Lisa Harrison Powell, or whatever name she now used. She tried to conceal her distress but he had seen it in her eyes. *Terror.* He could only imagine what was going through her mind with him standing next to her while she was tied to her hospital bed. He took a clean white towel and gently dried her face. "There you go. Better?"

He cocked his head to one side, looking at her as if she was a sick puppy. "I'm really glad to finally meet you," he said, "though, I'm not confident the feeling is mutual."

The Sheik had to give her credit, she didn't reply and the fire in her eyes wasn't from fear anymore. *Determination? Resolve?* It didn't really matter. She'd be dead within a week or so and there was nothing she could do about it.

"My men told me you killed a lot of people, Lisa," he said, his hand caressing her head and gently scratching her scalp. He sensed her body tense. She was a stunning woman, much more beautiful than Lidiya. And younger too.

"You've been a naughty girl, Lisa."

The Sheik abruptly moved his hand from her head to the wound just above her left knee. He squeezed hard. He wanted to know how she screamed. Now he knew. It was the loveliest scream of all. He weakened the pressure on her leg. Tears were running down her cheeks.

"You've taken so much from me, Lisa," he said in her ear while holding her head tightly in his hands. "Did you know that?"

He used his thumbs to dry her tears. "Don't cry, Lisa, don't cry," he said, his voice toneless. "You have nothing to cry about, yet. But it will come, I promise you. Be patient."

With that, he took one last look at her and exited the room. "Prep her," he ordered the doctor who'd been waiting outside. "We're leaving in two hours."

· · · · · · · ·

The Sheik had freaked her out. He was more savage than she'd thought. Monster was too nice a word to describe him. *You have nothing to cry about, yet,* he had said. What did he mean?

Lisa Walton tried to move her legs. An impossible task. Her left leg had undergone surgery to remove the bullet. As a trained medical doctor, she could see the signs that such an operation had taken place. But even if she had been able to move, both her legs and arms were tied to the bed with steel handcuffs. There was no way out, at least for now. Plus, she was sure it would be at least a couple of weeks before she could sit normally. The weight on her stomach was from the bullet she'd taken in the gut. The shot hadn't been fatal, but the damage to her abdominal muscles would take a while to heal.

The door opened and two people—probably doctors—entered. They didn't say a word. One of them prepared a syringe while the other held her in place. She didn't scream. She didn't even try to fight them off as the needle pierced her skin. She was too weak to do anything. She let herself slipped back into darkness, her mind holding on to images of Melissa and Mike.

CHAPTER 56

IMSI's Gulfstream, somewhere over Romania

Mike Walton allowed himself to relax. The last couple of days had been intense, much more than everybody had thought they would be while planning the intelligence-gathering mission back at the IMSI headquarters only a few days ago.

The two Russians had fallen asleep. Mike had forced them to take a couple of sleeping pills each. He had no idea what to do with them. He'd have to discuss their options with Mapother. They weren't bad guys *per se*, just a couple of crooked customs officials who'd messed with the wrong guys at the worst time. The Gulfstream was a superb aircraft. With a top speed of just over five hundred knots, it cleared Russia's airspace within ten minutes of taking off from the private aviation terminal. The first few minutes over Ukrainian airspace had been nerve racking, but once past Kiev they were pretty much home free to Bucharest, where they planned to refuel before continuing on to London.

"Mike," called St-Onge from the cockpit. "Charles Mapother's on the line. You wanna take it?"

He took one look at the Russians. They were both snoring loudly. They'd be out for at least another four hours. He headed to the cockpit where he accepted the satellite phone from St-Onge's outstretched arm.

"I'm here, Charles," he said.

"How are you feeling?" Mapother asked. "You're okay?"

Mike understood why Mapother was worried. If the roles were reversed, he'd be asking the same questions. Having an asset in the field was hard enough on a manager's brain; having one prone to panic attacks must have been a nightmare.

"I'm good, Charles," Mike replied. "Thanks for asking."

"I want you to sit down, my friend," Mapother said.

"I will. I promise. But we need to find Lisa—"

"That's not what I meant," interrupted Mapother. "That's a discussion for another time. I really need you to take a seat."

Mapother had him worried. *Did something happen to Lisa? Oh God, please no.* His legs were getting wobbly again. *I do need to sit down.*

He closed his eyes and took five deep breaths. "I'm listening, Charles," he said.

"We've found your father," Mapother said. "Actually, the Israelis and Zima did."

News of his father's whereabouts jolted Mike's mind into overdrive. *At last, some good news.* He didn't know if he was happier about the fact that his father had been found or because Mapother hadn't communicated bad news regarding his wife.

"Where is he?"

"Mykonos, Greece."

Mykonos? Why would Dad be in Mykonos? Wasn't he in Syria just yesterday?

"What's he doing in Greece?" he asked.

For the next ten minutes, Mapother explained the details. Mike winced when Mapother told him that Zima had badly injured her right hand. *Damn! On her first mission.*

"I want in," Mike said when Mapother was done. He had come so close to reuniting with his dad before. He didn't want to miss this opportunity. Plus, it would help keep his mind off Lisa while the IMSI figured out how to find her.

"Of course, that goes without saying," Mapother replied. "Let me talk to the pilots. I'll tell them to head to Tel Aviv."

Mike was about to hand over the phone to St-Onge when the issue about what to do with the two Russians popped into his mind. "There's one more thing, Charles," he said. "We have two unwanted guests of the Russian Federal Customs Service aboard the Gulfstream."

"Are they still alive?" Mapother asked.

What the hell? Why does everyone think I killed them?

"Of course they're still alive. What do you think?" he asked, a bit too loudly.

"I won't ask how that came to be, Mike," Mapother replied a second later. "I'll work it out with the Israelis. Now, let me talk with my pilots."

CHAPTER 57

Private airfield. Koltsovo, Russia

Lisa Walton was comfortable. *They probably shot me up with morphine.* With the severity of her injuries, there was no way she wouldn't be in pain unless they'd used morphine. Lots of it.

The ride from the hospital to the airport had been aboard a private ambulance. The medics had tried to bring the stretcher up the stairs and into the aircraft's cabin but it was too big. They had struggled down the steps and after a minute of consultation had decided to put her in a wheelchair. Even then she hadn't felt a thing, which wasn't necessarily a good thing. To bring the wheelchair up to the cabin level, they had to borrow a Mercedes-Benz Econic service vehicle, usually used to carry food in and out of airplanes.

Finally inside, Lisa saw that this wasn't any airplane. This was the private aircraft of someone beyond wealthy. The furniture matched what you'd find in the nicest hotels. Even the galley looked expensive, with high-end wood cabinets and a quartz countertop.

"Nice, isn't it?" asked the Sheik as he exited the lavatory.

Sight of him made her heart skip a beat. His mere presence repulsed her. He made her sick. "Do you know where we're going?" he asked with a smile. He shrugged when she didn't reply. "I wouldn't tell you anyway, Lisa. It's a surprise," he said, winking at her.

He walked to one of the two sofas and buckled his seat belt. She looked around the aircraft. There were two other people with them, excluding the two pilots. They all looked like military-type men in their late twenties or early thirties. One of them looked at her and smiled, as if he knew something funny was about to happen.

"I hope you . . . um . . . went to the bathroom, Lisa," the Sheik said, trying not to laugh. "Because it's a long flight, and um . . . well, your wheelchair won't fit in the lavatory, I'm afraid."

The two soldiers, or whatever they were, laughed out loud, mocking her. But she didn't mind. She'd just learned something important. They all understood English, even if they didn't speak it.

The engines started and the towing vehicle pushed the aircraft away from the gate seconds after the two medics climbed aboard. They didn't sit with the rest of the men and looked somewhat alarmed to be in the presence of the Sheik.

The plane rolled on the taxiway, heading toward the end of the runway. Lisa searched for something to hold. "You'd better fasten your seat belt, Lisa," the Sheik warned her in a sarcastic tone. As the plane turned on the runway, one of the medics changed place and sat next to Lisa. He buckled his seat belt and tried to hold Lisa's wheelchair as the plane accelerated.

The Sheik barked an order in Russian. She didn't have to understand the language to know he had just chastised the medic for helping her out. The medic looked at her and mouthed, "Sorry," in English. Realizing what was about to happen, she tried to hold on to him but he waved his arm away. The nose of the plane began to rise and Lisa's wheelchair rolled backward, gaining speed. Then one of the wheels hit something and she was thrown off the chair, flying in the air until her head slammed into something hard.

. . . .

The Sheik loved it. It was his way of blowing off some steam. The good doctor was going to die anyway. Why not have some fun while at it? It was juvenile, but he hated her. He hated her whole family, and Charles Mapother. Once he had dealt with the current situation, he'd send his son Igor to New York. He'd take care of Mapother. If he had one regret over this whole ordeal, it was that he had trusted Zakhar with something that was out of his reach. Not only had he lost a son, he had lost someone he trusted. And there weren't too many left of those in this world.

Prior to boarding the aircraft, and while the doctors were preparing Dr. Harrison Powell for her trip, he had made a stop at the Biopreparat facilities in Koltsovo. News of the death of Dr. Lidiya Votyakov had not yet reached her office. The Sheik figured it would take a few more days to concoct a plausible story pointing towards an assassination conducted by some Ukrainian rebels.

Since the Russian defense minister had personally called prior to his arrival at the Biopreparat complex, the Sheik had no problems gaining access to two of the five experimental doses of the new Marburg thread his former lover had created. Encased in a special Pelican case, the vials came with all the equipment that would be necessary to achieve what he had in mind.

Behind him Lisa groaned. The plane was still ascending so he kept his seatbelt secured, but he twisted around in his seat to watch the poor woman crawling towards him. She had a huge gash in her forehead, and even from a distance it was easy to see she was hurting. As the plane settled, the Sheik left his seat and picked up the wheelchair. He then asked the two Russian Spetsnazes to lift Dr. Harrison Powell off the floor of the cabin and set her back in the wheelchair. She wasn't so pretty anymore, was she? Her fall had reopened her wounds. Blood seeped through the bandages on her leg and stomach. She'd need medical attention if she were to survive the flight. He wasn't done with her. She still had a major role to play.

"Fix her," he ordered the two army medics before he himself approached the wheelchair. He bent next to her. "You know, Lisa, you could have simply locked the wheels," he said, pulling on the lock mechanisms located on the frame of each rear wheel. "Just like that."

CHAPTER 58

Tel Aviv, Israel

Mike Walton joined the pilots in the cockpit the moment the Gulfstream stopped at the gate to which it had been assigned. He congratulated them for the smooth landing.

"I have no idea how long I'll be here," Mike said, "but I need you to be on sixty minutes' notice."

"No worries," William Talbot replied, unstrapping himself from his seat. "We'll refuel and take care of business."

Mike followed Talbot out of the cockpit and both men walked to the cabin door. Mike unlocked the door and lowered the steps. A black minivan was parked twenty meters from the gate. When its side door slid open, Mike couldn't believe who came out.

Zima!

The first thing he noticed as she jogged toward him was the white bandage around her right hand.

"So sorry about your hand," he said, giving her a hug.

"A sniper shot my middle finger off," she replied, not missing a beat.

What? She must have sensed his dismay because she tapped his shoulder. "I'm good, Mike. Let's go," she said, pointing to the minivan. "Meir Yatom—he's a friend of Mapother—he wants to meet you."

She started toward the minivan but he called her back. "What about the two Russians?"

She turned to face him. "Yatom's men will take care of them," she explained, pointing back to the Gulfstream.

She was right. Yatom's men had woken up the Russians. They were being escorted down the stairs with opaque bags over their heads. "Let's go," his friend said. "We have lots to do."

Mike climbed into the van and Zima slid the door closed behind her.

"Meir Yatom," said the man in the front passenger seat, extending his hand.

Mike shook it. "Mike Walton."

"Now that we're friends," Yatom said, "please put these on."

In his hands were two opaque bags similar to those he had seen the Russians wear. "Is this really necessary?" Mike asked, not liking the idea.

"No at all," Yatom replied, a grin on his face. "You don't have to wear it if you don't want to."

Mike smiled, taking a liking to the old Israeli spy.

Next to him, Zima sighed. "Unbelievable."

"What?"

"Meir drugged me when he picked me up from the airport earlier today," she started. "Then, when we drove from wherever we were to here to pick *you* up, I had to wear one of these bags on my head."

Mike looked back at Yatom and raised his eyebrows. The Israeli shrugged. "What can I say? I like the drama," he said, laughing. Then to his driver, "Let's go. We've wasted enough time."

. . . .

Mike had traveled numerous times to Israel. It was a beautiful country. The first time he had set foot in the Jewish state was with the former Israeli ambassador to Canada. A member of the ambassador's close protective detail, Mike had spent a lot of time with the diplomat. They had quickly realized they had a lot in common. One thing led to another, and one night the ambassador invited Mike and Lisa to dinner at his private residence in Rockcliffe Park, a beautiful neighborhood in Ottawa. Their wives had hit it off right away, both being emergency physicians. The next summer, and knowing he and Lisa were history buffs, the ambassador had asked them to join him and his wife for a week in Tel Aviv. With both of them overdue for a vacation, they had gladly accepted. The ambassador had been a fantastic tour guide, taking them off the beaten path to see some spectacular sights. Mike's favorite part had been when the ambassador had given them a private tour of the Knesset, the Israeli parliament located in Jerusalem. They had then dined at the ambassador's private winery, a lovely twenty-minute drive away.

"You've been here before?" Yatom asked.

"Yes," Mike replied as they drove past another olive grove. "Good memories."

They spent the rest of the trip in silence, but Mike couldn't stop thinking about Zima's hand. What had really happened? He wished she'd been joking but knew it wasn't the case.

Zima's voice brought him back to reality. She was shaking his leg. "Time to wake up, Mike." He opened his eyes. They were in an underground parking garage. "How long was I out for?"

"About thirty minutes," she replied, sliding the door open. "But don't feel bad. Meir fell asleep too, and he snores much louder than you."

. . . .

Mike Walton was quickly introduced to Yatom's staff. Most of were younger than the personnel at the IMSI headquarters, but Mike had learned a long time ago that didn't mean they weren't as good. Their operation room reminded him of the IMSI control room but on a much smaller scale.

"We'll be joined shortly by the men that will accompany you during the assault," Yatom said. "They're the best."

Mike was dumbfounded. "Did you say 'assault'?"

"I don't know how they pulled it off, Mike, but Yatom's team received intelligence regarding your dad's whereabouts," Zima said.

"And it's good intel," Yatom continued. "You'll need to trust me on this."

They had come close to rescuing his dad twice now, but nobody had been able to pull it off. Mike was hesitant to trust anyone claiming he had intelligence regarding his dad's location. Probably seeing that Mike was doubtful, Yatom added, "Mapother does."

Good intel or not, they were here. So why not? He'd never forgive himself if he passed up on a good lead. "Why are you helping us?" Mike asked.

"Israel has very few friends right now," Yatom said. "Rescuing your dad, a former Canadian ambassador, would go a long way in helping us form a good relationship with the newly elected liberal government in Ottawa."

Mike couldn't fault Yatom's judgement. For the last decade, Israel had had the full support of the Canadian conservative government. The liberals, now forming a majority government, weren't as friendly toward the Jewish state. Bringing Ray Powell back safe and sound to Canada would bring Israel unconditional support.

"Plus, you guys helped us out in Croatia," Yatom added. "That counts for something too."

"Okay," Mike said. "I'll buy that. What do you know, and what's the plan?"

"I'll tell you what we know," Yatom said. "As for the plan, it will have to wait until the strike team arrives."

Mike nodded.

"As you know, your father was to return to Canadian custody in an exchange that was to take place in Damascus."

"I know that much," Mike said, accepting a hot cup of coffee from one of the analysts. "Zima was there."

"Yes, she was," Yatom conceded. "Would you like to see what happened?"

"You were there?" Mike asked.

"Someone was," Yatom replied. He pressed the play button. Mike watched in horror as the whole botched exchange played out on the flat screen in front of him. When it stopped playing, he said, "Again."

He watched the tape eighteen times, taking notes and drawing sketches. "Have you identified anyone?" he asked.

"The man Zima's talking to at the end of the video is Syrian General Fuad Younis, commanding officer of the Fifteenth Special Forces Division of the Syrian Army."

"He's the man who rescued my father from the Sheik's men four months ago," Mike said.

"Correct, which was confusing for us," Yatom replied.

"How so?"

"We always thought Younis's men were providing security for the Sheik's network in Syria."

"Maybe there was a falling out between them," Mike suggested. "The Sheik is known to turn against his allies."

"Maybe," Yatom said. "Or the general felt the momentum changing when we started bombing the hell out of ISIS, and he didn't want to be caught with his pants down supporting the losing side."

Mike was perplexed. "I thought the Syrian government was fighting ISIS. It doesn't make sense."

"Nothing makes sense in this part of the world, Mike," Yatom said. "You should know that by now. Alliances are built and destroyed in a day over here."

"Still," Zima interjected, "Younis's last words were that the Sheik was responsible for the ambush."

The Sheik. Always the Sheik. It had to end. This man was behind everything bad that had happened to him and his family in the last two and a half years.

"Did he say anything else?" he asked Zima.

"He died before I could get anything else out of him," Zima said. "But he didn't lie, Mike. I think he respected your father. Somehow."

"And how do you know these men, the ones responsible for taking my father, took him to Greece?" This time, his question was directed to Yatom.

"That's the part where you have to trust me, my friend," the Israeli replied.

Mike was about to say something when two armed men entered the small operation center. They were dressed in black combat uniforms. Their boots were dirty and so were their faces. The men looked tired.

Zima walked toward the tallest and, to his surprise, she jumped on him. The soldier caught her midair and gave her a hug. She whispered something in his ear. The man laughed and his eyes sparkled.

"Mike, this is Eitan,' she said, once the man had put her down. "I owe him my life."

She told him what had happened. Mike thanked the man profusely and shook his hand.

"And this is Ari," Zima continued, "the team leader."

"Thank you," Mike said. "Zima means a lot to me." Realizing what he had just said might be wrongly interpreted by Eitan, he quickly added, "And she's my wife's best friend."

"How's Zachary?" Yatom asked.

"He'll be fine," replied Ari. "He took one in the thigh. Rafael's with him."

"Okay, go get some rest. We'll reconvene right here to go over the tactical plan in three hours," Yatom said. Eitan and Ari left the room, but not before Eitan flashed a smile at Zima.

"Do we really have the luxury of waiting three hours?" Mike asked. He had no idea what condition his father was in. But if he was being tortured, three hours could make a huge difference.

"Let me explain something to you, Mike," Yatom said, taking a sip of his coffee. "What you're seeing here is, I believe, the Israeli equivalent of what you and Charles Mapother do. So I don't have access to unlimited personnel. Ari and his team are the best, but they won't do you or your father any good if they head to Greece tired and hungry. Wouldn't you agree?"

Mike nodded. Good men had been lost due to lack of sleep. If they were going head to head with the Sheik, or at least some members of his organization, they needed to be physically and mentally ready. And if he was honest with himself, he needed the sleep too.

"All right. See you here in three hours," Mike said.

Yatom seemed please he wouldn't have to argue with him. "Chaya will show you to your room."

He followed Chaya out of the operation center. "Aren't you coming?" he said to Zima as she headed in the opposite direction.

"I need to take care of something," she said, smiling.

Mike shrugged. He had more important things to do than to worry how she was going to spend the next three hours. Zima was a big girl.

His room had no windows but had a small shower attached to it. On a chair, next to his bed, was a black uniform identical to the one Yatom's men were wearing.

"There are socks in the drawer," Chaya said, pointing to a chest at the end of the bed. "And clean underwear."

Mike thanked her. He spent the next fifteen minutes under a hot shower. The water had never felt so good. He tried to relax but thoughts of his father and Lisa occupied his mind. They had to find Lisa. The thought of losing her forever deprived him of oxygen. He needed her. He'd give or do anything to get her back.

Anything.

CHAPTER 59

Tel Aviv, Israel

Zima ran her finger across Eitan's muscular chest. He was a god. She couldn't remember the last time she'd had such good sex. *Never. That's why you can't remember, girl. He's the best you ever had.* It all happened so fast. She didn't think they had exchanged more than a hundred words total between them before jumping all over each other. The memory of his fingers trailing over her breasts sent a small tingle low in her belly. The heat of his body tickled her skin. Her hand drifted lower and she was pleased with what she found.

"Don't you want to sleep for a few hours?" Eitan said.

"Sleeps overrated, don't you think?"

He grabbed her by the hips and placed her on top of him. His smoldering blue eyes burning into her own made her gasp as desire flooded her.

His thumbs caressed her cheeks gently then his hands moved down her waist, locking her in place. She found that extremely sexy.

"Doesn't that bother you?" she asked, looking at the bandage on her right hand.

"When I was tied to that chair, the only thing I could think about was you," Eithan said, the rasp of his voice enchanting her ears. "And I had known you for only—"

Zima pressed her finger against his lips. "Enough," she whispered, her lips only an inch from his. "I've heard enough."

"One more thing, though," Eitan said between two kisses. "I'd prefer if it was you next time, all right?"

"Me what?" she asked, out of breath.

"I'd prefer if it was you who'd tie me to a chair."

Zima smiled. She'd better watch herself, because this man she could fall for.

CHAPTER 60

Tel Aviv, Israel

Mike Walton woke up energized. It was hard to believe all the good a two-hour nap could do to the human body. Of course, he would have much preferred to sleep ten hours but it would have to wait. He dressed in the clothes provided and brushed his teeth with the toiletry kit he had found next to the sink. After looking at this reflection in the mirror, he decided he'd better shave too.

Ten minutes later, freshly shaved and wearing clean clothes, he headed back to the operations center. It was already buzzing with activity. The smell of freshly baked croissants, bagels and bread reached his nose. His eyes swept over the jars of preserves on a table tucked in a corner. The aroma of just-brewed coffee also made its way to him and his stomach gurgled in anticipation. Zima was already there, bent over a map next to Eitan, Rafael and Ari.

"Slept well?" Yatom asked, handing him a cup of coffee. "Serve yourself if you're hungry. Briefing starts in five."

"Thanks," Mike said, accepting the cup. *Five minutes.* That didn't give him much time to eat the number of pastries he was planning to.

. . . .

As Yatom had said, the briefing started five minutes later. Everyone had moved to the next room where someone had set up a projector and a large white screen. A seventy-inch flat-screen television had also been rolled in. Present for the briefing was Yatom's whole team of analysts and communication specialists. In addition, Ari's tactical team was there with Zima sandwiched between Eitan and Rafael.

251

The plan Yatom had concocted was simple but dangerous. Four operators—Mike, Ari, Eitan and Rafael—would be inserted into Mykonos by HALO—High Altitude Low Opening—somewhere on the northeastern tip of the island. From there, they would walk to a specific grid location where Zima would be waiting for them with transportation. Zima, who would arrive by commercial flight a couple of hours earlier, would be in charge of securing the landing zone. She'd be able to communicate with the team up to the point when they jumped. Then, if something happened, it was her job to take care of it. The rules of engagement for the insertion were clear. Under no circumstances were they allowed to engage Greek authorities. If the insertion went well, they would travel to the villa where Ray Powell was kept.

The next thirty minutes were spent analyzing satellite photos of said villa and the blueprints the Israelis had been able to come up with.

"How did you come up with these plans?" asked Mike.

"Our architects did," Yatom explained. "They looked at the structure, they analyzed it and that's the best they could do."

"So these schematics might not be a hundred percent accurate," Mike said.

"No," Yatom replied after a moment, conceding the point, "but I'm sure you'll be able to adapt."

If he was to believe the blueprints on the screen, the villa had four bedrooms on the second floor. Each bedroom had its own balcony and en-suite. A large living room, a dining room, a kitchen and a half-bath occupied the ground floor. The interior of the villa could be accessed via two doors. One was located at the front of the house while the other door could only be accessed from the large terrace facing the Aegean Sea.

Once everyone was familiar with the layout of the villa, Yatom continued with the details of the operation. He, Zima and Rafael were to be the assault team while Eitan and Ari would provide cover with their sniper rifles. Once they were able to establish exactly how many hostiles were present at the villa, they would launch the assault. Zima would drive the van, carrying Mike and Rafael in the back. The objective was to find Mike's father and to be in and out as fast as possible. They would leave the villa the same way they had come in while the two snipers covered their retreat. They would then exfiltrate Mykonos with the IMSI Gulfstream. Eitan and Ari would follow suit twenty-four hours later via two different commercial flights.

Mike had to agree that the plan might actually work. It was well thought out, and they had the element of surprise. The only thing he didn't look forward to was the HALO jump. He'd done a few when he was serving with the Canadian Special Operation Regiment but they weren't nice memories. He had never understood why some people's favorite hobby was jumping out of aircraft.

Two hours later, and with the briefing coming to an end, Yatom's cell phone chirped. Mike watched the Israeli's face turn pale. He wasn't the only one to notice because Ari asked, "What is—"

Yatom raised his hand to silence him. His eyes were glued to his smartphone. The room fell silent. Finally, Yatom said, "It appears that the Sheik might be on his way to Mykonos."

The Sheik.

"Do we know the timetable?" Mike asked.

"Not at this time. But it does change one thing," Yatom said. "Once you guys are in position, you won't move in before you have confirmation that the Sheik is on location."

They looked at each other. "You okay with this, Mike?" Ari asked.

Mike really appreciated the gesture. "I've waited for two and a half years for a shot at getting my father back. I'll wait for as long as it takes if it means we get to take the Sheik down. He started all this."

"All right then," Yatom announced. "Get ready."

Everybody moved out of the briefing but Mike stayed behind. "Where are you getting this intel, Meir?"

"Sorry, Mike," Yatom said. His firm voice left no room for negotiation. "This isn't something I'll share with you. You can walk out if that's your wish."

"You know I can't walk out, Meir," Mike said. "That's my father we're talking about."

"Then I suggest you get ready."

CHAPTER 61

Mykonos, Greece

Mike Walton was the first man on the ground. He collapsed his chute. The last time he had done this had been in Kosovo more than a decade ago while working with Jonathan Sanchez, then a Delta operator. The reason Yatom had wanted them to do a HALO jump was to minimize their exposure to potential ground observers and not, as had been the case when he jumped over hostile territory in Kosovo, to decrease their chances of being hit by enemy flak.

Just before he had jumped, the pilot had confirmed that the landing zone was secure. Prior to departure, it had been agreed that if Zima failed to communicate the LZ status or in case of any kind of problems, they would do another pass exactly sixty minutes later.

Rafael hit the ground next, followed by Eitan and then Ari. No one was hurt and Mike thanked God for that small miracle. Night jumps were always dangerous and he was glad they hadn't lost anyone due to an injury. In a regular army drop, there were hundreds, sometimes thousands, of paratroopers inundating a specific area. Even if ten percent were lost during the jump, you still had a combat force. Here, if they had lost even one member, it would have been a reduction of twenty percent. The whole operation assumed five assaulters. Four wouldn't do.

. . . .

Zima had no problem with the Greek customs officer that greeted her at the airport. He was all smiles and even a little too friendly for her taste. Nevertheless, he stamped her passport. The IMSI had provided her a solid cover and if anyone was to check her story, they'd find a room booked under her name at the Kouros Hotel & Suites. She picked up the keys to the Toyota HiAce van from the rental car counter outside the terminal. The HiAce was a large panel van that could sit three in the front but had room for another eight passengers in the back. However, the version the IMSI had booked had only two seats in front and none in the back. That specification would allow the rest of the assault team to carry their gear and remain somewhat concealed, as the side panels of the van had no windows.

Her first stop was the registration desk at the Kouros. She wasn't planning on using the room but needed to check in to avoid suspicion from the hotel staff. Even at night, the view from the lobby was exceptional, and Zima promised herself that one day, when she had the time and money, she'd come back to visit. *Maybe with Eitan?*

She went to check the room and it was gorgeous. Cozy but elegant. *Yes, definitely with Eitan.* She grabbed an apple and a water bottle and headed back up to where she had parked the HiAce.

The meeting point wasn't far from the hotel. A fifteen-minute drive at most. But Zima took her time and made a lot of detours to make sure the site was secure. Equipped with a powerful pair of night-vision binoculars, Zima scanned the surrounding area. Convinced the landing zone wasn't the site of an ambush, she contacted the pilot to let him know the site was green.

Twenty minutes later, she saw the first parachute. She'd never jumped out of a working aircraft but she had read somewhere that it was, indeed, dangerous. She caught herself holding her breath while she watched the three other chutes land close to each other. She gave the men three minutes to gather their stuff before she returned to the HiAce.

. . . .

Mike Walton saw the flashing lights and lead the way. They reached the van and Zima slid the side door open for them.

"Any issues?" Mike asked, dropping his gear in the back of the van.

"None. We're good to go," she replied.

Once they had all secured their equipment in the truck, Ari went over the plan one last time. He quizzed every one of them but they all knew the same thing—they were ready.

"Time to go to work," Ari said. Mike couldn't agree more. He hoped the intelligence they had received regarding the Sheik would hold true. He had to admit that, so far, the Israelis had been dead on. Clearly, Meir Yatom cared a lot about his source. But Mike didn't like acting on intel when he didn't know where it came from.

As Zima drove around the island, Mike and Rafael changed out of their jumpsuits and into civilian tactical clothes whereas Eitan and Ari put on their ghillie suits. Their first stop was about two hundred meters below Eitan's sniper nest. Using satellite imagery, Eitan had found his spot with the help of Chaya back in the operation room. It was located four hundred and twenty meters away from the villa and gave him an excellent view of the only road leading to the villa. Eitan would have to hike the rest of the way.

"Let's do a comm check before you're too far away," Mike said to Eitan as he exited the HiAce by its rear doors.

As soon as the doors were closed, the HiAce accelerated away.

"Ari from Eitan," Mike heard through his comm system. "Radio check, over."

"You're five by five, Eitan," Ari replied.

"Copy that, Ari. How do you copy, Mike?"

"You're five by five," Mike said.

"Got you loud and clear," Zima added.

"Same here," Rafael said.

"All comms are good," Eitan said. "Eitan out."

The next one out was Ari. His position was a little trickier than Eitan's. He'd have to walk for about two kilometers before reaching his position. Located about two hundred meters from the villa, his sniper nest was sandwiched between the villa's terrace and the ocean. "We'll get your dad out of there," he said to Mike.

"Stay safe," Mike replied.

Rafael and Ari banged their fists together. "Take care, brother."

The next stop was the staging area. It was about one kilometer away from the villa. This was where Zima would park the van and wait for Ari's word to go. Mike had butterflies. His mind traveled back to Benalmadena, where he, Lisa and Jasmine Carson had raided the Sheik's yacht. His mistake, his eagerness to go after his father and to catch the Sheik, had cost Jasmine her life. These thoughts brought tightness in his chest and his hands began to shake. He recognized it for what it was.

A panic attack.

As the panels of the HiAce closed on him, his mother's voice resonated in his head, telling him to be careful, to think about Lisa, and not to take unnecessary risks. But most importantly, she was telling him that she was proud of him and that everything would come out as it should.

"You're ready for this?" Rafael asked him, pulling him back to reality.

"Yeah," Mike mumbled, wiping the perspiration that had appeared on his forehead. *I have to be.* He grabbed a bottle of water and drank half of it before offering it to Rafael.

Ari's voice crackled in his earpiece. "In position," he said.

"Copy that," Mike replied.

Now we wait.

CHAPTER 62

Mykonos, Greece

L isa Walton's pain had become almost unbearable. The morphine was wearing off quickly. The medics had patched her forehead but the dressing was already soaked with blood. Since the impact, her vision had remained blurry. That sounded like a concussion to her.

She didn't know what hurt the most, her leg wound or her stomach. She was sure she had internal bleeding. She wouldn't be surprised if the doctors had only operated to make sure she'd live another three or four days. The agony she was in wasn't normal, even for a gunshot wound. That scared her because she was well aware that the main concern with a stomach wound wasn't the bleeding, or the pain for that matter, but the infections that resulted from the spillage of the contents of these organs. The deep burning from deep down seemed to confirm her biggest fear. It was entirely possible that the Russians doctors didn't know what they were doing and might have signed her death warrant when they removed the bullet. Maybe three or four days was too much to ask.

The plane landed without incident and rolled to a gate close to the end of the terminal. She closed her eyes. She was beyond tired but the pain caused her so much discomfort she couldn't sleep. Somebody picked her up. Through half-closed eyes, she could see it was one of the medics. He was strong. He carried her as if she weighed no more than a pillow.

The sun was rising and she forced herself to look around as the medic carried her down the stairs of the aircraft. She recognized the place immediately.

Mykonos.

She and Mike spent two weeks in Greece four years ago, and Mykonos had been one of their stops. It had been a fabulous trip. She remembered the beauty of Mykonos, its five sixteenth-century windmills, the enchanting sunsets and the intense nightlife they had taken advantage of. They had lost themselves more than once in the narrow, paved streets that had been built with the intention of confusing the pirates in the eighteenth and early nineteenth centuries. But the true highlight of their trip was when they had rented an ATV and crisscrossed the whole island in search of beautiful beaches. Elia Beach was the one they had finally decided to spend the day at. She could almost feel the sand between her toes and the cool touch of the pristine blue waters.

The medic sat her down in the backseat of a large SUV. She didn't have the strength to fight back. The medic probably knew that because they hadn't even bothered tying her hands together. She had done everything she could. Charles Mapother had given her a second chance, and she hoped she hadn't wasted it. She didn't think so. She had accomplished a lot. She truly believed the IMSI could make a difference. But she wasn't naïve, and as the pain continued to grow, she knew it was the end of the road for her.

She was fine with this. Mike would avenge her. He'd find the Sheik and he would rip him apart. He'd probably never forgive himself for letting her become an asset. She wished he would, though. Because it had been her way to seek justice. She couldn't have stood on the sideline while he traveled the world in search of the Sheik.

She must have dozed off, because when she opened her eyes she was in a wheelchair being rolled toward a beautiful villa. She shivered.

Fever.

In her own professional assessment, unless there was a capable doctor at the villa, she had a few hours to live, at most.

CHAPTER 63

Mykonos, Greece

Mike Walton checked his weapons for the hundredth time in the last hour. His leg holster carried a Glock 19 while his primary weapon was a Heckler & Koch UMP45. He had five spare twenty-five-round magazines in his tactical vest. Two hours ago, Eitan had reported one man patrolling the front of the villa while Ari had mentioned another one positioned on the terrace.

"Two black SUVs driving in tight formation are approaching the villa," Eitan said over their frequency. "They are four minutes away. Stand by for more info."

Mike's heart rate accelerated. He was ready. The toughest part for him was the wait. The wait was the silent killer. It was hard to remain focused for a long period of time.

Especially in the cargo area of a windowless panel van.

"In the first vehicle," started Eitan, "one woman in a wheelchair, with a bloody bandage on her forehead. I also count five men. At least two of them are armed."

Mike hoped the Sheik was part of this group. If he wasn't, he had no idea if Yatom would give the green light for the assault. He held his breath as he focused on Eitan's report.

"I see the Sheik. I repeat, the Sheik has arrived. Do I have the authority?"

Mike's heart sank. *No!* Ari couldn't give him the authority. That would be a death warrant for his father, if he was really inside.

"Negative," came in Ari. "Authority comes from Meir. Standby."

Ari's voice broke the frequency five minutes later. "Get ready. We're moving in four minutes."

Mike smiled. *At last.*

CHAPTER 64

Mykonos, Greece

Ray Powell was stuck in his room. At least they hadn't beaten him up and he had access to his own bathroom. A luxury he didn't have while the Sheik had sequestered him in the shithole in Syria. But he wasn't naïve enough to think he was out of trouble. They had a plan for him. He just didn't know what it was.

His captors had made no secret that he was being watched. Not that he cared that he had no privacy, but it made it difficult to find a weapon he could use.

The door to his room opened and someone in a wheelchair was rolled in. At first, he didn't recognize her. But then he did. And he started crying.

· · · · · · · ·

Lisa was lifted from her wheelchair and laid down on a comfortable bed. It was soft and nice. *Heaven?* Someone tried to lift her shirt. *No. Not this.* She tried to push the hands away but she wasn't strong enough. Warm tears filled her eyes. I'm going to be raped. *Oh God, please let me die in peace. Not like this!*

"Lisa, it's me, Ray," a voice said, making its way through her foggy mind. *Ray?* She forced her eyes open. Mike's dad was standing next to her, crying but smiling. She couldn't believe it. That wasn't possible. His hands were carefully removing the dressing she had on her stomach. She let him clean her wound with a damp towel. Lisa had never been so confused. She honestly couldn't tell if she was dreaming or not.

"What have they done to you?" Ray said, his voice cracking. "What on earth have these bastards done to you?"

CHAPTER 65

Mykonos, Greece

The Sheik held his son in his arms. "You've done well, Igor."

"I always do," Igor replied.

"Are your men ready?" he asked, heading toward the dining room.

"For what? Our instructions were to wait for you here."

That was good to know. That meant that Vienamin Simonich had kept his part of the bargain. He wouldn't be interfering with *his* plan.

"I don't know what the president told you, son, but we've suffered some setbacks in Russia," he started as they took seats at the large dining table.

"What kind of setbacks are we talking about?" Igor asked, sharply looking up from the cup of coffee one of his men had just brought to him.

"Simonich has lost plausible deniability," the Sheik said. "A full-scale attack is now out of the question, but we'll use the ambassador and the woman to achieve our objective." The Sheik sensed his son didn't like what he had just said, so he added, "We'll still be able to strike at our enemies."

"Who's enemies, Qasim?" Igor's eyes were inquisitive. "Yours or Russia's?"

If his son's intention was to offend him, it worked. He felt his blood pressure rise. *How dare this little shit say something like that to me, his father, the Sheik?*

"I respect you," Igor continued, "but my loyalty is to Russia—"

The Sheik burst out of his chair and shouted, "And mine is to you, your mother and the family that was taken away from us. Don't you get this?"

His son didn't reply. He looked stunned. His father had never talked to him in such a way. The soldier who had served them coffee stopped moving. He was looking at Igor, waiting for instructions.

"I know," Igor finally said. "I never doubted it."

The Sheik sat back down. When he spoke, it was as though his recent outburst had never happened. "The woman, the one in the wheelchair, she's part of the team that took out Omar in Benalmadena."

That caught his son's interest.

"She's part of Charles Mapother's team?"

"Yes, she is," he said. "She's the wife of Mike Walton, one of Mapother's minions."

His son took his time to digest the news. "What do you want to do?"

"On my way here, I stopped by Koltsovo to meet with your mother," he lied. "On Simonich's order, she gave me two doses of the new Marburg virus she created."

When his son didn't reply, he continued, "We'll inject Ray Powell with the virus, and then we'll let him escape."

"When?"

"As soon as we're done here," he said.

"What about the woman?"

"I originally wanted to do the same thing with her but she won't live long enough," the Sheik explained. "I have something else in mind for her. But trust me, son, she'll pay for her sins too."

CHAPTER 66

Mykonos, Greece

Ray Powell did his best to treat Lisa's wounds, but there wasn't much he could do with only a couple of wet towels. With the seriousness of her injuries, he was surprised she hadn't passed away. But she was here, and he'd do everything in his power to keep her alive for as long as he could.

The Sheik's henchman, Omar Al-Nashwan, had told him his whole family had died. He had even shown him the story about Mike's heroism, and his subsequent death at the hands of the terrorists who had attacked the Ottawa airport. If Lisa had survived, if the story about her death had been false, was there any chance that his son was alive?

His thoughts were cut short by the arrival of three men, one of them the Sheik.

The hope he had just felt was replaced by a surge of pure hatred. The Sheik, the man who had ruined his life and broken his family apart, was standing, hands in his pockets, less than ten feet away from him. Powell wanted to run at him and smashed his head against the wall. But he couldn't. Not just because of the two goons standing next to him, but also for Lisa. She needed him.

"I see you guys are getting reacquainted," the Sheik said. "How nice."

Powell never saw the tranquilizer gun. The only thing he felt was a sharp pain just above his left nipple. He looked at the dart protruding from his chest. His legs became wobbly and he fell to his knees.

. . . .

The Sheik pushed Powell with his foot and watched him fall to his side. He sensed movement to his right. Lisa had turned her head.

Her eyes were on him and they carried the same revulsion Ray Powell's had moments ago.

The Sheik accepted the Pelican case his man gave him. He kneeled beside the unconscious former ambassador and opened the case, making sure to explain to Lisa what he was doing.

"This syringe contains a new virus. I'm told it is extremely painful and becomes highly contagious seven to ten days after it is administered. Isn't that exciting?"

Lisa muttered something. "I can't hear what you're saying, my dear," the Sheik said. "Are you wondering if you'll get the virus too?" He didn't wait for an answer. "As tempting as it is, I'm afraid you won't get it. I have another plan for you," he said, as the tip of the needle pierced Powell's skin. Once he was sure the whole dose was in Powell's system, he looked up at Lisa. "See? He didn't mind."

"You . . . You're a . . . sick . . . fuck," Lisa said.

"Don't you want to know your surprise, Lisa?" he asked.

"Fuuuuck. . . you."

"Well, all right, then. I'll tell you." He paused for effect. "You, my dear, I'll burn alive."

CHAPTER 67

Mykonos, Greece

His father's plan had impressed him. And it could work. With a little luck, they would pull it off. He imagined Ray Powell at the head table of a gala organized in his honor. Politicians, business leaders and intelligence officials all fighting to get his attention and the opportunity to take a photo with him. And who knows, maybe Powell would get an invitation to the White House. That would be great. Powell would become Russia's Trojan horse.

But for that, Igor had to make sure that his escape looked authentic. He headed to the security room to discuss this very issue with his second-in-command.

"How are things?"

"Something funny just happened," his man said. Igor gestured him to start talking. "I've detected a transmission going out of the villa."

Igor scratched his head. He had ordered his men not to communicate with anyone outside the villa until further notice. It was probably one of his father's men, but this hypothesis didn't last long.

"And it can't be the Sheik or his men."

"Why's that?"

"Because there was another burst before he had even arrived."

That didn't make any sense to Igor. He trusted his men with his life. They had all fought together for years. Except for one. *Grigory.* Grigory had been forced into his team by someone higher up in the chain of command to replace one of his men who had been killed during a training exercise a little less than a year and a half ago. But Grigory was his best man, the fiercest fighter he had ever seen. He was merciless, and had proven himself in Ukraine. Still, he had to make sure.

"Can you trace back the number to where it originated? Igor asked.

"No, sir. The only thing I can tell is that these communications aren't phone calls. They're encrypted text messages."

"Okay, where's Grigory?"

"Camera six," his man replied. "He went out to conduct a patrol."

Igor left the security room and found Grigory smoking a cigarette on the terrace.

"How are things, Grigory?"

Even though Igor was his commanding officer, the men under his command were pretty relaxed around him. And as long as they did their jobs, he didn't mind. Like most special operation forces around the world, the discipline within his unit was different than that in regular army regiments. Grigory threw his cigarette butt on the ground and extinguished it with his foot.

"No complaints. The view is great, and the weather's nicer here than in Ukraine," he said, turning toward the ocean.

By the time Grigory turned to face him again, Igor had his pistol pointed at his chest.

"Igor?" Grigory asked. He took a step back and raised his hands. "What's going on?"

"Don't play with me. I know." Igor said. "To whom have you been sending these text messages?"

"Text messages? Igor, I don't know what you're talking about," Grigory replied. "I really don't."

He really looked distraught but Igor kept the pressure on. "Stop lying, Grigory," Igor shouted. "You're better than that."

"What the fuck do you want me to say?" Grigory yelled back. "You believe me or you don't. I have nothing to do with these text messages."

Igor could see his man was pissed and he was momentarily caught off guard when Grigory removed his tactical vest and let it fall on the ground. "If you don't trust me anymore, Igor," Grigory said, his voice shaking, "then shoot me, my friend, because you're like a brother to me. I'd never, never betray you."

This wasn't the reaction Igor expected. Either Grigory was the best stage actor in Russia, or he wasn't the one communicating with the outside world.

Igor brought his weapon down. If it wasn't Grigory, then who?

. . . .

Igor returned inside the villa and saw his father walking with a jerry can in hand.

"What are you doing?" Igor asked.

"I'm about to set someone on fire," his father replied. "Would you like to watch?"

"You already took care of Powell?"

His father nodded. "I'll bring the woman outside. I'm actually thinking about grabbing a spare tire from one of the SUVs—"

"Don't," he interjected. "Why don't you just shoot her and be done with it?"

His father looked at him as if he had gone mad. "After everything she's done to us, you want me to *just shoot her*?"

Igor raised his hands in surrender. "Do what you wish. I have something I need to take care of."

His father cocked his head. "Problems?"

Igor pondered how much he should tell his dad. "I'll take care of it," he said, and started walking away.

His father grabbed his arm with his free hand and dug his fingers into his biceps. "What is it?"

Igor looked at his arm. "Get your hand off me." His father still had his strength.

"Not before you tell me what's the problem."

Igor pivoted ninety degrees and lifted his arm in the air before bringing it back down hard on the inside of his father's forearm.

His father's face twitched in anger. The Sheik wasn't used to people who fought back. Igor wasn't impressed and dug his index into his father's chest. "Don't you ever do that again," he said before walking away.

He didn't look back. Aware that his father had killed men for less, he half expected to be shot in the back and was rather surprised when he reached the security room in one piece. To his dismay, the door of the security room was open. He was about to reprimand his man but quickly realized it wouldn't be necessary. His second-in-command lay face first on his keyboard, blood pouring out of a giant gash in his throat.

Shit! Igor keyed his mic. "All, this is One, report," he said over the air. Right away, his men started to report. Within twenty seconds, he had the location and the status of all except one. Grigory.

"Grigory, from Igor, status check, over." Nothing. Where the hell was he? Igor pushed over the dead body of his second-in-command to gain access to the video feeds of the cameras. But he had no luck. The keys of the keyboard were flooded with blood. There was nothing he could do from this end. Did Grigory play him?

He ordered one of his men to check on the prisoners and to search for Grigory. He had turned on them.

There was one more thing he needed to do before joining his men. He took his secured phone from the left pocket of his tactical vest and called the man he was working for.

Vienamin Simonich answered on the first ring. "Igor?"

"Sir, we have a problem," he started. "I have one man down and I believe an attack might be imminent—"

"What?"

"Sir—"

"Stop talking, Major Votyakov, and listen to what I have to say," Simonich ordered.

"I'm listening, sir," Igor replied.

"Did the Sheik take care of his business with Ray Powell?"

"Yes, he did," Igor said. "He told me so himself."

"Very well. Now, do you love your country, Major?" Simonich asked. His voice indicated he was about to say something unpleasant.

What kind of question was that? President of the Russian Federation or not, Vienamin Simonich should know better than to ask stupid questions like these.

"Yes, sir. I do."

"Then I want you to kill the Sheik."

That, he didn't expect. He felt as if he had been sucker punched. "Sir?" he managed to say.

"I trust you'll do your duty, Igor," Simonich said. "Your father has betrayed the confidence of the Russian people."

"But—"

"There is no but," Simonich replied. "Look at your inbox and do as you're ordered. You'll call me once it's done."

I want you to kill the Sheik. He wasn't sure he could. His phone chirped in his hand. Simonich had sent him a video. He pressed play. Halfway through the video, Major Igor Votyakov threw up.

CHAPTER 68

Mykonos, Greece

M ike Walton was growing impatient. It didn't make any sense to wait. "What the hell are we waiting for?" he asked Rafael. The Israeli shrugged, as if it was no big deal. "It doesn't matter. We wait."

"Assault team for Ari, you're on in two minutes,"

"Assault team copy," Mike replied, relieved the wait was over.

"We got confirmation that there are two hostages," Ari said. "They're both in the same room. Male is confirmed to be Ray Powell."

Ari continued with his briefing but Mike wasn't listening anymore. His father was there, only a few hundred meters away. It was hard to believe after all these years. Rafael kicked his boot. "Mike?"

"Yeah?"

"Did you get that?"

"What?"

"Get your shit together, Mike," Rafael warned him. "There are twelve people in the villa, two hostages, nine hostiles, counting the Sheik, and one friendly."

"One friendly?"

"He's one of ours. Deep cover. He'll be wearing a green bandana on his left arm. He took care of one tango for us, so there are eight left."

"Got it," Mike said, holding himself steady by pushing against the side of the van with his feet. Zima was driving like a maniac.

"Five hundred meters," she yelled from the driver's seat.

Then Eitan was on the air. "I got one tango exiting the front door. Can I engage?"

"Engage at will," Ari replied.

271

Two seconds later they heard, "Tango down. Seven left."

Then Zima yelled again, advising them they were one hundred meters away. Mike braced himself for a rapid deceleration, which came moments later. As soon as the HiAce came to a stop, Rafael opened the rear door and jumped out of the van. Mike was a little disoriented but when he saw Rafael go left, he followed right behind him.

They were thirty meters from the front door when they were engaged. Bullets whizzed past him and Rafael yelled out in pain as he was knocked down by numerous hits. Mike dove to the ground, unsure where the fire was coming from.

"Two tangos spotted, second-floor balcony. Angle isn't right. I have no shot," Mike heard Eitan said.

Mike saw one of them and fired three two-round bursts at the silhouette, but the man had already ducked behind a balustrade. Behind him, Rafael was groaning. Mike fired five more two-round bursts and jumped to his feet. He grabbed the Israeli by the drag handle of his tactical vest and started to pull him out of the danger zone. Bullets kicked up dirt all around them and Rafael was struck again, this time in the thigh. Another round grazed Mike's neck, leaving a painful furrow behind his left ear.

Fuck! They wouldn't make it.

· · · · · · · ·

Zima Bernbaum tried to get out of the van as soon as she had put it in park but couldn't. She had forgot to unbuckle her seat belt. *Stupid!*

The moment she set foot out of the vehicle, someone started to engage them. Zima dropped behind the engine block as round after round went through the windshield. She heard Eitan call out the shooters and heard Mike's silenced UMP45 return fire. Things weren't starting the way they had hoped. Being pinned down less than ten seconds after they had started the assault wasn't a sure way to win the battle.

Taking two deep breaths, Zima rose from behind the engine block with the butt of her MP5 firmly into her shoulder. She looked through the weapon's sight. One of the tangos had just stepped out from behind the balustrade he used as cover and was shooting at

Mike and Rafael. Zima pulled the trigger and the man went down in a mist of blood and bones.

"Cover me, Zima," Mike yelled. "Rafael's hit."

"Covering," Zima yelled back, continuing to pump rounds at the second-floor balcony.

. . . .

Thanks to Zima, Mike was able to pull Rafael to relative safety behind the HiAce. He quickly assessed Rafael's injuries. He could see at least three hits, none of them fatal.

"I'll be fine," Rafael said through his teeth. He tore open his own trauma kit. "Go."

Mike nodded. "Hang on, I'll be back."

He then joined Zima who was in the process of inserting a new magazine into her MP5. When she was done, Mike did the same, and then he tapped her shoulder to let her know he was ready. Just as they were about to advance, Ari came on the air.

"Assault team from Ari."

"Go ahead," Mike replied.

"SITREP."

"Rafael's hit. We have another tango down, six left," Mike replied, while scanning for any threats. "We're about to advance."

"I'll join you on the assault," Ari said, out of breath. It sounded as though the Israeli team leader was running. "You won't make it if you're only two. Let me surprise them with a dynamic entry through the rear door." That wasn't a bad idea. "Give me thirty seconds," Ari added.

"Copy that, thirty seconds," Mike replied, looking at his watch.

"Mike," came in Eitan," you're clear to advance to the front door. I'll cover your movement."

"Copy," Mike said. He looked at Zima. "You're ready?"

She was smiling. "I've been ready all my life."

Good girl. He was happy to have her by his side. "Let's go."

They dashed across the driveway and reached the front door without being shot at.

"Tango down," Eitan announced. "Five left. Got the other guy on the balcony as he was trying to get back inside."

"Assault team copy. Five tangos are left," Mike said. He took three deep breaths as he visualized what was about to happen. He had breaching charges in his kit but they wouldn't be necessary. The first hostile Eitan had killed had left the door open an inch.

"On my authority," he heard Ari say. "Three, two—"

CHAPTER 69

Mykonos, Greece

Ray Powell opened his eyes with a jolt. One of his Russian captors was bent over him. He had his pistol in one hand while the other was shaking him. The Russian's eyes weren't on him, though. They were looking toward the door. Acting on instinct and out of anger, Powell punched the man in the head. The Russian fell to one knee, clearly stunned by the sudden strike.

The door of the room opened and Powell watched as Igor barged in and shot his man twice. The Russian dropped to the floor, moaning in pain. He tried to reach the pistol he had dropped but Igor was already on him and kicked the gun away.

"Who's coming, you piece of shit?" Igor screamed.

Powell was puzzled. Why were they turning on each other? He had never seen Igor upset. He'd always been so calm and collected. Why was he acting so erratically?

Suddenly, a series of shot rang out. When Igor turned toward the sound of gunfire, Powell knew it was now or never. He jumped out of bed and lunged at Igor who was standing less than five feet away. But the tranquilizer drug slowed him down and Igor easily ducked under his left hook. The Russian counter-punched him in the solar plexus and brought down the butt of his pistol between his shoulder blades. Powell crashed to the floor, struggling for breath. He raised his head in time to see Igor aim his pistol at his head.

He had already started to pull the trigger when the Sheik rushed into the room and screamed at Igor to stop.

CHAPTER 70

Mykonos, Greece

The Sheik was furious. They were under attack and his son was about to kill the only man who could guarantee the virus would reach American soil, instead of fighting the assailants. And what about his man writhing on the floor? Had he shot him too?

"What are you doing?" he yelled. "We need Powell. Join your men and fight!"

Igor turned to face him. His son's eyes were clouded by hate and resentment. He had never seen him like that. What had Ray Powell said to anger his son so much?

"How could you do that?" his son roared, advancing toward him.

"Calm down, Igor," the Sheik pleaded. "We have to go. Now."

That seemed to push his son over the top. "You killed my mother, you fuck," Igor said, aiming his pistol at the Sheik's head with one hand.

His heart twisted in pain as he realized that his son knew the truth. How could he? Then it came to him. Vienamin Simonich. The Russian president had played him. Like a fool. The bastard. He had turned the last of his family members against him. Simonich would pay dearly for this. Nobody insulted him and lived to tell about it. It wouldn't be different for Simonich. But first he had to defuse this situation.

"This isn't the truth, son," the Sheik said, making sure his tone of voice wasn't threatening. "Simonich lied to you, just like he lied to me."

"I saw you do it, you pathetic liar, I saw you do it," his son hissed, showing him the phone in his other hand. His eyes had gone wild. "Simonich recorded the whole fucking thing, you sick bastard. How could you do this? How could you betray your own family?"

They were losing way too much time arguing. This operation was falling apart. They had to get out of the house now and leave Ray Powell behind. But what about Powell's daughter-in-law?

"Hey! I'm talking to you." Igor's voice brought him back.

The Sheik looked at his son. "I did what I had to in order to win, Igor. Just like you did when you killed your own brother."

His son shook his head in disgust but held the pistol steadily toward him. "I trusted you," he murmured.

If Simonich had really recorded the ordeal, he'd never be able to get his son back. Not after he had watched him murder his mother. There was only one way out of this.

The Sheik looked at Ray Powell and yelled to his son, "Watch out!"

As his son turned around to face what he thought was an incoming threat, the Sheik raised his small Kel-Tec P32 and shot his last family member in the head.

. . . .

Ray Powell knew this crisis was coming to an end. The firefight outside the room had intensified. People were coming. But time was running out. The Russian soldier Igor had shot was still alive and was slowly crawling toward his gun while a trail of blood followed his progress. Then Powell saw the Sheik raise a small pistol to Igor's head and fire at point blank range. He fired three more times. He then turned the pistol toward Lisa who was still lying on the bed. Using the last of his energy, Powell got to his feet and jumped on top of Lisa a millisecond before the Sheik fired.

Powell's body jerked once. There was a sharp pain in his back, then nothing. It was weird, really. As if he was having an out-of-body experience. Lisa was watching him. She was screaming his name. For some reason, he couldn't move his legs and felt himself slide off the bed and onto the floor. Then he heard another gun go off. It had a different sound than the pistol the Sheik had been using. From the corner of his eye, he saw the Sheik disappear into the hallway.

Breathing was more difficult now. His thoughts were with Lisa. He hoped she was okay.

CHAPTER 71

Mykonos, Greece

Mike Walton was the first in and saw a man running up the steps in front of him with a jerry can. He opened fire just as he was struck twice in his side and knocked off his feet. Zima fired her MP5 as two more rounds lodged into the wall inches from her head.

Fuuuuck! He had committed the ultimate sin. He hadn't cleared his corner coming in. His mistake had nearly cost him and Zima their lives.

"You're okay?" Zima asked, scanning left and right.

"I fucked up," he replied. The bullets had hit his vest. One of them had smacked into his combat knife while the other had struck one of his spare magazines.

The sound of a silenced MP5 came from the living room.

"One tango down in the kitchen," Ari said. "Four left."

"We got one more in the foyer," Zima said. "Three left."

"Copy that," Ari said. "Living room, dining room, kitchen and half-bath cleared. Coming in."

Ari joined them in the foyer and saw the pain in Mike's eyes. "You're good?"

Mike nodded. His pride had taken a hit. "Follow me," he said, heading up the stairs. "Let's get these bastards."

CHAPTER 72

Mykonos, Greece

Igor Votyakov pressed his hand against in his head. The amount of blood pouring out of his wound was scary. He couldn't believe his father had shot him. He tried to get up but only managed to get up on one knee. He was dizzy and his vision was blurred. His chest hurt too, and when he looked down he realized he'd been shot another three times in his upper body. His vest had stopped the bullets but it still hurt like hell.

Behind him, Grigory lay motionless on the hardwood floor, though his chest was still heaving. Somehow, Grigory had managed to retrieve his pistol. Igor searched for his own weapon but grabbed Grigory's when he didn't immediately find his.

"Looking for this?"

Igor turned around and looked in disbelief at the woman standing in front of him. She was holding *his* pistol in *her* hands. He sighed loudly. *The bitch.*

He had time to curse his father one more time before she pulled the trigger.

· · · · · · · ·

Lisa watched in satisfaction as the Russian's hands shot up to his neck. Her target fell to his knees, blood escaping from between his fingers. His eyes showed confusion, and she watched him die. Gunfire close to her made her jump.

Ray Powell yelled a warning but it was too late. By the time she started pivoting, the Sheik was already on her. He punched her hard on the head and she collapsed. She felt his hands on her ankles as

279

he dragged her back to the bed. He lifted her up and laid her on top of the mattress. A loud explosion shook the entire floor but the Sheik didn't pay any attention. She raised her head but he punched her again. And again. She tasted blood, and the throbbing in her mouth told her that the last punch had broken her jaw. Then he poured something on her. The pungent smell hit her first. *Gasoline.*

The Sheik move closer to Ray Powell and splashed some gasoline on him too. "I hate you," he said. He reached for something in his pocket and her heart sank. She knew what he was looking for. In desperation, she screamed.

CHAPTER 73

Mykonos, Greece

If Mike were to trust the blueprints the team had studied back in Tel Aviv, the second floor had two bedrooms on the left and another two on the right. With two tangos plus the Sheik left, they had to be careful. The element of surprise was long gone and three bad guys were more than enough to screw them all over.

Mike had just set foot on the last step when he heard a single gunshot coming from one of the bedrooms on the right. The shot hadn't been directed at them so either his dad or the other hostage was in trouble. *Or the Israeli deep cover is taking numbers.*

Whatever it was, Mike had no choice. He had to go right. He cleared the corner, knowing Ari would go left to cover the other side of the corridor while Zima would follow him. He hadn't reached the first bedroom before someone opened fire from behind them. Bullets zipped past him and smacked against the wall at the other end. By the time Mike spun around, Ari was on his side firing his MP5.

"I'm hit," Ari screamed as he continued firing his weapon.

"Zima, stay put," Mike ordered, while moving closer to Ari. He took a knee next to the Israeli.

"Last bedroom to the right," Ari said, changing magazines.

Mike brought his weapon up and kept it tight against his shoulder while using his right hand to prep a stun grenade. When he was three feet away from the bedroom door, he threw the grenade in.

The detonation shook the entire floor and Mike moved in, scanning the room with the muzzle of his UMP45. There was another door in the far right corner. *The en suite.* Mike fired through the wall, hoping to catch whoever was hiding by surprise. He fired two-round bursts, moving right to left. While firing, Mike continued to advance toward the en suite. He was ten feet away when a frag grenade dropped at his feet and the door of the en suite closed.

The world stopped. His heart caught in his throat when he realized he had no cover. Mike acted on instinct and rushed to the en suite, ramming its wooden door with his shoulder. The door split open and Mike barged in. For the briefest moment, he made eye contact with the bewildered Russian hiding in the shower. He hit the floor just as the grenade went off, scattering shrapnel around the bedroom. He rolled to his side and transitioned to his Glock. The Russian had just started to raise the muzzle of his submachine gun when Mike fired the Glock in quick succession, hitting him multiple times in the upper body. Once the Russian was down, Mike took half a second to aim his last shot. His round hit the Russian half an inch above his nose.

Mike rose painfully and assessed himself for injuries. Two of his ribs were on fire but that was from downstairs. He inserted a fresh magazine into his pistol and replaced it in its holster.

"Coming out," he said to Zima and Ari to let them know he was exiting the bedroom and that it would be appreciated if they didn't shoot at him.

"Two left," he told them, showing them two fingers. Ari's right arm was covered in blood. "You're good?" Mike asked him.

"Bullet went through my bicep. I'll patch it later."

Mike nodded. "Let's go."

They had been on the second floor for just over thirty seconds now. *Too long.* Mike pushed forward and Zima followed him while Ari took the rear. Mike heard someone scream. *A woman.* It came from the last bedroom. They were running out of time.

Going against everything he had learned in the past, Mike bypassed the next bedroom and headed directly to the last one where he had heard the scream. A strong odor of gasoline emerged from that room. The door was open and Mike made the turn. What he saw stopped him dead in his tracks.

Two bodies were on the floor; one had a green bandana attached to his arm. The other, from which most of the blood seemed to come, lay motionless on his back. Worse yet, Lisa lay on the bed and was soaked in gasoline. And last, his father was crawling around the bed using only his elbows, his hair drenched with the same gasoline.

Standing in the middle of this mess was the Sheik. He was pulling a gold Zippo lighter out of his pocket. Knowing a gunshot could potentially ignite the whole room, Mike let go of his UMP45 and darted across the room and over the bed. He crashed into the Sheik and the Zippo slid across the floor. Both men rolled. Still attached by a strap across his shoulder, Mike's UMP45 dug into his already tender ribs and he yelled in pain. He jumped on the Sheik as he was trying to reach for the Zippo. He flipped the Sheik to his back and effortlessly blocked his weak attempt at a punch. Mike kneed him in the groin with such force that one of his testicles exploded. Mike did it again, and the Sheik's eyes rolled up into his head. But Mike wasn't done. In a fit of rage, he grabbed the Sheik by the collar of his shirt and by his belt and lifted him into the air. He then threw him against the wall. The Sheik crashed to the floor. He tried to raise his head but Mike kicked it like a soccer ball during a penalty. Mike heard something crack and the Sheik went limp. Mike watched him for a few seconds. He was still breathing.

CHAPTER 74

Mykonos, Greece

Lisa Walton felt the strong arms of her husband around her. She touched his face. He was crying and saying mostly unintelligible things. She put her fingers on his lips. "Your dad," she whispered. "He saved my life."

. . . .

Zima was next to Ray Powell holding his hand. Mike glanced at his dad. He kissed his wife on her forehead and went to kneel next to his dad. Blood poured from under him. It really looked bad. Zima left him alone with his father and went to handcuff the Sheik.

Mike shook his head in disbelief. It had been two and a half years since his father's capture at the hands of the Sheik. That was a hell of a long time to be in captivity. He took his father's hand in his own.

. . . .

Ray Powell's eyes lit up at the sight of his son. He would have given everything to see him again. It looked as if he had been granted his miracle. He was so proud of his son. Unfortunately, he also knew this was the end of the road for him. At least one bullet had lodged in his spine. His pain was great but he didn't want his son to remember him being in agony, so he did his best to look serene. But by the look on his son's face, he knew the situation was dire.

"I thought you were dead," he said to his son.

"I'm so sorry, Dad," Mike replied. Tears rolled down his cheeks. "I've been looking for you. I never stopped. I've—"

"I'm just so happy to see you, Mike," he said as tears welled up in his eyes. "But you have to go now."

"No, dad, we'll bring you with us."

"You can't do that. I've been infected. That's what the Sheik wanted all along."

"What are you talking about?"

"Lisa told me what the Sheik did to me while I was out," he explained. It was important that his son understood that he couldn't be moved anywhere, even as a corpse, until personnel properly trained in hazardous substances showed up. "The Sheik injected me with a new thread of the Marburg virus."

. . . .

Mike understood. "Fuck!"

Then Eitan came on the radio. "Two police cars are approaching. They're three to four minutes away. You guys need to go."

"Assault team copy," Mike replied.

His father's hand touched his leg. "I still can't believe you're alive, Mike," his dad said weakly. "The Sheik . . . The Sheik, he showed me newspapers. He told me you were dead."

"No, Dad," he said. "I'm here."

"Your mom?"

"She's alive and well, Dad," Mike lied. It broke his heart to do so, but his dad didn't need to know the truth. "All lies, Dad. Just a bunch of lies to break you."

His father suddenly started to shake uncontrollably. "Dad? Dad?"

His dad squeezed his hand. "I love you."

"I love you too, Dad. Keep fighting."

"I'm proud of you. Thanks for . . . Thanks . . ." His father's eyes closed gently.

Mike checked for a pulse. There was none. He started CPR but on the first chest compression, a ridiculous amount of blood came out of his father's mouth. It was over.

Fuck! I didn't even thank him for saving Lisa's life . . .

Ari tapped on his shoulder. "We need to go, Mike. I'm sorry for your loss."

Mike took one last look at his father and swore that one day he'd bring back his body to Canada, so he could lay him to rest next to his wife and grandchildren. "I'll come back for you, Dad. I promise."

Mike carefully picked up his wife from the bed.

"I've got you, Lisa."

His wife was obviously in great pain, but she didn't make a sound. Even with an injured arm, Ari was able to put the Sheik on his shoulder. Zima led the way to the HiAce while Mike silently prayed for it to start. With the number of bullets that had flown in its vicinity, he wouldn't be surprised if a couple of rounds had found their way to the engine block.

Eitan was already waiting at the HiAce. "We'll have a few minutes extra," he said, climbing in the back. "I've disabled the two police cars."

"Was that a good idea?" Ari asked. "They'll close the airport."

"They would have closed it anyway," Zima said, coming to Eitan's defense.

"She's right," Mike said. "I'll make a call."

He watched as Ari raced back into the villa. "What are you doing?"

His question was answered when Ari came back carrying the soldier with the green bandana on his arm. "We owe him much," Ari said.

CHAPTER 75

IMSI Headquarters, New York

Charles Mapother was in his office with Jonathan Sanchez when Mike called.

"Yes," he replied. "Meir Yatom kept me apprised of your progress all along."

Mike informed him that Lisa and Rafael both needed immediate medical attention, and that they had the Sheik in custody. That he hadn't known.

"What do you need from me?" Having the Sheik in custody was a major bargaining chip. He could ask his friend DNI Richard Phillips pretty much anything, and he would get it.

Getting a medevac for his and Yatom's operatives wouldn't be an issue. Smoothing things out with the Greeks would require a little more work, but it wasn't Mapother's problem to solve.

CHAPTER 75

Over the Aegean Sea, Greece

Mike Walton was glad Charles Mapother had come through with his promise to evacuate them rapidly. The private air ambulance that picked them up from Mykonos was a piece of art. It carried all the equipment a real intensive care unit would have. Mike was impressed.

The three onboard doctors were great and they had already started to treat Rafael's wounds. As for the mystery Israeli with the green bandana, there was nothing the doctors could do. Lisa's situation was more critical than Rafael's but she was now stabilized.

Mike was holding her hand, trying to console her.

· · · · · · · ·

Lisa never expected she would kiss her husband again. When the Sheik had soaked her in gasoline, she had thought it was all over. The idea of being burned alive had freaked her out. She wasn't sure if she was made for this kind of work anymore. With the Sheik in shackles, she had her vengeance.

Now she felt another kind of pain. Something sharper.

Guilt.

Why did Mike's father jump on top of her? Why did he sacrifice himself? Those bullets had been meant for her.

For me.

CHAPTER 76

IMSI's Gulfstream, just outside Greek airspace

Zima couldn't stop gazing at Eitan. She really liked him. He smiled at her. She waved back.

Stop it, girl. You ain't twelve anymore.

Still, his grin melted her heart.

They had all boarded the IMSI Gulfstream without incident. She believed Charles Mapother or Meir Yatom might have played a role ensuring there wouldn't be any problems. Ari had decided to come with them, even though he had been offered a place on the air ambulance. The bullet that had torn through his bicep was still there, and Zima assumed it was painful. He had told Zima and Eitan that he preferred to be treated in Tel Aviv rather than Athens. Zima thought the real reason was that he thought his wingman Eitan needed a chaperone.

Mike had given the Sheik a pretty good beating. One that he would remember all his life, Zima was sure. Mike's last kick to the head had cost the Sheik his left eye and half a dozen teeth. But he'd get the best treatment in the United States. Zima had no clue what they'd do with him. Would they send the Sheik to a secret prison to be interrogated for the next five years? Would they put a bullet in his head? Would they want him to stand trial? These questions were way above her pay grade. She'd let someone else worry about them. For now, the Sheik had been sedated and he wouldn't open his good eye until they were in the United States.

Their final destination was New York, but they would make a quick stop in Tel Aviv to drop off Ari. Eitan had volunteered to stay with her for the final leg. *Smart move.*

EPILOGUE

Miami, Florida

Mike and Lisa were on their balcony watching the sun go down. Since their return to the United States four weeks ago, they hadn't set foot inside the IMSI. Mike made sure to speak with Mapother or his buddy Jonathan Sanchez once every week, but that was it. They both needed the time off. Mike had been told that the Sheik was now being interrogated by a special joint task force of investigators from the United States, Canada and Israel.

Lisa's doctor stopped by every day. So far, she was happy with Lisa's recovery, but she had told Mike this morning that Lisa's worst injuries weren't the visible ones.

Mike hoped his wife had had enough of the field, but he wasn't going to initiate the discussion. It would have to come from her. To change her mind, he had invited Mapother, Sanchez, Zima and her new boyfriend Eitan for dinner at their newly acquired condo. Miami was an easy flight from New York City, and going away a couple of weekends a month would help him deal with his own issues. Time would tell.

Their guests arrived at six and they had a marvelous lobster dinner that continued late into the night. Nobody talked business, and Mike was glad to see his wife smiling and laughing. She even blew him a kiss at one point.

They were all half drunk when Mapother's phone rang. Mike knew something was very wrong when he saw Mapother's face turn white. "Of course, sir. I understand," the IMSI director finally said.

Everybody had stopped talking. All eyes were on Mapother. "What is it?" Mike asked.

"Party's over, I'm afraid," Mapother replied, walking to the living room. "Mike, you're heading to Paris tomorrow morning."

Was this a joke? "Why would I want to go to Paris?"

"Turn on the TV."

Mike did. And they all watched in horror as coordinated terror attacks killed scores of people in Paris. *Again.*

"That's why, Mike. That is why."

Notes

[1] Charles Mapother's bodyguard Sam Turner did what he had to do. It wasn't by luck that he was able to detect the threat lurking behind him and his protectee. Scanning to the rear is something that is taught to us from the first day of the national bodyguard course. Awareness and observation are the cores of any security initiative. Any well-trained close protection officer will constantly scan the environment he's in and apply effective awareness techniques to identify any potential threats to his protectee.

A single-man detail isn't the strongest formation, since the bodyguard is responsible for the entire 360-degree perimeter that surrounds him and his client. Normally, the single bodyguard will place himself to the left or right rear of the person he's protecting but will adjust his position as the environment dictates. Staying within an arm's reach of the protectee is ideal. If he discovers a threat, the bodyguard will position himself between it and his protectee. But here's the tricky part; at least it was for me: instead of adopting a tactically sound firing position, the bodyguard needs to make himself as big and tall as possible in order to shield his protectee from the threat. This is much more difficult than it sounds, especially for former counterterrorism guys like me who've been trained to seek cover—if possible—or to adapt a fighting stance while engaging a target. When more than one bodyguard is available, the recommended firing position for the bodyguard who stays behind to engage the threat is the Isosceles Stance. That means the bodyguard will face his target squarely with his feet set shoulder width. The bodyguard's arms are extended and form an isosceles triangle. Not only is it a stable firing position, but it also offers the retreating bodyguard and the protectee the best protection possible.

. . . .

[2] When I submitted *A Red Dotted Line* to my editor, one of his notes was, "He would really shoot like that in a crowded place?"

Valid question. The answer is yes. Mike Walton definitely would. That doesn't mean every cop or federal agent would, though. There's an important distinction between law enforcement officers or military personnel belonging to specialized units and those who aren't. Here's why:

- Most police officers only shoot once a year for their annual qualification. If they're lucky, they'll fire one hundred rounds per year at a fixed paper target. Some officers are still excellent shots. Having said that, I've seen many of my former colleagues uncomfortable with their own firearms. Would they shoot at a moving target in a crowded place like the Grand Central Station? I think not.
- In contrast, officers assigned to a specialized section like the counterterrorism unit I was with will sometimes shoot hundreds of rounds of ammunition in a single day. We will fire at moving targets and our firing drills are exponentially more advanced than the ones regular officers use. Firing at a target twenty meters away from him—even in a crowded place— was no biggie for Mike Walton.

· · · · · · · ·

[3] In my debut novel *The Thin Black Line* I mentioned that Mike Walton had worked closely with JTF2 during his military career. But what is JTF2? JTF2 stands for Joint Task Force 2 and is the tier 1 special operations unit of the Canadian Forces. The unit was created in 1993 and has continuously evolved to meet modern-day threats.

JTF2 operators are the product of a nation that values training rather than advancement by weapon technology alone. The unit gained famed while operating with Task Force K-Bar under the command of Rear Admiral Bob Harward, a US Navy Seal. The K-Bar coalition forces are rumored to have killed more than one hundred Taliban and Al Qaeda leaders. Admiral Harward professed that the JTF2 members were his first choice for any "direct action" mission.

JTF2 operators were often tasked with the protection of Canadian ministers while they were visiting Afghanistan. This is why I decided to use them to protect CSIS deputy assistant-director Joachim Persky in *A Red Dotted Line*.

· · · · · · · ·

[4] In this chapter, Lisa finds herself in an impossible situation. She's injured and on her knees with two armed bad guys behind her. One of them is about to handcuff her while the other one is covering his

partner by keeping his pistol trained on her. She knows it's the end if she gets caught. She needs to get out.

Thankfully, I've never experienced this out in the field. However, I was trained on how to escape similar situations. Mind you, the chances of success aren't high. In fact, I can't remember one single occasion when I was able to successfully disarm the person trying to handcuff me and neutralize his partner before getting peppered with Simunition FX rounds...

. . . .

[5] Mike Walton has to engage four men at close range. He's armed only with his pistol. His only advantage is that he has the element of surprise. In order to keep it, he needs to neutralize all the threats in a short period of time. Within three seconds, he fires ten rounds and then one more half a second later. He knows he's getting low on ammo, and he is still uncertain if there are any threats left to deal with. He can't afford to throw away any rounds, so he performs a tactical magazine change or "tactical reload." What is it?

A tactical magazine change is the action of reloading a weapon—in Mike's case it's his pistol—that has only fired a few rounds out of its magazine and keeping the original for later use. To execute a tactical reload, the shooter must grab a spare magazine with the thumb and forefinger of his support hand and bring it to the weapon. He then ejects the partially depleted magazine between the index and middle finger of his support hand before inserting the new magazine into the magazine well. The partially used magazine is then secured for later use.

I know my military and law enforcement friends are currently scratching their heads. A lot of people criticize this technique. It is true that there are disadvantages to using it. It takes longer that a speed reload, and it is highly dependent on manual dexterity. And we all know what happens to our dexterity while under extreme stress. In a normal firefight, I personally wouldn't do a tactical reload, either. But since Mike is in Russia with no backup and no additional ammunition available to him, I decided the tactical reload was the way to go for this specific situation.

294

Acknowledgements

I have the greatest job in the word, and I wouldn't have it without you. I read every email, Facebook post, or Tweet you send my way, and I do my absolute best to respond right away. I love interacting with my readers and I always welcome comments or suggestions. If you aren't following me on Facebook yet, you definitely should. Find me at Facebook.com/SimonGervaisAuthor and on Twitter at @GervaisBooks. There are lots of cool prizes to win and you'll get frequent updates on my upcoming novels.

I'd like to thank my editor Lou Aronica for believing in me. It's good to know that I have someone talented like you in my corner. Your availability means a lot. Thanks to my fantastic literary agent Eric Myers at Dystel & Goderich. Eric and I have become good friends. Signing with him gave me the boost I needed to really believe in my work. Thanks for your support, my friend. I owe you one!

I'd like to show my gratitude to *New York Times* bestselling author Nelson DeMille for his kind words. His support and encouragement means a great deal. I'm in your debt, sir. A big thank you is also due to my friend and *New York Times* bestselling author Mark Greaney, who took time away from writing his own series and the next Tom Clancy book to read *A Red Dotted Line*. Another thank you goes to my friend and #1 international bestselling author Peter James and his lovely wife Laura for their tremendous support. Thank you to *New York Times* bestselling author Grant Blackwood for reading my book in less than two days. I'm also thankful to my friend and *New York Times* bestselling author Marc Cameron for our long chats on Facebook and for having my back in NYC. I couldn't be more appreciative. If you enjoy my Mike Walton series and for some reason you've never read these fabulous authors, you really should pick up their books. They are all exceptional.

Most of all, I'd like to thank my beautiful wife who juggles being a doctor, businesswoman, wife, and mother to our two wonderful children. You inspire me every day. I love you.

About the Author

Simon Gervais is a former federal agent who was tasked with guarding foreign heads of state visiting Canada. Among many others, he served on the protection details of Queen Elizabeth II, US President Barack Obama, and Chinese President Hu Jianto. He has also protected the families of three different Canadian prime ministers. Prior to this, Simon spent five years in an anti-terrorism unit and was deployed in many European and Middle Eastern countries. He now writes full-time and is a member of the International Thriller Writers organization. He is the author of one previous Mike Walton novel, *The Thin Black Line*, which was an international bestseller, and the Mike Walton novella, *A Long Gray Line*. He lives in Ottawa with his wife and two children. Find Simon online at SimonGervais-Books.com, facebook.com/SimonGervaisAuthor, and Twitter.com/GervaisBooks.